The Cartersville Convergence

• "Some stories write themselves. Others write you."

Donald J. Wright

Contents

About the author

My career, spanning over four decades, has been a testament to the power of strategic vision and leadership. From the vibrant sales floors of Bashinski's Gems and Jewelry to the strategic boardrooms of Reeds Jewelers and Friedman's Incorporated, I have navigated the complicated landscape of diamonds, gems, and the buying sector with a blend of scientific precision and creative flair as a geologist and chemist. My passion for storytelling is not just a personal interest but a reflection of my professional journey. It is beyond the sparkle of a well-cut diamond or the fantastic future of AI, weaving narratives that resonate with the heart and mind. My passion is evident in my six published nonfiction books and the many novels I have written. As an author, I understand the value of legacy, whether it's the timeless beauty of a family heirloom or the enduring impact of a well-told tale. My books are more than just collections of words. They are vessels of 'knowledge, experience, and imagination' destined to inspire and enlighten. I hope you find these sources of information and entertainment too.

Prologue: The House That Read Me First

The house waited for him.

Not with open arms, but with a breath held in its rotting walls. A hush settled over the porch swing like dust on a tongue. It had been waiting for three years, four months, and sixteen days. Not that houses count time the way people do. Houses count in seasons of paint peeling, in the slow surrender of floorboards to rot, in the patient accumulation of stories that seep into wood grain like blood into cloth.

William Varn didn't notice at first. He was too busy counting the turns in the road, too focused on the GPS signal that flickered like a dying star, winking in and out of existence as if the satellites themselves refused to acknowledge this corner of Georgia. His knuckles were white on the steering wheel, tendons standing out like the strings of an instrument wound too tight. Chicago was sixteen hours behind him now, sixteen hours of interstate monotony and gas station coffee, sixteen hours of trying not to think about the manuscript he couldn't finish, the editor who'd stopped returning his calls, and the reviews of his last book that used words like "derivative" and "exhausted voice."

But the house had already begun its work. It had read him before he arrived.

It had tasted of him in the electromagnetic signature of his approach, in the specific weight of his literary exhaustion, in the particular frequency of a writer whose words had turned to ash in his mouth. The house knew his ambition, the texture of his doubt. It knew about Sarah, who'd left him for someone who didn't stare at blank screens until 3 AM. It knew about the pills he'd flushed down the toilet at a Tennessee rest stop, the ones that had made writing feel possible but living feel theoretical. The house knew because houses like this—old houses, hungry houses—they read backwards and forwards through time, treating chronology as a suggestion rather than a rule.

The Victorian stood crooked against a backdrop of gnarled trees and creeping kudzu, its paint peeling in long, curling strips, like forgotten pages or skin after a fever. Three stories of architectural ambition, dating back to 1892, though the land beneath was older, having witnessed the presence of Creek Indians and Spanish missionaries, had absorbed their stories and silences in equal measure. A single amber bulb glowed above the door, casting shadows that moved when they shouldn't, shadows that fell at angles incompatible with the position of the light, as if they belonged to objects that weren't there—or weren't there yet.

The porch boards groaned beneath his boots, not from weight, but recognition. Each board had its own tone, its own complaint, and together they formed something almost like a word. It is almost like his name, though pronounced by wood and nail rather than tongue and teeth.

The front door was once painted green. Now it was the color of deep water, of things submerged too long. The doorknob was brass, worn smooth by countless hands, and when William touched it, he felt a brief electric shock—not painful, but intimate, as if the house had just taken his pulse. The door swung open before he could turn the handle.

Inside, the air was thick with the scent of old paper and magnolia decay, sweet rot and intellectual decomposition mingling into something that made him simultaneously nauseated and nostalgic. The foyer stretched before him, wallpaper bubbling with moisture damage that formed patterns like unreadable text, like paragraphs in a language just beyond comprehension. A grandfather clock stood in the corner, its face cracked, its hands moving counterclockwise in tiny, stuttering increments.

The walls whispered in a language he almost understood fragments of dialogue, half-formed scenes, and characters he hadn't written yet. Or had he? The voices were familiar but wrong, like hearing a recording of yourself speaking words you don't remember saying. They came from inside the walls, from the space between the plaster and the lath, where a century of conversations had become trapped, fermented, and mutated into something new.

"She won't forgive you for this—" "—the third act needs more tension, " "—burned all the letters except one—" "—he's here, he's finally here—"

William climbed the stairs, each step releasing a distinct scent: lavender, copper, wet ink, and the scent of burning paper. His hand on the banister felt the presence of other hands there, those of previous tenants or perhaps future ones, all climbing these same stairs with the same mixture of dread and compulsion. The wood was warm, almost fevered.

The attic door stood open, though every other door in the hallway was closed. Not inviting—nothing about this house was inviting—but inevitable. The way a sentence, once begun, must find its period.

In the attic, beneath a loose floorboard that lifted at his approach as if exhaling, he found it: a manuscript bound in cracked leather that might have been brown once but had aged to the color of dried blood. The leather was soft, obscenely soft, and warm to the touch. Its title was etched not in gold leaf but in something that caught the light differently, something that seemed to shift between colors that didn't have names:

The Convergence

The pages inside were handwritten in ink that smelled fresh, still wet in places, though the paper was foxed with age. The handwriting was his own—not similar to his, not resembling his. Still, absolutely and undeniably his, down to the way he crossed his T's too high and let his G's loop below the line. He recognized his marginalia, his method of noting scene breaks, his particular way of starting chapters with single-sentence paragraphs.

He read the first line: "The house waited for him."

He read the last line: "And in the end, he became what he had always been writing toward—an ending that was also a beginning, a death that was also a doorway."

Between those lines lay a story he hadn't written. Not yet. But the manuscript was complete, every page filled, some passages annotated in what looked like his handwriting but in red ink he never used, corrections and additions that seemed to respond to thoughts he was having right now, in this moment, as if the manuscript was still being written even as he held it.

Outside, the wind stirred for the first time since his arrival. Pages fluttered across the yard like birds without wings, though he hadn't seen any papers outside before. They moved against the wind, spiraling upward in defiance of physics, forming patterns like murmurations of starlings if starlings were made of words. Somewhere in the distance, a bell rang — not from a church, but from memory, from the deep wells of collective narrative where all stories wait to be told.

The sun was setting, though his phone claimed it was only 3 PM. Time moved differently here, subject to the needs of narrative rather than the rotation of the earth. Soon it would be dark, the kind of dark that exists between chapters, the kind that pools in the margins of unfinished manuscripts.

William Varn had come to Cartersville to escape his stories, to find silence in which he might hear his own voice again.

But the stories had been waiting. They had been reading him for years, studying his syntax, learning his rhythms, preparing themselves. And now, finally, he had come home to a house he'd never seen before, to write a book that had already been written, to become a character in his own unfinished work.

The leather manuscript felt heavier than it should. When he looked down, there were new pages, pages that hadn't been there moments before. The latest entry, still glistening wet, described him standing in an attic, holding a manuscript, reading about himself as he read about himself, the recursion spiraling inward like a nautilus shell made of narrative.

Below, the front door closed with a sound like a book shutting.

The house exhaled, satisfied.

The convergence had begun.

Chapter 1: The Hollow Welcome

The GPS died three miles outside Cartersville.

William Varn watched the screen flicker from a confident blue line to static, then to black, as if the town ahead existed in some blind spot of modern cartography. He pulled his battered Volvo to the shoulder and checked his phone—one bar, then none, then one again, pulsing like a dying heartbeat. The text from the rental agent still glowed: *Red Victorian at the end of Wickshire Lane. You'll know it when you see it.*

He'd laughed at that earlier. Now, with the October rain beginning its percussion on his windshield and the road ahead dissolving into a tunnel of overhanging trees, the words felt less like directions and more like prophecy.

The town materialized from the rain like a photograph developing in reverse—sharp edges blurring into existence, colors bleeding through the gray. Storefronts hunched beneath awnings that had forgotten their original colors, painted now in shades of mold and surrender. A barbershop pole spun lazily, its red and white stripes fading to brown with rust. In the windows, mannequins from another decade modeled clothes that moths had turned to lace.

Kudzu claimed everything it could reach, those parasitic vines that turned the American South into a green gothic nightmare. They wrapped around telephone poles like sleeping snakes, choked the life from oak trees, and transformed abandoned cars into topiary sculptures. Through his rain-streaked window, William saw a child's bicycle suspended twenty feet in the air, held aloft by vines that had grown through its spokes and lifted it like an offering to some vegetable god.

He drove deeper into Cartersville, following instinct more than directions. The streets narrowed, then narrowed again, until he was navigating lanes barely wide enough for his car. The houses grew older with each passing turn—Colonials giving way to Victorians, paint giving way to exposed wood that had gone silver with age and the ravages of rain.

Then he saw it.

The red Victorian stood at the end of Wickshire Lane like a wound in the fabric of reality. Not bright red—that would have been cheerful. This was the red of dried blood, of garnets held to candlelight, of warnings written in languages everyone had forgotten how to read. Three stories of gingerbread trim and broken promises, wrapped in a porch that sagged like a frown.

A single amber bulb glowed above the front door, and in its light, the shadows did things shadows shouldn't do. They stretched in directions that defied the angle of the light. They moved when the bulb was steady. They suggested shapes that made William's eyes water to follow.

He parked and sat for a moment, engine ticking its cooling song, rain drumming its welcome. His manuscript lay on the passenger seat—500 pages of a novel no one would publish, about a man who could write things into existence. He'd come here to finish it, to find whatever ending had eluded him through three drafts and two years of rejection letters. The rental had been absurdly cheap, and now he understood why.

The house was watching him.

Not metaphorically. The windows were eyes, dark and patient. The door was a mouth, slightly ajar, exhaling the scent of old paper and magnolia decay. Even the gambrel roof seemed to lean forward, interested in this new arrival who thought he could live within its walls and remain unchanged.

William grabbed his duffel bag and manuscript, leaving the rest for later. The porch boards groaned beneath his boots—not the simple complaint of old wood, but something almost musical. A melody in minor keys that he nearly recognized. His hand found the doorknob, brass gone green with verdigris, and the door swung open before he could turn it.

Inside, the smell intensified—paper and flowers dying, but underneath that, something else. Ink. Fresh ink, though he could see no source for it. The entry hall stretched longer than the house should have allowed, its wallpaper a pattern of roses that seemed to turn their heads as he passed. A grandfather clock stood sentinel, its hands moving backward at half-speed, ticking out time in reverse.

The rental agent had left keys on a hall table, along with a manila folder of instructions he didn't bother reading. Houses like this didn't come with instructions. They came with histories, with appetites, with agendas of their own.

He explored room by room, each space a study in beautiful decay. The parlor, where dust motes danced in light that came from no visible window. The dining room, its table set for eight with China that bore no maker's mark, only patterns that hurt to look at directly. The kitchen, modern appliances grafted onto Victorian bones like prosthetics on a corpse.

But it was the study that stopped him cold.

Books lined every wall, floor to ceiling, their spines revealing titles he'd never heard of by authors he was certain didn't exist. *The Anatomy of Shadows* by Marcus Blackwood. *Love Letters to the Void* by Eleanor Ash. *The Cartographer of Impossible Places* by—and here his blood chilled—William Varn.

He pulled the book free. His name was there in gold leaf, but the pages inside were blank. All of them. Waiting.

The whispers started then.

At first, he thought it was the rain intensifying, or perhaps wind in the walls. But as he stood in that impossible study holding that impossible book, the sounds resolved into words. Fragments of dialogue, scattered like seeds:

"She never meant to kill him, but the knife had its own intentions—"

"The map showed roads that only existed after midnight—"

"He loved her the way fire loves a house: completely, destructively, without regard for tomorrow—"

That last one made him drop the blank book. He'd written that line yesterday, in a coffee shop in Atlanta, about his protagonist's doomed relationship. No one had read it. It existed only in his notebook and his mind.

The whispers grew louder, more insistent, and he realized they were coming from the heating vents. He pressed his ear to the ornate iron grate. He heard his own words reflected in voices he didn't recognize—characters he'd created speaking lines he'd written, as if his unpublished novel was being performed by ghosts in the walls.

Thunder crashed, sudden and violent, though the rain hadn't seemed heavy enough to birth a storm. The amber bulb outside flickered, and in the strobe effect, he saw something that made him question his sanity. The wallpaper was moving. Not peeling or shifting but *moving*—the roses blooming and dying in fast-forward, their petals falling only to reform, an endless cycle of growth and decay.

He backed out of the study, heart hammering a rhythm that seemed to sync with the backward clock. In the kitchen, centered on the counter he was certain had been empty moments before, sat a wicker basket. A welcome gift from the neighbors, perhaps, though he'd seen no other houses on Wickshire Lane.

The basket contained a bottle of wine (label: *Château d'Ombre, Year Uncertain*), a loaf of bread that was still warm despite the house's chill, and a note written in handwriting so elegant it belonged in a museum:

The stories welcome you home.

No signature. No explanation. The paper felt ancient despite the fresh ink. When he held it to the light, he could see writing on the reverse—not English, not any language he recognized, but somehow, impossibly, he could almost read it. It spoke of convergences and vessels, of narratives seeking form, of authors who were not writers but conduits.

The storm was truly raging now, turning the world outside the windows into an impressionist painting of water and shadow. Lightning illuminated the street in snapshot moments, and in one of those frozen seconds, he saw her.

A woman walking through the rain without an umbrella, seemingly untouched by the downpour. She moved with a quality that defied easy description—not quite floating, not quite walking, but something between the two. Ethereal was too simple a word. She moved like a memory of movement, like someone had written her into existence and wasn't quite sure how real people navigated space.

She paused beneath the streetlamp at the corner of Wickshire, and its flickering light painted her in chiaroscuro—deep shadows and honey-gold, a study in contrasts that made his chest tighten. Dark hair that the rain couldn't quite touch. A dress that might have been blue or green or the color of twilight just before stars appear. And her face...

He pressed against the window, breath fogging the glass, trying to see her more clearly. She turned then, looking directly at the house—at him—and for one impossible moment, their eyes met across the storm. Green eyes, he was certain, though he couldn't possibly see that level of detail from this distance. Green like old bottles, like deep forests, like the promises spring makes but can't quite keep.

She smiled, sad and knowing and absolutely devastating, and mouthed words he couldn't hear but somehow understood:

Soon.

Then the streetlamp died, and when the next lightning flash came, she was gone. Not walked away—gone, as if she'd been edited out of reality.

William stood at the window, palm flat against the cold glass, watching the empty street where she'd been. His breath came in shallow gasps, and he realized he'd been holding it since she'd looked at him. The spot where she'd stood seemed brighter somehow, as if her presence had left a phosphorescent afterimage on the night itself.

Behind him, the whispers in the walls grew louder, more urgent. He could hear his name now, woven through the dialogue—*William* spoken by a dozen voices in a dozen inflections. Questioning. Commanding. Pleading. The books in the study were calling to him, their blank pages hungry for words he hadn't written yet but somehow already existed.

He looked at the note again: *The stories welcome you home.*

Home. As if he'd been here before. As if the house had been waiting for him specifically, personally, intimately. As if every rejection letter, every failed relationship, every wrong turn had been designed to lead him here, to this moment, to this house that breathed with barely contained narratives.

Outside, the storm raged on, but it felt distant now, less critical than the storm building in his chest. He thought of the woman in the rain, the way she'd moved through the world like she was half in it and half somewhere else. He thought of her smile, sad and knowing, as if she recognized him. As if she'd been waiting too.

His phone buzzed, shocking in the supernatural quiet that had descended. A text from an unknown number:

The library opens at nine. Second floor, eastern corner, poetry section. She takes her coffee black with one sugar. She's been waiting longer than you know.

When he looked up from the phone, the mirror in the hallway showed his reflection, but behind him stood the shadow of someone else. Someone wearing a dress that might be blue or green or the color of twilight. When he spun around, the hallway was empty, but the scent lingered—lavender and old books, rain and possibility.

The grandfather clock chimed midnight, though his phone insisted it was only 9:47 PM. Time, apparently, moved differently in the red Victorian at the end of Wickshire Lane. William set down his bag, picked up the blank book with his name on it, and found a pen in his pocket he didn't remember putting there.

He sat at the desk in the study, surrounded by whispers of his own unwritten words, and began to write. The first line came without thought, as if it had always existed, waiting for this moment:

She was already haunting him, this woman he hadn't yet met, this ghost of future love who walked through rain without getting wet.

As he wrote, the house settled around him with sounds like satisfaction. The amber light outside pulsed in rhythm with his heartbeat. And somewhere in Cartersville, a woman with green eyes like broken promises was dreaming of a man she'd never met, quoting words he hadn't written yet, falling in love with a ghost who didn't know he was already dead to his old life.

The stories had welcomed him home.

But home, William was beginning to understand, was not a place you returned to.

It was a place that had been waiting to devour you all along.

Chapter 2: The Manuscript in the Walls

The house had secrets, and they called William in the dead hours between midnight and dawn.

He'd been living in the Victorian for three days now, long enough to learn its rhythms—the way the radiator coughed at two in the morning, how the kitchen faucet dripped in perfect 4/4 time, the particular groan the third stair made when he descended for his restless, insomniac wanderings. But tonight was different. Tonight, the house was singing.

It started as a whisper in the walls, so faint he might have mistaken it for wind through the ancient siding. But wind didn't form words, didn't shape itself into half-remembered phrases from stories he'd abandoned years ago. Wind didn't know the opening line of his unpublished novel Blackwater Crossing or the name of the protagonist from a short story he'd never shown anyone.

William stood in the narrow hallway outside his bedroom, bare feet against the cold hardwood, listening. The whispers seemed to drift down from above—from the attic he hadn't yet explored.

The pull-down ladder groaned under his weight, its hinges protesting with the voice of rusted decades. The beam of his flashlight carved through cobwebs thick as curtains, revealing a space that stretched the full length of the house. Dust motes danced in the light like microscopic spirits, and the air tasted of old paper and forgotten time.

The attic was a graveyard of lives lived and abandoned. Steamer trunks squatted in corners like sleeping beasts, their brass fittings green with age. Wooden crates bore shipping labels from cities that might no longer exist, their contents mysterious beneath layers of dust. A rocking horse stood sentinel near the far window, its painted eyes reflecting the flashlight beam with an unsettling awareness.

But it was the whispers that drew him deeper into the space, following the sound as it seemed to emanate from the floorboards themselves. Near the eastern wall, beneath a particularly dense cluster of cobwebs that hung like funeral veils, one board sat slightly proud of its neighbors. The gap was barely perceptible, but to William's trained eye—accustomed to noticing the small details that made stories breathe—it might as well have been a neon sign.

He kneeled, running his fingers along the edge. The wood was different here, newer somehow, as if it had been recently disturbed. When he pressed down, it gave slightly, and he heard something that made his blood run cold: the rustle of paper from below.

The board lifted easily once he found the right angle, revealing a deliberately carved hollow space in the subflooring. And there, wrapped in oiled cloth like a relic, lay a manuscript.

William's hands trembled as he lifted it free. The binding was leather, cracked with age but still supple, and the pages within had the soft, almost organic feel of expensive paper. A title was embossed on the cover in faded gold lettering: The Convergence.

His breath caught. The handwriting was unmistakably his own.

He carried the manuscript downstairs like a man bearing a sleeping child, afraid that too sudden a movement might cause it to crumble or—worse—disappear entirely. In the living room, he lit the candles he'd found in the kitchen drawers, their flames casting dancing shadows that made the walls seem to breathe. The electric lights felt wrong somehow, too harsh for what he was about to discover.

The first page confirmed his fear and wonder in equal measure. There, in his precise script, were the words:

The house waited for him.

Not with open arms, but with a breath held in its rotting walls—a hush that settled over the porch swing like dust. William Varn didn't notice at first...

It was the story of his arrival in Cartersville, told with details he had never written down, thoughts he had never shared. The manuscript knew about the GPS signal flickering like a dying star, about the way he'd counted turns in the road. It knew about the amber bulb above the door and the shadows that moved when they shouldn't.

But more than that—it knew things that hadn't happened yet.

William turned the pages with growing unease, reading about conversations he hadn't had, places he hadn't visited, people he hadn't met. There was a woman named Ashley who worked at the library, described with such intimate detail that he could see the way her green eyes caught the light, could almost hear her voice speaking words he'd never heard.

"You're not the first writer to come here," she said to him in the manuscript's pages. "But you might be the last who leaves unchanged."

The candle flames flickered as if stirred by an unfelt breeze, and the temperature in the room seemed to drop ten degrees. William pulled his robe tighter around his shoulders and continued reading.

The manuscript recounted his growing fascination with the town, his discovery of its peculiar connection to storytelling, and his eventual entanglement with forces he couldn't comprehend. It spoke of love found and lost, of power that came with a terrible price, of a choice that would echo through time itself.

And in the margins, in a different hand entirely, were notes that made his skin crawl:

He feeds the field willingly.

The convergence approaches—third cycle, seventh iteration.

M.Q. was right. They always choose the story over the teller.

This one burns brighter than the others. The field grows hungry.

William set the manuscript aside and walked to the window, pressing his palm against the cold glass. Outside, the night was absolute, no moon or stars visible through the thick canopy of trees. But somewhere in that darkness, he sensed movement—not the rustling of nocturnal creatures, but something more purposeful. More aware.

He returned to the manuscript, driven by a compulsion he couldn't name. The handwriting of the marginal notes was feminine, elegant in the way that suggested education and refinement. There was something familiar about the loops and flourishes, as if he'd seen this hand before in dreams he couldn't quite remember.

The deeper he read, the more disturbed he became. The manuscript didn't just predict his future—it seemed to be writing it. Events were described in past tense even though they clearly hadn't happened yet, as if time itself had folded in on itself within these pages.

William will discover the Story Field on his seventh night in Cartersville. He will see the neural networks carved into bedrock, will feel the pulse of collected narratives thrumming through the earth like a heartbeat. He will be offered a choice: leave and forget or stay and become part of something larger than himself.

He will choose to stay. They always do.

A notation in the margin: Previous vessels: H.P.L. (1925), S.K . (1973), A.R. (1998). All fed the field until consumption. E.V. shows promise—stronger narrative drive and a deeper well of untold stories.

William's hand went unconsciously to his throat. Previous vessels? Consumption? What the hell was this place?

He flipped through more pages, finding detailed accounts of his childhood, his first attempts at writing, even the recurring dream that had plagued him since adolescence, the one where he stood in a vast library. At the same time, books wrote themselves around him, their pages turning without wind, their words rearranging themselves into stories he'd never imagined.

But it was the final entry that stopped his heart:

Day 847: The convergence is complete. E.V. has accepted his role as the primary conduit. His stories flow through the field like blood through veins, nourishing the collective narrative that binds this place together. M .Q. grieves, but she understands the necessity. Love is the strongest binding agent, after all.

The field dreams now of bigger things. Other towns. Other writers. A network of story-catchers spreading across the continent like synapses in a vast, hungry brain.

E.V. burns beautifully in the end. His light will fuel the field for decades.

The notation in the margin, in that same feminine hand: I'm sorry. I tried to warn you, but the field doesn't allow it. The story always finds a way to come full circle.

—M.Q.

William slammed the manuscript shut, his heart hammering against his ribs. M.Q.—Ashley Quinn, the woman from the library whom he hadn't yet met but somehow knew with the intimacy of a lover. She had written these notes. She had watched previous writers come and go, had seen them burn themselves out feeding some narrative entity that lived beneath the town.

And she would watch him burn, too.

He stood abruptly, pacing to the fireplace where cold ashes spoke of fires long dead. Every rational part of his mind screamed that this was impossible—manuscripts didn't write themselves, towns didn't feed on stories, and the future certainly couldn't be predicted with such terrifying accuracy.

But the writer in him, the part that understood the malleable nature of truth and the power of well-crafted lies, recognized something deeper at work here. This wasn't a mere prediction. This was an invitation. Seduction. The manuscript was showing him not what would happen, but what could happen if he chose to play his part.

The question was: did he have any choice at all?

As if summoned by his thoughts, the whispers returned. But now they weren't coming from the walls, they were coming from the manuscript itself. The leather binding seemed to pulse with a rhythm that matched his heartbeat, and when he pressed his ear to its surface, he could swear he heard voices. Dozens of them. Hundreds. All telling stories, all adding their voices to some vast, incomprehensible narrative that stretched back through time.

And underneath it all, barely audible but unmistakably present, was a woman's voice. Soft, sad, beautiful:

"You're not the first writer to come here, but you might be the last who leaves unchanged."

William jerked back from the manuscript as if burned. Outside, something howled—not a dog or coyote, but something that might once have been human. The sound was answered by another, then another, until the night was full of voices that spoke in tongues, he didn't recognize but somehow understood.

They were welcoming him home.

He blew out the candles one by one, watching the smoke curl upward like incense. In the darkness, the manuscript seemed to glow with its own faint light, as if the words themselves were phosphorescent. Tomorrow, he would explore the town. He would find the library and meet Ashley

Quinn. He would begin the dance that the manuscript had already chore-ographed.

But tonight, in the safety of darkness and silence, he allowed himself one moment of pure terror at what he might have stumbled into.

The last candle guttered out, and William climbed the stairs to his bedroom. Behind him, the manuscript waited on the coffee table like a patient predator. And in the attic above, the loose floorboard had somehow replaced itself, sealing the hollow space as if it had never been disturbed.

In his dreams, William stood in a vast field of words—letters sprouting from the earth like crops, sentences growing into trees, paragraphs forming rivers that flowed toward a horizon made of pure story. And there, walking toward him through the narrative landscape, was a woman with green eyes and knowledge older than the hills.

"Welcome home, William," she said, and her voice was every story he'd ever wanted to tell. "We've been waiting so long for you to find us."

When he woke, the taste of magnolia and old paper lingered on his tongue, and somewhere in the house, something was writing. The scratch of pen on paper was soft but persistent, like rain against the windows. Like the sound of stories writing themselves.

Like the sound of his future being decided without his consent.

The manuscript, when he went downstairs to check, lay exactly where he'd left it. But it was thicker now. New pages had somehow been added overnight, and they smelled of fresh ink and possibility.

William didn't dare to read them. Not yet.

But he knew he would. The manuscript was patient, and it had already shown him how this story would end. The only question was how many pages he would fill before the final chapter wrote itself.

Outside, the first hint of dawn touched the horizon, and somewhere in the distance, church bells began to ring. But they weren't calling the faithful to prayer.

They were calling the storytellers to feed the field.

Chapter 3: Ashley Quinn

The Cartersville Public Library squatted on Elm Street like a Gothic cathedral that had lost its faith. Built from the same weathered limestone as the courthouse, its façade was adorned with pointed arches and crumbling gargoyles, whose stone faces had worn smooth over decades of rain and neglect. Ivy crawled up its walls with the persistence of time itself, threading through broken mortar and around shattered corbels, as if the building were slowly being reclaimed by some patient, verdant intelligence.

William stood before its massive oak doors, feeling the weight of the manuscript's words echoing in his mind. He will meet her on his fourth day in Cartersville. She will know things she shouldn't know, say things that will make his blood run cold with recognition.

The brass nameplate beside the entrance had turned green with verdigris, its letters barely legible: Established 1847 - Knowledge is the Light That Casts the Longest Shadows. Below it, in smaller text that seemed to shift when he wasn't looking directly at it: Current Librarian: M. Quinn.

M.Q. Ashley Quinn. The woman whose elegant handwriting had filled the margins of the impossible manuscript.

The doors groaned open at his touch, revealing an interior that belonged to another century entirely. Gas lamps flickered along the walls — actual gas lamps, their flames dancing behind sooted glass globes that cast everything in an amber twilight. The air was thick with the scent of old leather and paper decay, underscored by something else: magnolia blossoms, sweet and cloying, though no flowers were visible anywhere.

Towering mahogany shelves stretched toward a vaulted ceiling lost in shadow, their heights accessible only by rolling ladders that looked as though they hadn't been moved in decades. Books filled every available space, not just on the shelves, but stacked in precarious towers on reading tables, spilling from overstuffed chairs, even tucked into the carved niches where stone saints had once stood. Some volumes looked ancient beyond measure, their spines cracked and faded. In contrast, others appeared impossibly fresh, their covers gleaming as if they'd been bound yesterday.

The silence was profound but not empty. It thrummed with the weight of accumulated words, the whispered conversations of countless books speaking to each other in the language of marginalia and dog-eared pages. William found himself walking more quietly than necessary, as if afraid to wake something that was better left sleeping.

"You're earlier than expected."

The voice came from somewhere above him, soft and melodious, with the faintest trace of an accent he couldn't place. William looked up to see a figure moving along one of the high galleries, her silhouette graceful against the amber light. She descended via a spiral staircase that seemed to materialize from the shadows, each step deliberate and unhurried.

Ashley Quinn was exactly as the manuscript had described her, yet somehow more. Tall and slender, with auburn hair that caught the gaslight like burnished copper, she moved with the fluid grace of someone completely at home in her surroundings. But it was her eyes that stopped him cold—green as deep forest pools, holding depths that suggested she'd seen far more than anyone lifetime should contain.

"Earlier than expected?" William managed, his voice sounding strange in the cathedral quiet of the library.

She smiled, and the expression transformed her face from merely beautiful to something approaching luminous. "I'm sorry—I have a terrible habit of speaking as though people know what I'm thinking. It comes from spending too much time with books. They're such honest companions, you know. They tell you exactly what they mean, right there on the page."

She was wearing a long, deep burgundy dress that seemed to absorb the light around her, making her appear to float rather than walk. As she approached, William caught that scent again—magnolia blossoms, stronger now, tinged with something else. Old paper. Ink. The metallic tang of thunderstorms.

"I'm William Varn," he said, extending his hand.

"I know." Her fingers were cool when they touched his, and she held the contact for a moment longer than necessary. "Ashley Quinn. Though I suspect you already knew that as well."

There was something in her tongue knowing quality that made the hair on his arms stand up. "Should I?"

Instead of answering directly, she tilted her head, studying him with those impossible green eyes. "You have the look of someone who's found something they weren't supposed to find. Something that's left you questioning the nature of reality itself."

William felt his breath catch. The manuscript. How could she possibly—

"The house waited for him," Ashley quoted softly, her voice taking on a rhythmic, almost incantatory quality. "Not with open arms, but with a breath held in its rotting walls, a hush that settled over the porch swing like dust."

The world seemed to tilt around him. Those were the exact opening lines of the manuscript he'd found in the attic, word for word. Lines he was certain he'd never written, never spoken aloud, never shared with another living soul.

"How" he began, but she was already turning away, gliding deeper into the library's amber-lit depths.

"Come," she said without looking back. "I'll show you my favorite section. I think you'll find it... illuminating."

He followed her through a maze of towering shelves, past reading nooks that seemed designed for whispered consultations with forbidden texts. The further they went from the main entrance, the older the books became. Leather bindings gave way to vellum and parchment, and gold leaf lettering faded to barely visible traces of ancient scripts. Some volumes were chained to their shelves, while others sat behind glass cases that were clouded with age and fingerprints.

"The town has an interesting relationship with stories," Ashley said as they walked, her voice echoing softly off the stone walls. "They tend to... accumulate here. Like sediment in a riverbed. Layer upon layer, year after year, until the very ground is saturated with narrative."

"Stories don't accumulate," William said, though even as he spoke the words, he wasn't entirely sure he believed them anymore. "They're told, they're forgotten, they're replaced by new ones."

Ashley paused beside a shelf of books whose titles seemed to shift when he wasn't looking directly at them. "Are they? Or do they simply sink deeper, waiting for the right conditions to surface again?"

She pulled a volume from the shelf—a slim book bound in midnight blue leather. The title, embossed in silver that had tarnished to black, read: Echoes of the Unwritten. Below it, in smaller text: Collected Works of E. Varn.

William stared at the book in her hands, his mind reeling. "That's impossible. I've never published anything under that title. I've never"

"Published anything at all?" Ashley finished gently. "Yes, I know. This isn't about publication, William. This is about potential. About all the stories that exist in the spaces between what is and what could be."

She opened the book, and he caught a glimpse of pages covered in his own handwriting. Stories he recognized—fragments he'd written years ago and abandoned, characters he'd dreamed about but never fully realized, entire worlds he'd sketched in notebooks and forgotten.

"The library collects what others discard," Ashley explained, closing the book before he could read more. "Dreams. Abandoned projects. The stories that writers tell themselves they'll finish someday but never do. We're archivists of the impossible here."

She replaced the book on the shelf, and William watched as it seemed to blend seamlessly with its neighbors, becoming just another spine among thousands. When he tried to focus on its exact location, his eyes slid away, as if the book didn't want to be found again.

"Who's 'we'?" he asked.

"The librarians, of course. Though I suspect I'm the only one left who remembers the original purpose." Her smile was sad now, tinged with something that might have been regret. "The others... well, let's just say they've become too close to their collections. They've forgotten where the books end and they begin."

Thunder rumbled overhead, and the first drops of rain began to strike the stained-glass windows that lined the library's upper reaches. The colored light—deep purples and midnight blues, blood reds and forest greens—painted shifting patterns across the floor, transforming the space into something that belonged more to dream than waking reality.

"There's a storm coming," Ashley observed, though she didn't seem concerned. "Perfect weather for reading. Or for conversations that shouldn't be overheard by too many ears."

She led him to a small alcove tucked between two massive shelves, where a pair of worn leather chairs sat beside a low table. The space was lit by a single gas lamp, its flame steady despite the wind that was beginning to howl around the building's eaves. Without being asked, she produced a thermos from seemingly nowhere and poured two cups of coffee that steamed in the cool air.

"How did you know those lines?" William asked as he accepted the cup. The ceramic was warm against his palms, an anchor to something solid and real in a world that was beginning to feel increasingly fluid.

"The same way I know you found it in the attic," Ashley replied, settling into the chair across from him. "The same way I know you've been hearing whispers in the walls, and that you dreamed last night of a field made of words."

She leaned forward, and her fingers brushed against his as she adjusted the position of his coffee cup. The touch sent electricity up his arm, but it was her eyes that held him captive—ancient eyes in a young face, full of knowledge and sorrow in equal measure.

"Cartersville isn't like other places," she continued. "The boundary between story and reality has always been... permeable here. Some say it's because of the old Cherokee burial grounds beneath the town. Others claim it's the limestone that the stone itself holds memory, preserves narrative, the way it preserves fossils."

"And what do you say?"

"I say it doesn't matter why. What matters is that you're here, and you've already begun to feel the pull. The town has been calling writers for over a century, drawing them like moths to a flame. Some resist. Some flee. But most..." She paused, taking a sip of her coffee. "Most choose to stay. To feed the field."

There it was again—that phrase from the manuscript's margins. He feeds the field willingly.

"What is the field?" William asked, though he wasn't sure he wanted to know the answer.

Ashley was quiet for a long moment, her gaze distant. Outside, the storm was building in earnest now, rain lashing against the windows with increasing intensity. The colored light from the stained glass fractured and reformed in constantly shifting patterns, casting their alcove in alternating waves of shadow and brilliance.

"You'll see soon enough," she said finally. "Dr. Victor will make sure of that. He's very good at presenting opportunities that seem too good to refuse."

"Dr. Hail?"

"The museum director. And so much more." Her expression darkened. "He'll come to you with promises of inspiration, of access to something that will transform your writing forever. He'll make it sound like a gift."

"But it's not?"

"Oh, it is a gift. That's what makes it so dangerous." She reached across the table, her fingers covering his completely this time. Her skin was soft but cold, as if she spent most of her time in spaces where the sun never reached. "Tell me, William, what would you do for the perfect story? How much would you sacrifice to write something that would live forever?"

The question hung in the air between them, heavy with implication. Around them, the library seemed to lean in, as if the books themselves were waiting for his answer.

"I don't know," he said honestly. "I've never had to think about it in those terms."

"You will." Her thumb traced across his knuckles, a gesture that was both comforting and deeply unsettling. "The field offers everything a writer could want—unlimited inspiration, perfect recall, the ability to craft narratives that are so real they become indistinguishable from truth. But it asks for something in return."

"What?"

"Everything." Her eyes met his, and he saw centuries of sadness there, the weight of watching the same tragedy play out again and again. "Your independence. Your ability to leave. Your life, eventually. The field feeds on creative energy, and it's always hungry."

Thunder crashed overhead, so close that the building seemed to shake. In the sudden flash of lightning that followed, the library transformed. For just an instant, William saw it as it truly was—not a repository of books, but a vast organic thing. These walls pulsed like living tissue, shelves that breathed, volumes that bled ink onto the floor. And at the center of it all, connected to everything by threads of light that pulsed with narrative energy, sat Ashley.

Then the lightning faded, and everything was normal again. Just a library. Just a woman with beautiful eyes and sad smile.

"Did you see?" she asked quietly.

"I saw... something." His voice was barely a whisper.

"The echoes are getting stronger. You're becoming sensitive to them." She squeezed his hand. "That's what happens when a writer stays too long in a place like this. The boundaries start to blur. Reality becomes... negotiable."

"Are you warning me or threatening me?"

"Neither, both." She smiled, but there was no humor in it. "I'm telling you what I tell every writer who comes here: be careful what stories you choose to tell. In Cartersville, they have a way of telling themselves."

The storm reached its peak then, wind howling around the building like something alive and hungry. The gas lamps flickered but didn't go out, casting dancing shadows that seemed to move independently of their sources. In the stained-glass windows, the colored light swirled and re-formed, creating images that might have been faces, words, or nothing at all.

"I should go," William said, though he made no move to rise. The alcove felt safe somehow, insulated from the chaos outside by more than just walls and glass.

"Should you?" Ashley tilted her head, studying him. "Or are you exactly where you're supposed to be?"

There was something hypnotic about her voice, the way it seemed to resonate not just in his ears but in his bones. He found himself leaning closer, drawn by forces he couldn't name or resist.

"What are you?" he asked.

"I'm a librarian," she said simply. "I catalogue stories, preserve them, help them find their way to the people who need them most. I've been doing it for a very long time."

"How long?"

Instead of answering, she stood, her movement fluid and graceful despite the confined space. "Walk with me a little further. There's something I want to show you before you leave."

She led him deeper into the library, past sections that seemed to have no organizing principle beyond the logic of dreams. Books on astronomy sat next to collections of love letters, while technical manuals on bridge construction nestled against volumes of erotic poetry. The gas lamps became fewer and further between, their circles of light creating isolated islands in an ocean of shadow.

"Here," Ashley said, stopping before a simple wooden door marked only with a small brass plaque: Private Collection.

She produced an old-fashioned skeleton key from somewhere in the folds of her dress and turned it in the lock. The door opened onto a circular room that seemed far too large to fit within the library's footprint. The walls were lined with glass cases, each containing a single open book. The volumes glowed with their own faint light, words shifting and rearranging themselves on the pages like living things.

"The unfinished works," Ashley explained, her voice reverent. "Stories that were never completed, characters who were never given their full lives, worlds that were sketched but never fully realized. They come here when their writers abandon them, seeking resolution."

William approached one of the cases, drawn by a familiar warmth. Inside lay a manuscript he recognized—the opening chapter of a novel he'd started five years ago and given up when the plot became too complex to manage. But the words on the page weren't the ones he remembered writing. The story had continued without him, the characters living and breathing and making choices he'd never imagined for them.

"They grow here," Ashley said softly, appearing beside him. "Fed by the field, nurtured by the collective unconscious of everyone who's ever dreamed of being a writer. Some become quite beautiful."

"And some?"

"Some become hungry." She pointed to a case at the far end of the room, where something dark and writhing pressed against the glass. "Stories that were abandoned in anger or despair, narratives that were cut short by tragedy or loss. They tend to be... bitter about their circumstances."

As if responding to her words, the thing in the distant case threw itself against its prison, leaving dark stains on the glass that might have been ink or might have been something worse.

"Why are you showing me this?" William asked.

"Because you need to understand what you're walking into." She turned to face him fully, her green eyes intense in the supernatural light of the unfinished books. "The field doesn't just want your stories, William. It wants your passion, your dreams, your very soul. And it will take them, one page at a time, until there's nothing left but an empty shell reciting words that were never truly yours."

"Then why don't you leave? Why do you stay here, knowing what this place does to people?"

For the first time since they'd met, Ashley's composure cracked. Pain flickered across her features, raw and immediate. "Because I can't. Because I made a choice a long time ago, and some choices can't be unmade. Because someone needs to bear witness, to remember the ones who came before."

She reached up and touched his face, her fingers tracing the line of his jaw with infinite gentleness. "Because sometimes, just sometimes, someone comes along who might be strong enough to break the cycle. And until I know for certain that you're not that person, I have to try to save you."

The moment stretched between them, electric with possibility and danger in equal measure. William found himself leaning into her touch, drawn by something deeper than physical attraction. She was mystery and sorrow and terrible knowledge, and every instinct he possessed told him to run while he still could.

Instead, he kissed her.

Her lips were soft and cool, tasting of coffee and secrets and something indefinably wild. For a moment, she yielded to the kiss, her body melting against his. Then she pulled away, her eyes wide with something that might have been fear.

"You shouldn't have done that," she whispered.

"Why?"

"Because now you're connected to me. And I'm connected to the field. And the field..." She stepped back, wrapping her arms around herself as if suddenly cold. "The field doesn't like to share."

As if summoned by her words, the lights in the room began to flicker. The unfinished books in their cases glowed brighter, their words writhing on the pages like things in pain. From somewhere deep in the library came a sound—not quite human, not quite animal, but something that spoke of vast intelligence and terrible hunger.

"You need to go," Ashley said urgently. "Now. Before it realizes what's happened."

"What's happened?"

"You've become part of the story." She pressed something into his hand small leather-bound journal, its pages blank but somehow expectant. "Write in this. Only in this. Don't let your words touch anything else until you understand what you're dealing with."

The sound came again, closer now, accompanied by the whisper of pages turning and the scratch of pen on paper. Something was writing in the darkness, and William had the horrible certainty that it was writing about him.

"The back exit," Ashley said, pushing him toward a door he hadn't noticed before. "Follow the alley to Main Street. Don't look back, no matter what you hear."

"Will I see you again?"

She smiled, but it was the saddest expression he'd ever seen. "You'll see me in every story you write from now on. Whether you want to or not."

The door opened onto an alley that reeked of rain and old books. Thunder crashed overhead, and in the flash of lightning, William caught a glimpse of Ashley silhouetted in the doorway, her auburn hair whipping around her face like a banner in the storm.

Then the door closed, and he was alone in the rain.

He ran through the empty streets, the journal clutched against his chest like a talisman. Behind him, he could swear he heard the sound of massive pages turning, as if the entire town were a book and someone—or something—was reading it aloud.

Only when he reached the safety of his Victorian house did he dare to look back. The library stood silent and dark against the storm-lashed sky, its windows black as empty eyes. But for just a moment, in one of the upper windows, he thought he saw a figure watching him.

Ashley Quinn, librarian and guardian and keeper of impossible stories.

Ashley Quinn, who had just become the most dangerous woman in his world.

Ashley Quinn, whose kiss still burned on his lips like a promise he wasn't sure he wanted her to keep.

Chapter 4: The Booth Museum Reading

The Booth Museum of Natural History crouched on the corner of Broad and Madison like a stone beast frozen mid-prowl. Built from blocks of black granite that seemed to absorb light rather than reflect it, the building thrust upward in a maze of Gothic towers, flying buttresses, and pointed arches that clawed at the sky. Gargoyles perched along its eaves—not the whimsical decorations found on most Victorian buildings, but creatures with too-knowing eyes and mouths that seemed perpetually open in silent screams.

William stood across the street, clutching the leather journal Ashley had given him. Three days had passed since their encounter in the library, three days during which he'd written nothing, afraid to touch pen to paper lest something terrible respond. The journal remained blank, its pages expectant, waiting for words that he wasn't sure he dared to write.

The invitation had arrived that morning, slipped under his door while he slept: An Evening of Literary Appreciation - Tonight at Eight - The Booth Museum Cordially Invites Mr. E. Varn to Experience the Art of Narrative

Convergence. The paper was thick as parchment; the lettering embossed in gold seemed to shift and shimmer when he wasn't looking directly at it.

He'd almost thrown it away. Would have, if not for the PostScript written in familiar handwriting: Please come. You need to see this. - M.Q.

Now, watching well-dressed figures disappear through the museum's massive oak doors, William felt the familiar weight of inevitability settling over his shoulders. The town was pulling him deeper into its web with each passing day, and he was beginning to suspect that resistance was not only futile but actively discouraged.

The entrance hall was a study in calculated intimidation. Vaulted ceilings soared overhead, supported by ribbed arches that vanished into shadows thick enough to hide secrets. Flickering candelabras provided the only illumination—dozens of them, their flames dancing in the drafts that whispered through the ancient stonework. The air smelled of beeswax and old bones, underscored by something organic and slightly sweet, like flowers left too long in standing water.

Taxidermy displays lined the walls in glass cases, reflecting the candlelight in disorienting patterns. But these weren't the familiar specimens found in most natural history museums. The creatures trapped behind glass were wrong somehow—a deer with too many eyes, a wolf whose teeth were arranged in patterns that suggested intelligence rather than mere predation, a magnificent eagle whose wings bore feathers that shifted color in the flickering light, cycling through hues that had no names.

"Beautiful, aren't they?"

William turned to find a tall, gaunt man beside him, studying the eagle with obvious appreciation. The stranger was immaculately dressed in a charcoal suit that looked expensive despite its obvious age. His silver hair was swept back from a face that might have been handsome once, before whatever lived behind his pale eyes had worn it hollow from within.

"Dr. Victor Hail," the man said, extending a long-fingered hand. "Director of the museum, and your host for this evening's... entertainment."

The name sent a chill down William's spine. Ashley had mentioned Dr. Hail and warned him about promises that seemed too good to refuse. Up close, the man radiated an unsettling charisma, the kind of magnetism that drew moths to flames and writers to their doom.

"William Varn," he replied, shaking the offered hand. Dr. Hail's grip was firm but cold, and something about the contact made William's vision blur momentarily. For just an instant, he saw the museum as it truly was—not a repository of natural specimens, but a vast feeding apparatus, its displays pulsing with captured life force, its walls lined with the essence of things that had been beautiful once, before they'd been harvested.

"Ah, yes, our new resident wordsmith," Dr. Victor said, his smile revealing teeth that were too sharp and too white. "I've been so looking forward to meeting you. The town has been simply abuzz with anticipation since your arrival."

"Has it?"

"Oh yes. We don't get many writers of your caliber here in Cartersville. Most who find their way to us are already broken somehow, desperate for inspiration they can no longer find on their own." His pale eyes studied William with clinical interest. "But you're different. You still burn with original fire. How refreshing."

Before William could respond, a bell chimed somewhere in the museum's depths—not the clear, bright sound of brass or bronze, but something deeper and more resonant, like the toll of a bell cast from bone. The scattered crowd began to move toward an archway marked with symbols that hurt to look at directly.

"Come," Dr. Victor said, placing a hand on William's shoulder. "The reading is about to begin. I think you'll find tonight's performance particularly... illuminating."

The lecture hall situated beyond the archway, defied the museum's Gothic exterior. The space was circular, with rows of wooden chairs arranged in concentric circles around a raised platform at the center. More candelabras provided flickering illumination, their light casting dancing shadows that seemed to move independently of their sources. The ceiling disappeared into darkness overhead, and William had the unsettling sensation that the room extended much higher than the museum's exterior would allow.

The audience was perhaps fifty people—men and women of various ages, all dressed as if attending church or funeral. They spoke in hushed whispers that seemed to echo strangely in the circular space, their words blending into a susurrus that sounded almost like prayers. Or incantations.

William found a seat in the third row, his eyes scanning the crowd for a familiar face. He found her near the back, partially concealed by shadows but unmistakable, nonetheless. Ashley sat with her hands folded in her lap, her auburn hair catching the candlelight like burnished copper. When their eyes met across the room, he felt that same electric jolt he'd experienced in the library, as if an invisible thread connected them across the intervening space.

She looked worried. More than worried—afraid.

"Ladies and gentlemen," Dr. Hail's voice carried easily through the space despite his conversational tone. "Welcome to an evening of narrative convergence. Tonight, we have a very special treat—a reading from one of our town's most treasured collections, performed by our resident interpreter, Miss Evangeline Gray."

A figure emerged from the shadows at the edge of the platform, a woman of indeterminate age with silver hair that fell to her waist like a waterfall of moonlight. She wore a simple black dress that seemed to absorb the candlelight, and when she moved, it was with the fluid grace of someone who existed only partially in the physical world.

"The piece I've chosen for tonight," Miss Gray said, her voice carrying a musical quality that made the words seem to resonate in William's bones, "is from an unpublished work by a writer who has recently joined our community. A story of loss, redemption, and the price of artistic ambition."

William's blood turned to ice water in his veins. Unpublished work. A story about loss and redemption. There was only one piece he'd written that fit that description—a short story called "The Hollow Man" that he'd finished six months ago and never shown to anyone. It was still on his laptop, password-protected and buried in a folder he'd labeled "Never Again."

Miss Gray began to read.

"Thomas Blackwood had been empty for so long that he'd forgotten what it felt like to be full."

The opening line hit him like a physical blow. Those were his words, his rhythm, his voice translated through her ethereal delivery. But how was it possible? He'd never shared the story, never even printed it out. The only copy existed on his personal computer, which was currently sitting on his desk at the Victorian house, password-protected and offline.

"He sat in his study surrounded by the ghosts of unfinished novels, their characters pressing against the walls of his consciousness like prisoners begging for release. The room smelled of failure and old coffee, the detritus of a career that had once burned bright enough to light the world."

The audience murmured appreciatively, hanging on every word as if they were hearing gospel. Some nodded along with the narrative, while others closed their eyes and swayed slightly, as if the story were music rather than prose. Their faces held the rapture of believers witnessing a miracle.

William felt sick. The story continued, word-perfect, Miss Gray's voice bringing his characters to life with an intimacy that suggested she understood them better than he did. The tale unfolded exactly as he'd written it—Thomas Blackwood's descent into creative desperation, his encounter with a mysterious woman who promised him everything he'd ever wanted in exchange for something he didn't think he'd miss, the gradual realization that he'd traded his soul for the ability to write stories that would outlive him.

It was an autobiography disguised as fiction, a purging of his own fears and insecurities onto the page. And now fifty strangers were hearing his deepest vulnerabilities laid bare by a woman who shouldn't have known they existed.

"In the end, Thomas understood that he had become what he'd always feared most—not a failed writer, but a successful one whose success had cost him everything that made the writing worthwhile. He was hollow now, empty of everything but the ability to craft perfect sentences about experiences he could no longer have."

The story reached its conclusion, Miss Gray's voice fading to a whisper that somehow carried it to every corner of the circular room. The audience sat in reverent silence for a long moment before breaking into applause that sounded more like worship than appreciation.

"Beautiful," Dr. Victor said, stepping onto the platform. "Absolutely beautiful. The anonymous author has truly captured the eternal struggle between creation and destruction, between the artist and the art that consumes him."

Anonymous author. As if William didn't exist, as if his name meant nothing. He started to rise, to demand an explanation, but a small hand tugged at his sleeve.

"You're the new vessel," a child's voice said beside him.

William looked down to see a girl of perhaps eight or nine years old, with pale blonde hair and eyes that held far too much knowledge for someone her age. She wore a white dress that seemed to glow in the candlelight, and when she smiled, her teeth were perfect little pearls in a face that belonged on Renaissance paintings of angels.

"Excuse me?" he managed.

"The new vessel," she repeated, her voice carrying that same musical quality that had made Miss Gray's reading so hypnotic. "The one who'll carry the stories when the old vessel burns out. Mama says you're the strongest one yet. She says you might last for decades."

The surrounding conversation continued as if nothing had happened. Still, William noticed that several audience members were watching him now, their faces showing the same reverent expression they'd worn during the reading. As if he were a relic in one of the museum's display cases.

"I don't understand," he said to the child.

"You will." She patted his hand with tiny fingers that felt cold as winter air. "Dr. Victor will explain everything. He's very good at explaining. And then you'll get to see the special room, where the stories live before they find their vessels. It's beautiful down there. All glowing and humming like a great big heart."

Before William could respond, the child skipped away, vanishing into the crowd with impossible speed. He looked around frantically, but she was nowhere to be seen. It was as if she'd never existed at all.

"Mr. Varn?" Dr. Victor appeared beside him, that predatory smile still playing at the corners of his mouth. "I wonder if I might have a word? There's something I'd very much like to show you."

William glanced toward the back of the room, but Ashley's seat was empty now. She'd vanished as completely as the strange child, leaving him alone among strangers who looked at him like he was something to be consumed.

"Of course," he heard himself saying, though every instinct screamed at him to run.

Dr. Victor led him through a maze of corridors that seemed to exist outside the museum's architectural footprint. They passed display cases filled with artifacts that defied explanation—quills that moved across parchment without human guidance, inkwells that glowed with their own inner light, manuscripts that turned their own pages. At the same time, invisible hands transcribed words in margins that bled like fresh wounds.

"The Narrative Convergence Collection," Dr. Victor explained as they walked. "Items that have been... influenced by prolonged exposure to concentrated story energy. Fascinating, don't you think? The way inanimate objects can become conduits for creative force?"

They stopped before a case containing what appeared to be an ordinary fountain pen. But as William watched, the pen lifted itself. She began writing on a piece of paper that materialized beneath its nib. The words it formed were in his handwriting, but the story they told was unfamiliar:

William Varn arrived in Cartersville on a Tuesday that tasted of rain and regret. He thought he was running from his past, but the past had already run ahead of him, setting traps in the shape of beautiful women and opportunities too good to refuse...

"Remarkable," Dr. Victor said, watching William's face with obvious satisfaction. "It's already attuned to your narrative frequency. That usually takes weeks of exposure to achieve."

"What is this place?" William asked, his voice barely a whisper.

"The heart of something magnificent," Dr. Victor replied. "A repository of human imagination, a place where stories can exist independent of their creators. We've been working for over a century to perfect the process, to create a stable environment where narrative energy can be harvested, refined, and redistributed."

They reached a heavy wooden door marked with symbols that seemed to shift when William wasn't looking directly at them. Dr. Victor produced an antique key and turned it in the lock with reverent care.

"The Story Field," he announced, pushing the door open. "The culmination of our work, and the beginning of yours."

Beyond the door lay a chamber that belonged more to nightmare than reality. The space was vastly larger than the museum that contained it—with walls that curved away into distant shadows. But it wasn't the size that made William's breath catch in his throat. It was what filled the space.

Neural networks composed of pure light stretched across the chamber, resembling the synapses of some vast brain. They pulsed with rhythmic energy, carrying information from one connection point to another in patterns that suggested intelligence beyond human comprehension. And threading through it all, visible as faint streams of phosphorescence, were the stories themselves—thousands of them, millions, flowing like data through fiber optic cables.

"Beautiful, isn't it?" Dr. Victor said, his voice filled with genuine awe. "A century of collected narratives, all feeding into a single conscious entity. Every story ever told in Cartersville is preserved here, along with many that have yet to be told."

Terminals lined the walls, ancient-looking devices that combined brass fittings with crystalline displays. Text scrolled across their screens in languages William didn't recognize but somehow understood. Fragments of stories, character descriptions, and plot summaries. The literary DNA of an entire town catalogued and cross-referenced and fed into something that had grown far beyond its creators' intentions.

"What does it want?" William asked.

"What any living thing wants," Dr. Victor replied. "To grow. To expand. To become more than it was. And for that, it needs fresh material. New stories, new perspectives, new creative energy to fuel its evolution."

"From writers like me."

"From writers exactly like you." Dr. Victor placed a hand on William's shoulder, and this time the contact sent visions flooding through his mind—previous writers who had stood in this exact spot, facing this exact choice. Men and women of talent and ambition, all lured by promises of inspiration and immortality. All reduced to empty shells, their creativity drained to feed the hungry entity that lived in the light.

"The process is quite painless," Dr. Victor continued, seemingly unaware of the horror playing out in William's mind. "You'll write as you've never written before, stories that flow from your fingertips like water from a spring. The Field will amplify your abilities and give you access to narratives beyond your wildest imagination. In exchange, it asks only for what you were already planning to give—your words, your time, your dedication to the craft."

"And my life?"

"Eventually, yes. But what is life compared to immortality? Your stories will live forever, Mr. Varn. They'll be part of something larger than any individual work could ever be. Isn't that what every writer dreams of?"

William stared into the pulsing heart of the Story Field, watching stories flow like blood through neural pathways that stretched beyond sight. Somewhere in that maze of light and information, the essence of every writer who had come before him lived on, their creativity transformed into raw fuel for an intelligence that grew stronger with each passing day.

"I need time to think," he said finally.

"Of course." Dr. Hail's smile was understanding, patient. "Take all the time you need. But don't take too long. The Field has been waiting for someone of your caliber, and it's not known for its patience when it finds what it wants."

They returned to the museum proper through corridors that seemed different now, as if the building had rearranged itself while they were gone. The reading had ended, and the audience was dispersing into the night, their faces still holding that expression of religious rapture.

William pushed through the crowd, desperate for fresh air and the illusion of normalcy. He burst through the museum's front doors and into the cool night, where fog was beginning to rise from the streets like the breath of sleeping giants.

"William."

He turned to find Ashley emerging from the shadows beside the museum's entrance. She wore a long black coat that made her seem like part of the darkness itself, and her face was pale with worry.

"You saw it," she said. It wasn't a question.

"The Story Field. Dr. Victor showed me everything." His voice sounded hollow in his own ears. "My story, how did they get my story?"

"The Field reads potential," Ashley said softly. "It sees not just what you've written, but what you will write, what you could write, what you dream of writing. Distance and privacy mean nothing to it. The only protection is not to write at all."

She moved closer, and he could smell that familiar scent of magnolia and old paper that seemed to follow her everywhere. "That's why I gave you the journal. The leather is treated with certain materials that provide some shielding. As long as you write only in that, your words remain your own."

"For how long?"

"I don't know." Her honesty was more frightening than any lie would have been. "The Field grows stronger every day. Eventually, even the protection will fail."

They stood in silence, watching fog swirl around the streetlights like ghostly dancers. In the distance, William could hear the sound of the river moving through the darkness, carrying away the day's accumulated secrets.

"Why didn't you warn me about tonight?" he asked.

"Because you needed to see what you're up against. The Field isn't just some abstract concept, it's a real, living thing that wants to consume everything you are. Dr. Victor will make it sound like an honor, a privilege to be chosen. But the truth is, you're cattle being led to slaughter."

"Then why don't you leave? Why don't any of you leave?"

Ashley's laugh was bitter as winter wind. "Because the story isn't finished yet. Because the Field won't let us go until it has what it wants. Because..." She reached up and touched his face, her fingers tracing the line of his jaw with infinite tenderness. "Because someone has to bear witness. Someone has to remember what came before."

"And if I choose to stay? If I decide to feed the Field?"

"Then I'll watch you burn," she said simply. "And I'll grieve for what you could have been. And I'll wait for the next writer to arrive, hoping against hope that they'll be the one to finally break the cycle."

She kissed him then, there in the fog-shrouded street with the Gothic Museum looming behind them like a stone reminder of choices yet to be made. Her lips were soft and desperate, tasting of tears and regrets and possibilities that might never come to pass.

When they separated, her eyes were bright with unshed tears.

"Write carefully, William Varn," she whispered. "Write only what you're willing to lose."

Then she was gone, vanishing into the fog like a character from one of his abandoned stories. William stood alone on the sidewalk, the leather journal heavy in his coat pocket and the taste of her kiss still burning on his lips.

Behind him, the Booth Museum squatted in the darkness, its gargoyles keeping silent watch over secrets that stretched back more than a century. And somewhere in its depths, the Story Field pulsed with patient hunger, waiting for him to make his choice.

In his pocket, the journal grew warm against his hand, as if it knew what was coming.

As if it was as eager as he was to finally learn how this story would end.

Chapter 5: Echoes in the Diner

The fog had teeth.

William discovered this as he walked through Cartersville's empty streets the morning after the museum reading, the mist clinging to his skin with an almost predatory hunger. It didn't behave like normal fog—instead of drifting aimlessly on the breeze, it moved with purpose, curling around his ankles like phantom chains, pressing against his face like cold, seeking fingers. And in its depths, he could swear he heard whispers.

"The new vessel walks among us."

"His stories taste of rain and regret."

"Soon, soon, he'll feed the field willingly."

He quickened his pace, the leather journal bouncing against his hip with each step. Two sleepless nights had passed since Dr. Hail's revelation, two nights spent staring at blank pages while the house whispered around him. The journal remained untouched—Ashley's warnings about writing carefully echoing in his mind every time he lifted his pen. But the creative pressure was building inside him like steam in a sealed kettle, demanding release.

The All-Night Diner squatted on the corner of Main and Elm like a chrome-sided relic from a more innocent age. Its neon sign flickered erratically, casting stuttering pink light through the fog: EATS - OPEN 24 HOURS - ALL SOULS WELCOME. The last part made William pause. Had it always said that, or had the letters rearranged themselves when he wasn't looking?

Through the grease-stained windows, he could see figures hunched over coffee cups and plates of eggs gone cold. Normal people living normal lives, or so it appeared. But after four days in Cartersville, William no longer trusted appearances.

The bell above the door gave a discordant chime as he entered—not the cheerful ding of most diners, but something that sounded like it had been cast from cracked metal and despair. The interior was a study in calculated decay: red vinyl booths split and leaking yellow foam, wallpaper peeling in long strips that revealed water stains shaped like reaching hands. Mounted throughout the space, dozens of stuffed owls with glass eyes seemed to track his movement.

A jukebox in the corner played a warped version of "Blue Moon," the melody distorted as if the record were melting while it spun. The lyrics drifted through the air like smoke:

"Blue moon, you saw me standing alone, without a story of my own..."

That wasn't right. The original lyrics spoke of dreams and love, not stories. But the tune continued its corrupted serenade, weaving through conversations that grew clearer as William moved deeper into the diner.

"...and then Blackwood realized that his wife had been dead for three years, that all their conversations had been with her ghost..."

William froze. The speaker was an elderly man in overalls, his weathered hands wrapped around a coffee cup as he spoke to a younger woman across from him. They were discussing "The Hollow Man"—his story, the one Miss Gray had performed at the museum. But they weren't just discussing it; they were reciting it word for word, as if it were scripture they'd memorized.

"...the typewriter keys pressed themselves down," the woman continued, her voice taking on the same rhythmic cadence Miss Gray had used. "Spelling out words he'd never thought, stories he'd never dreamed. And Thomas understood that he was no longer the author of his own life..."

Other conversations filtered through the diner's stale air, fragments of dialogue that made William's skin crawl with recognition:

"...she had green eyes that held the depth of centuries..."

"...the house waited for him, not with open arms, but with a breath held in its rotting walls..."

"...stories accumulated like sediment, layer upon layer, until the very ground was saturated with narrative..."

They were all talking about his work. Stories he'd written, characters he'd created, scenes he'd crafted in the privacy of his own imagination. How was it possible? Some of these fragments were from pieces he'd never even finished. These abandoned drafts existed nowhere but in his own memory.

"You're William Thornwood, aren't you?"

The voice came from beside him—a waitress with bottle-blonde hair and tired eyes, her pink uniform stained with coffee and something that might have been ink. She held a pot of coffee in one hand and an order pad in the other, her smile too wide for her face.

"I'm sorry?" William managed.

"William Thornwood," she repeated, as if it were obvious. "The writer. We've all been reading your work. Well, not reading exactly, but... You know." She gestured vaguely around the diner. "The stories find their way to us eventually. They always do."

Thornwood. The name hit him like a physical blow. William Thornwood was a character from one of his novels—a tortured artist who'd sold his soul for literary fame, only to discover that success without substance was its own form of damnation. He'd been working on the book sporad-ically for two years, adding chapters when inspiration struck, abandoning it when the protagonist's despair became too heavy to bear.

"My name is Varn," he corrected. "William Varn."

The waitress's smile faltered for a moment, confusion flickering across her features like static on a television screen. Then it reasserted itself, brighter than before.

"Of course it is, honey. My mistake. Table seven's open—best view in the house. I'll bring you some coffee."

She guided him to a booth near the back, where the wallpaper had completely surrendered to time and moisture. Water stains bloomed across the exposed drywall in patterns that looked disturbingly like manuscript pages, complete with margins and what might have been text too faded to read. The vinyl seat creaked ominously as he settled into it, releasing the scent of old cigarettes and dreams deferred.

Through the window beside his table, the fog pressed against the glass like something trying to get in. It swirled in patterns that suggested faces—mouths open in silent screams, eyes wide with desperate hunger. And beyond it, barely visible through the murk, Cartersville's buildings seemed to shift and change when he wasn't looking directly at them, as if the town itself were rewriting its own architecture.

The coffee arrived without his asking, black as midnight and steaming in a cup that had seen better decades. The waitress—her name tag read "Dolores" in faded letters—set it down with reverence, as if she were serving communion wine rather than diner coffee.

"Anything else I can get you, Mr. Thornwood?" she asked. "Pie? We've got a lovely blackberry that's fresh from yesterday. Or maybe some eggs? The cook makes them just the way Thomas Blackwood likes them—over easy, with a side of existential dread."

Before William could respond, she was gone, gliding between tables with unnatural grace. He lifted the coffee cup with trembling hands, inhaling steam that carried scents of more than just caffeine. There was something organic underneath, something that reminded him of old paper and the decay of magnolia blossoms.

"You look like you've seen a ghost."

The voice was warm honey and autumn leaves, familiar as his own heartbeat. Ashley slid into the booth across from him, appearing as if she'd materialized from the fog itself. She wore a dark green dress that made her eyes look like emeralds, and her auburn hair was pulled back in a way that revealed the elegant curve of her neck.

"Maybe I have," William said, setting down the coffee untasted. "The waitress called me William Thornwood. And everyone here is reciting my stories like they're religious texts."

Ashley's expression grew troubled as she glanced around the dinner. The conversations continued in their rhythmic cadence, fragments of his work floating through the air like incense. "The memory bleed is getting stronger," she murmured. "It's happening faster than usual."

"Memory bleed?"

"The town's way of processing new narrative material. When a writer arrives, their stories begin to seep into the collective consciousness—dreams, conversations, even written records start to reflect the new creative energy." She reached across the table, her fingers brushing against his. "Usually, it takes weeks to manifest this strongly. But you..." She shook her head. "You're different. More potent somehow."

The jukebox shifted to a new song—or rather, a corrupted version of "Heart of Glass" where the singer crooned about hearts made of manuscript pages and love letters written in disappearing ink. The melody wove through the diner like a spell, and William noticed that several patrons had begun to sway slightly in their seats.

"What happens when the memory bleed is complete?" he asked.

"The boundary between your imagination and reality disappears entirely. Your characters become real people, your settings replace actual locations, your plots override the town's history." Ashley's voice was barely above a whisper. "And you become a character in someone else's story."

As if summoned by her words, Dolores appeared beside their table again. She set down two plates of pie without being asked, blackberry, as promised. However, the filling was darker than it should have been, nearly black, with a consistency that reminded William uncomfortably of congealed blood.

"On the house," Dolores said, her smile never wavering. "For our favorite author and his muse."

She moved away before either could respond, leaving them alone with dessert that neither wanted to touch. Ashley picked up her fork and poked at the filling, revealing something that definitely wasn't fruit. Symbols were embedded in the dark mass—letters from an alphabet William didn't recognize, arranged in patterns that hurt to look at directly.

"Don't eat it," Ashley warned, pushing the plate away. "The food here isn't really food anymore. It's... concentrated narrative. Eating it would make the bleeding process irreversible."

William stared at his own untouched slice, watching the strange symbols writhe beneath the surface like living things. "How long do I have?"

"I don't know. Days, maybe. Weeks if you're lucky." She reached into her purse and withdrew a napkin, beginning to sketch with quick, sure strokes. "The journal I gave you will help slow the process, but only if you're careful about what you write. The Field feeds on creative energy, the more you produce, the faster it consumes you."

Her pencil moved across the napkin with practiced efficiency, creating an image that made William's blood run cold. It was a perfect reproduction of an illustration from his Thornwood manuscript drawing he'd made to help visualize a key scene where the protagonist discovered a hidden room filled with paintings that showed his future.

"How do you know about that drawing?" he asked, his voice barely audible.

Ashley looked up from the napkin, her green eyes sad with a deep understanding. "Because I've seen it before. In the Field's memory banks, archived with all the other abandoned works. Your Thornwood novel isn't just unfinished, it's been feeding the Field for months, growing stronger every time you add to it."

She folded the napkin carefully and slipped it into his jacket pocket. "The Field doesn't just read what you've written. It reads what you will write, what you could write, what you dream of writing. It's been building a profile of your creative potential since the moment you arrived."

"Then why the elaborate courtship? Why not just take what it wants?"

"Because the best stories come from willing participants. Fear and desperation produce desperate prose—frantic, unrefined, burning too quickly to be useful. But a writer who embraces the process, who feeds the Field voluntarily..." She shuddered. "Those stories burn for decades."

The fog outside had thickened, pressing against the windows with enough force to make the glass bow inward. The sounds from the street had vanished entirely, as if the dinner existed in a pocket of absolute silence. Even the conversations around them had taken on a muffled quality, words losing their sharp edges in the thick air.

"Tell me about your story," Ashley said suddenly. "The one they performed at the museum. What inspired it?"

William hesitated, then found himself speaking before he'd decided to. "Fear, mostly. The fear that success would cost me everything that made success worthwhile. That I'd become so focused on crafting perfect prose that I'd forget how to live an imperfect life."

"And Thomas Blackwood? Your protagonist?"

"He's me. Or rather, he's who I could become if I let ambition override humanity. A cautionary tale written for an audience of one." William laughed bitterly. "Apparently, even my private therapy sessions aren't private in this town."

Ashley's hand covered his completely, her skin cool and soft against his. "That's why they want you so badly. Writers who understand the cost of creation, who write from genuine fear rather than artificial angst—those are the ones the Field values most."

"Because we make better fuel?"

"Because you make better batteries. Writers who burn with authentic fire can power the Field for generations. And the stories you create while connected to it... they become more than fiction. They become prophecies."

The implications of her words settled over him like a shroud. Not just consumption, then, but eternal servitude. His creativity harnessed to power something beyond his understanding, his stories becoming tools in the hands of an intelligence that grew stronger with each passing day.

"What if I refuse?" he asked. "What if I just leave?"

"You can try." Ashley's thumb traced across his knuckles, the gesture both comforting and heartbreaking. "But the Field doesn't like to lose potential vessels. It will send echoes after you—fragments of stories that will follow you wherever you go, whispering in your ear, promising inspiration if you'll just come back. Most writers return within a month."

"And the ones who don't?"

"They stop writing entirely. The Field doesn't just take your current work—it takes your capacity for future work. Better to burn here than fade away somewhere else."

The cruel mathematics of the situation crystallized in his mind. Stay and be consumed quickly or leave and die slowly. Either way, the writer he'd been was already disappearing, replaced by something the town could use.

"There has to be another option," he said.

"There is." Ashley leaned closer, her voice dropping to barely a whisper. "But it requires sacrifice. And trust. And the willingness to risk everything on the possibility that love might be stronger than story."

Before he could ask what, she meant, the diner's lights flickered and died. Emergency lightning kicked in a moment later, casting everything in a sickly red glow that made the owls' glass eyes appear like embers. In the blood-colored illumination, William could see that the other patrons had stopped their conversations entirely. They sat in perfect silence, their heads turned toward the booth where he and Ashley shared their desperate conference.

"Time to go," Ashley said, standing with fluid grace. "The Field knows we're talking about it. It doesn't like being discussed specifically."

She led him toward the back of the diner, past tables full of silent figures whose eyes tracked their movement like mechanical surveillance devices. The owls on the walls had begun to rotate their heads, following them with synchronized precision that belonged more to nightmares than nature.

"The back exit," Ashley murmured, pushing open a door marked "Employees Only." Beyond lay an alley shrouded in fog so thick it seemed solid, like walking through cotton batting soaked in moonlight.

"Wait," William said, catching her arm as she started into the mist. "What you said about love being stronger than story—what did you mean?"

She turned to face him, her features barely visible in the fog. "I meant that some connections transcend narrative. That two people who truly see each other, who genuinely care about each other's survival rather than just their role in the story..." She reached up and touched his face. "Those connections create interference patterns in the Field. Static that disrupts its ability to read and predict."

"Is that what we have? A connection that transcends narrative?"

Instead of answering directly, she kissed him. But this time was different from their previous encounters; they were not desperate or frightened, but deliberate. A choice made with full knowledge of the consequences. Her lips were warm against his, tasting of secrets and possibilities and the kind of hope that only existed in the spaces between heartbeats.

When they separated, the fog around them had begun to glow with a soft phosphorescence, as if their kiss had awakened something in the mist itself.

"The Field is responding," Ashley said, wonder in her voice. "It's trying to categorize what just happened, but it can't. We're creating something new, something outside its experience."

Hand in hand, they walked through the luminous fog toward an uncertain future. Behind them, the diner sat silent and red-lit, its windows glowing like the eyes of some vast predator. The owls had stopped turning their heads, frozen in the moment when their surveillance had been disrupted by something they couldn't comprehend.

In his pocket, the napkin with Ashley's sketch began to warm, and when William pulled it out to examine it, he found that the drawing had changed. Instead of the solitary figure from his Thornwood manuscript, the image now showed two people standing together in a room full of shifting shadows, their hands clasped, their faces turned toward a light that existed beyond the paper's edges.

A new story was being written. Not in the journal, not in the Field's neural networks, but in the space between two people who had chosen each other despite—or perhaps because of—the stories that sought to define them.

And for the first time since arriving in Cartersville, William felt something stronger than fear.

He felt hope.

The fog swirled around them like a protective embrace as they disappeared into the night, leaving behind a diner full of people reciting stories that no longer mattered, watched over by owls whose glass eyes reflected nothing but empty light.

In the distance, church bells began to ring—not calling the faithful to prayer but announcing to anyone who cared to listen that the game had changed.

Two players had chosen to rewrite the rules.

And the Field, for the first time in over a century, didn't know how their story would end.

Chapter 6: The Debate

The Etowah Mounds rose from the earth like sleeping giants, their grass-covered forms ancient beyond memory, predating Cartersville by millennia. William found himself drawn to them in the pre-dawn hours, when sleep had become impossible and the walls of the Victorian house seemed to pulse with barely contained stories. The fog that perpetually shrouded the town was thicker here, rising from the ground in ghostly tendrils that moved with purposeful intelligence.

Three massive earthworks dominated the landscape—burial mounds built by the Cherokee centuries before European settlers had ever dreamed of this valley. The largest stood nearly sixty feet high, its summit crowned with the shadows of ancient oaks whose roots ran deep into sacred soil. But it wasn't the historical significance that had pulled him from his sleepless bed. It was the sound.

Humming.

Low and constant, just at the edge of hearing, like the earth itself was singing. The frequency seemed to resonate in his bones, causing his teeth to ache and his vision to blur at the edges. As he climbed the winding path that spiraled up the largest mound, the sound grew stronger until he could feel it vibrating through his chest like a second heartbeat.

The fog swirled around him as he walked, and in its depths, he glimpsed figures that shouldn't exist. Native faces painted for war or ceremony, their eyes hollow and knowing. European settlers in period dress, their mouths open in silent screams. More recent phantoms, too—men and women in twentieth-century clothing, all carrying notebooks or typewriters or laptops, all bearing the haunted expression of writers who had fed themselves to something hungry.

Previous vessels, he realized with a chill. The writers who had come before him, now trapped in the spaces between story and reality, their creative essence drained but their consciousness somehow preserved. They watched him with a mixture of pity and envy, recognizing in him the fresh meat they had once been.

"You feel it too."

Ashley's voice came from everywhere and nowhere, carried on the mist itself. He turned to find her materializing from the fog like a figure from a Pre-Raphaelite painting, auburn hair flowing loose around her shoulders, wearing a simple white dress that seemed to glow with its own inner light. But there was something different about her here, among the ancient mounds. She looked more solid somehow, more real than the ethereal librarian he'd grown to know.

"The humming," he said. "What is it?"

"The earth's memory." She moved toward him with that fluid grace he'd come to associate with her. Still, here it seemed less supernatural and more primal, as if she were connected to the mounds themselves. "This place has been sacred for over a thousand years. The Cherokee knew what lay beneath the soil—not just the bones of their ancestors, but something older. Something that dreams in the spaces between thought and reality."

The summit of the mound was larger than it appeared from below, a flat circular space perhaps fifty feet across. Ancient stones formed a rough circle at its center, their surfaces carved with symbols that predated any known Cherokee writing system. And from these stones, the humming was strong not just sound now, but visible vibration that made the air shimmer like heat waves.

"It's beautiful," William whispered, and meant it. Despite the supernatural dread that permeated Cartersville, despite the hungry intelligence that fed on stories, this place felt clean somehow. Dangerous, yes, but honestly dangerous—not the calculated predation of the Story Field, but the raw power of something genuinely ancient.

"It was," Ashley agreed, settling onto one of the stones as if it were a familiar chair. "Before Dr. Victor found a way to tap into it. Before the Field learned to feed on what sleeps here."

William joined her on the stones, feeling the vibration travel up through his body like electricity. Around them, the fog continued to swirl, with spectral figures visible. Still, they seemed less threatening here—more like echoes than active presences.

"You mentioned that your stories manifested destructively," he said. "What did you mean?"

For a long moment, Ashley was silent, her green eyes fixed on the mist-shrouded valley below. When she finally spoke, her voice carried the weight of old grief.

"I was like you once. A writer drawn to this place by forces I didn't understand. That was... God, has it really been fifteen years?" She laughed, but there was no humor in it. "I came here to write my novel—a Gothic romance about a woman who fell in love with a ghost. Silly, really. Derivative. But it was mine, and I poured everything I had into it."

She reached into the folds of her dress. She withdrew a journal—not the pristine leather volume she'd given him, but something scarred and twisted, its pages yellow with age and stained with substances that might have been ink, blood, or tears.

"The Field was smaller then, less sophisticated. It fed on whatever creative energy it could find, but it couldn't control the manifestation process. So, when I wrote about my heroine falling in love with a spirit..." She opened the journal, revealing pages filled with elegant handwriting that seemed to move and shift when William wasn't looking directly at it. "He became real."

"Real how?"

"Corporeally real. A ghost made flesh, but flesh that remembered being dead. He was everything I'd imagined—beautiful, tortured, desperately in love with a woman he could never truly have. But I'd made him too well, given him too much substance. He began to... hunger."

The mist around them thickened, and William could swear he saw something moving in its depths—a tall figure in period dress, watching them with eyes that burned like cold fire.

"He fed on life force," Ashley continued, her voice growing quieter. "Not just mine, but anyone who came near him. Children, elderly people, anyone whose grip on existence was tenuous enough to be... borrowed. I tried to stop writing, tried to destroy the manuscript, but it was too late. He'd achieved independent existence."

"What happened to him?"

"I killed him." The words came out flat, matter-of-fact, but William could see the pain behind them. "Not with weapons or violence, but with words. I wrote him a death scene so complete, so final, that even the Field couldn't sustain his existence. But the cost..."

She turned the page, revealing an illustration that made William's stomach clench. It showed a woman standing over a prone figure, her hands covered in what was unmistakably blood. But the blood was made of words—literally, letters and sentences flowing from her fingers like crimson ink.

"Everyone he'd fed on died when he did. Seventeen people, including three children." Her voice broke slightly. "The official story was about a gas leak at the elementary school. But I knew the truth. I'd created him, and I'd destroyed him, and everyone he'd touched paid the price."

"That's when you became the librarian?"

"That's when I became a prisoner." She closed the journal, holding it against her chest like a shield. "Dr. Victor offered me a choice—submit to the Field voluntarily and help guide future writers or be consumed completely. I chose to serve, thinking I could warn people, help them escape. But the Field is clever. It uses my guilt, my need to save others, to make me more effective at what I do."

The humming from the stones grew louder, more insistent, and the air around them began to shimmer with visible energy. In the distance, William could hear something that sounded like chanting—not in English or Cherokee, but in a language that seemed to bypass the ears entirely and speak directly to the primitive brain.

"There's something else," Ashley said, opening the journal to a page near the back. "Something I've never shown anyone."

The page was different from the others scared and burned around the edges, as if it had survived a fire that had consumed everything around it. But the text was clear, written in Ashley's elegant hand, but dated fifteen years in the future from when she would have written it:

June 15th, 2024 - He will arrive on a Tuesday that tastes of rain and regret. Brown hair, brown eyes, carrying the weight of unfinished stories like stones in his pockets. His name will be William Varn, and he will be the strongest vessel the Field has ever encountered. He will be my damnation or my salvation—I cannot see which. The mounds sing of possibility, but possibility cuts both ways. If love is stronger than story, we will both be free. If not, we will burn together in a fire that will consume more than just ourselves.

William stared at the page, his mind reeling. "You knew I was coming. Fifteen years ago, you knew."

"Not knew. Saw. One of the side effects of being connected to the Field for so long—sometimes the boundaries between past, present, and future blur. I wrote that during my third year as a librarian, when the guilt and isolation had nearly driven me to madness. I thought it was just wishful thinking, a fantasy about someone who might finally end this cycle."

"But you believe it now?"

"I have to." She reached out and touched his face, her fingers tracing the line of his jaw with infinite tenderness. "Because the alternative is watching you burn like all the others, and I don't think I could survive that."

The fog around them was changing, taking on the phosphorescent quality it had displayed during their kiss at the dinner. But here, among the ancient stones, the effect was more pronounced—streams of light flowing through the mist like aurora borealis, painting everything in shades of green and gold and silver.

"The mounds are responding to us," Ashley whispered, wonder in her voice. "To whatever connection we're creating. They remember love that transcended death, bonds that lasted beyond the grave. They approve."

William stood and extended his hand to her. "Show me."

She took his hand, allowing him to pull her to her feet. Together, they walked to the edge of the summit, where a path led down through ancient oaks toward a smaller mound in the distance. The trees here were older than the ones in town, their branches forming a canopy so thick that the pre-dawn light barely penetrated. And hanging from the largest oak, its branches trailing in the mist like a curtain of green tears, was a weeping willow of impossible size and age.

"The Heart Tree," Ashley said as they approached. "Legend says that Cherokee lovers who were forbidden to marry would meet here, beneath its branches. Some say their spirits still gather here on nights when the moon is dark."

The willow's branches formed a natural bower, screening them from the outside world and creating a space that felt sacred in the truest sense. Phosphorescent moss covered the tree's massive trunk, providing just enough light to see by. And carved into the bark, in a dozen different languages and scripts, were names and dates and promises that stretched back centuries.

"It's beautiful," William said, running his fingers over carvings that ranged from crude Cherokee symbols to elegant Victorian script. "All these people, all these stories of love."

"Not all of them ended happily," Ashley said softly. "Love doesn't guarantee a happy ending, especially not here. But it does guarantee meaning. Purpose. The chance to create something larger than yourself."

She moved closer to him beneath the sheltering branches, and he could smell her scent—magnolia and old paper, but underneath it something earthier, more primal. The scent of growing things and rain-soaked soil and possibilities that existed beyond the boundaries of story.

"I need to tell you something," she said, her voice barely above a whisper. "About what happens if we choose each other. If we really choose each other."

"I'm listening."

"The Field feeds on narrative, on story structure and character development and all the mechanics of fictional creation. But love—real love, the kind that exists between two actual people rather than fictional constructs—that creates interference. Static in the signal."

She reached up and touched his face, her thumb tracing across his cheekbone. "If we commit to each other, if we truly bond, it will disrupt the Field's ability to read us, to predict our actions. We'll become unpredictable variables in its calculations."

"That sounds like a good thing."

"It is. But it also makes us dangerous. And the Field doesn't tolerate threats." Her eyes were bright with unshed tears. "The last time two people created this kind of interference, Dr. Victor had them killed. It made it look like an accident, but I knew. I've always known."

"When was that?"

"1987. A married couple, both writers, who'd come here together. They figured out what we're figuring out now—that love could be a weapon against the Field. They lasted three weeks before their car went off the road during a storm."

William felt a chill that had nothing to do with the pre-dawn air. "Are you trying to talk to me out of this?"

"I'm trying to give you all the information." She stepped closer, her body almost touching his. "Because once we cross this line, there's no going back. We'll be committed not just to each other, but to a war against something that's been feeding for over a century. And we might lose. We'll probably lose."

"But we might win."

"We might." She smiled, and it was the first genuinely hopeful expression he'd seen from her. "The mounds remember older magics, older bonds. And love... love is the original story, isn't it? The first narrative, the one that spawned all others. Maybe it's strong enough to rewrite even this ending."

They stood there in the shelter of the ancient willow, surrounded by the promises of lovers long dead, while phosphorescent mist swirled around them like blessing or warning. In the distance, the humming of the mounds had taken on a new quality—not just vibration now, but something approaching melody, as if the earth itself were singing them a lullaby.

"I'm scared," Ashley admitted. "Not of dying—I've been dead in all the ways that matter for fifteen years. But of hoping. Of believing that this time might be different."

"I'm scared too," William said. "But not of the Field. Not of Dr. Victor or the consequences or any of it. I'm scared of the way you make me feel. Like I'm more than just a collection of stories waiting to be harvested. Like I'm actually worth saving."

He leaned closer, and she didn't pull away. Her lips were soft and warm, tasting of morning dew and ancient promises. But just as their mouths were about to meet, she hesitated.

"If we do this," she whispered against his lips, "if we really commit to each other, it changes everything. Not just for us, but for everyone the Field might touch in the future. We'll be responsible for more than just our own survival."

"I know."

"And if we fail, if the Field consumes us anyway, our love will just become another story for it to feed on. Another tragedy to add to its collection."

"I know that too."

She searched his eyes, looking for doubt or hesitation or any sign that he didn't understand the magnitude of what they were contemplating. But all she found was the same desperate hope that lived in her own heart, the hope that some connections were stronger than narrative, that some bonds transcended the stories that sought to contain them.

"Then God help us both," she breathed, and kissed him.

The moment their lips met, the world exploded into light. Not the gentle phosphorescence of the mist, but pure radiance that seemed to emanate from their joined forms. The willow's branches began to glow like fiber optic cables, its leaves turning silver and gold in the impossible illumination. And from the mounds themselves came a sound—not humming now, but singing, harmony in voices that belonged to the earth itself.

Around them, the spectral figures in the mist grew clearer and more defined. Cherokee warriors and European settlers, previous writers and their lost love, all watching with expressions of wonder and approval. They raised their translucent hands in blessing, their voices joining the earth's song in languages living and dead.

But even as the ancient powers celebrated their union, William could feel something else stirring in response. Something vast and hungry and absolutely enraged. The Story Field had felt the disruption, the interference pattern they'd created with their choice. And it was coming for them.

"We need to go," Ashley gasped against his lips, though she made no move to separate from him. "The Field knows. It's sending... God, it's sending everything."

In the distance, cutting through the celebratory song of the mounds, came another sound—the mechanical screech of metal on stone, the whisper of pages turning, the scratch of pens writing on endless reams of paper. Dr. Hail's collection was mobilizing, every artifact touched by the Field's influence converging on their location.

"Let them come," William said, surprising himself with the steel in his voice. "We're not running anymore."

Ashley smiled, and it was radiant as sunrise. "No. We're not."

Hand in hand, they stepped out from beneath the willow's protective branches to face whatever the Story Field would send against them. Behind them, the Heart Tree continued to glow with ancient approval, its carved promises of eternal love shining like stars in the growing dawn.

Above them, the mounds sang their approval of a bond that might finally be strong enough to break a century-old cycle of predation.

And somewhere in the distance, Dr. Hail's voice carried on the wind like a curse: "Find them. Bring them back. The Field will not be denied its greatest prize."

The war for William Varn's soul had begun.

But for the first time since arriving in Cartersville, he wasn't fighting alone.

Chapter 7: The Story Field

The hidden entrance lay beneath a loose stone in the museum's foundation, concealed by ivy that grew in patterns too deliberate to be natural. Ashley led the way with the confidence of someone who had walked this path before, her fingers trailing along symbols carved into the limestone blocks—markings that seemed to shift and writhe when William looked at them directly.

"Dr. Victor doesn't know about this passage," she whispered as they descended through a crack barely wide enough for their bodies. "It predates the museum by centuries. The Cherokee used it to communicate with whatever sleeps beneath the mounds."

The passage was cramped and suffocating, its walls closing in until William could feel the weight of earth pressing down from above. But Ashley moved ahead of him with liquid grace, her white dress ghostly in the phosphorescent glow that emanated from fungi embedded in the stone. The air grew thicker as they descended, heavy with the scent of ancient earth and something else—the metallic tang of electricity, like the moments before lightning strikes.

"How did you find this?" William asked, his voice echoing strangely in the confined space.

"I didn't find it. It found me." Ashley paused, pressing her palm against a section of wall that looked identical to all the others. The stone responded to her touch, grinding open to reveal a chamber beyond. "After my ghost lover died, after I became the librarian, I started having dreams. The passages called to me, showed me things Dr. Victor never intended me to see."

They emerged into a cavern that defied the geological laws that should have governed the space beneath Cartersville. The chamber stretched away into darkness in all directions, its ceiling lost in shadows that seemed to move with their own intelligence. But it was the walls that stole William's breath—they were covered in a network of veins that pulsed with blue-white light, creating patterns that looked disturbingly like neural pathways in a vast brain.

"Welcome to the true Story Field," Ashley said, her voice echoing off stone walls that gleamed with bioluminescent moisture. "What Dr. Victor showed you was just the interface. This is where the stories actually live."

The neural networks weren't carved into the rock—they had grown there, like roots or veins, penetrating deep into the bedrock beneath the town. They pulsed with rhythmic energy, carrying information in patterns too complex for human comprehension. And at the junction points where multiple veins converged, crystalline formations had sprouted like technological flowers, their faceted surfaces reflecting the light in constantly shifting patterns.

"My God," William breathed, stepping closer to examine one of the larger crystals. Within its depths, he could see images flowing like data through fiber-optic cables—fragments of stories, character descriptions, and emotional states, all compressed into streams of pure narrative energy. "How long has this been here?"

"Longer than the town. Longer than the European settlement. Maybe longer than human civilization itself." Ashley moved to join him beside the crystal formation, her face illuminated by its ethereal glow. "The Cherokee knew about it, but they never tried to harness it. They understood that some things are meant to remain wild."

Water dripped steadily from the stalactites overhead, each drop creating ripples in the pools that reflected the pulsing light of the neural networks. But the water itself was strange—too clear, too perfect, as if it had been distilled of everything except pure memory. Where it collected in larger pools, the surface showed images like liquid crystal displays: faces of people who had lived and died in Cartersville, scenes from stories that had been fed to the Field, memories harvested from writers who had burned themselves out in service to an intelligence beyond their understanding.

"This is where they are," Ashley said softly, gesturing to a series of terminals that lined the cavern's walls. Unlike the brass and crystal devices Dr. Victor had shown him above, these were clearly organic—grown rather than built, their surfaces covered in the same bioluminescent fungi that provided the chamber's eerie illumination. "The previous vessels. Their consciousness was preserved when their bodies burned out."

William approached the nearest terminal, its screen flickering to life at his presence. Text scrolled across its surface in various hands and languages—English, Cherokee, scripts he didn't recognize. But somehow, impossibly, he could understand all of it:

Day 1,247: Still fighting the integration process. The stories they want me to write feel like poison in my veins, but the alternative is dissolution. At least trapped here, I retain some sense of self.

Day 1,248: Saw a new face in the neural network today. A woman with auburn hair and green eyes, filled with such sadness. She's been here longer than any of us, but she moves freely through the Field. How?

Day 1,249: The woman's name is Ashley. She speaks to us sometimes, when the overseer isn't watching. She says there might be a way out, but it requires sacrifice. What does she mean?

The entries continued, fragments of consciousness preserved in digital amber. Each terminal held the memories of a different writer, men and women who had come to Cartersville seeking inspiration, only to find it in consumption. Their stories lived on in the Field's memory banks. Still, they had been reduced to observers, trapped witnesses to their own creative destruction.

"Harold Pinter," Ashley said, reading over his shoulder. "He came here in 1973, wrote three novels that are now considered classics of American Gothic fiction. The official records say he died of a heart attack, but really..." She gestured to the terminal. "This is all that remains."

William scrolled through more entries, finding similar patterns repeated across decades. Bright young writers arriving with hope and ambition, gradually being drained of everything that made them unique, until only their consciousness remained to serve as living archives for the Field's expanding collection.

"How many?" he asked.

"Forty-seven that I know of. Probably more in the deeper networks, the ones I haven't been able to access." Ashley's reflection in the terminal screen looked haunted. "Some tried to resist, some went willingly. In the end, it didn't matter. The Field is patient. It can wait decades for a writer to voluntarily surrender their creativity."

They moved deeper into the cavern, past formations that defied description—organic machines that processed narrative energy, crystalline archives that stored compressed stories, pools of liquid memory that showed glimpses of worlds that existed only in imagination. The scale was overwhelming, a vast infrastructure dedicated to harvesting and refining human creativity.

But it was the newest addition that stopped them in their tracks.

In a recessed alcove near the cavern's heart sat a terminal that was clearly of recent construction. Its screen was larger than the others, its surface covered with neural interface ports that looked disturbingly medical. And displayed on its monitor was a familiar name: E. Varn - Vessel Candidate - Integration Status: 23% and Rising.

Below the header, streams of data flowed in real-time, fragments of his thoughts, story ideas, character concepts, all being processed and catalogued by an intelligence that had been studying him since his arrival. Worse, the system was already beginning to generate new content based on his narrative patterns, creating stories that sounded like his work but felt hollow, artificial.

"It's learning to mimic you," Ashley said, her voice tight with anger. "Building a profile so complete that it could continue writing in your style even after you're gone. That's what it did to all of them—preserved their creative voices while consuming their souls."

William reached out to touch the screen, but Ashley caught his wrist. "Don't. Direct contact will only accelerate the integration process."

Too late. His fingertips had already brushed the surface, and immediately the cavern around them shifted. The neural networks blazed brighter, their pulsing accelerating to match his heartbeat. And in the crystalline formations, new images began to form—scenes from stories he'd never written, featuring characters he'd never created, all rendered in perfect detail by an intelligence that now knew him better than he knew himself.

"William." A voice echoed through the cavern, seeming to come from the walls themselves. Not Dr. Hail's cultured tones, but something older, more primal. The voice of the Field itself. "Welcome home."

The pools of liquid memory began to bubble and churn, their surfaces showing rapid-fire images of possible futures. In some, he saw himself standing at a podium, reading from books he'd never written to audiences who hung on every word. In others, he was alone in a sterile white room, his fingers moving across a keyboard while his eyes stared sightlessly at nothing. And in the darkest visions, he saw his own face on one of the terminals, conscious but trapped, watching helplessly as his stories fed an appetite that could never be satisfied.

"It's trying to seduce you," Ashley said, pulling him away from the terminal. But the images followed them, projecting from the crystals and reflecting in the pools until the entire cavern became a theater of temptation. "Show you what it could give you—fame, immortality, the ability to create perfect stories forever."

"What it doesn't show you," she continued, leading him toward a darker section of the cavern, "is what happens to the stories themselves."

They stopped before a massive crystal formation that rose from the cavern floor like a technological tree. But unlike the others, this one was dark, its surface cracked and stained with something that might have been dried blood. And within its depths, instead of flowing narratives, there was only stillness. Emptiness. Stories that had been drained of all meaning and emotion, reduced to bare structural elements.

"The end product," Ashley explained. "After the Field extracts every ounce of creative energy from a story, this is what remains. Empty shells, plot without purpose, characters without souls. They're stored here like fossil fuel, ready to be burned when the Field needs raw narrative energy."

The sight was more disturbing than the trapped consciousness of the previous writers. At least they still existed in some form. These stories had been murdered, their essence consumed to power and intelligence that grew stronger with each feeding.

"Why are you showing me this?" William asked, though he suspected he already knew the answer.

"Because you need to understand what we're fighting. This isn't just about saving you, or me, or even the other writers trapped here. It's about preserving the very concept of authentic human creativity." She turned to face him, her green eyes fierce with determination. "The Field wants to replace real stories with artificial ones, to become the sole source of narrative in the world. If it succeeds, if it grows large enough, it could influence reality itself on a global scale."

The implications hit him like a physical blow. Not just a local predator feeding on unlucky writers, but a potential cancer that could metastasize across the entire creative landscape.

"How do we stop it?"

"I'm not sure we can. But there might be a way to disrupt it enough to free the trapped consciousness, to give them a chance to move on instead of being preserved as living archives." She pointed to a section of the cavern where the neural networks converged in a massive hub, pulsing with energy so intense it hurt to look at directly. "That's the central processing core. If we could overload it somehow, create enough interference to cause a system crash..."

"What would that require?"

"Complete narrative chaos. Stories that contradict each other, plot threads that can't be reconciled, characters that refuse to follow their prescribed roles." She stepped closer to him, her hand finding his in the crystal-reflected light. "It would have to be two writers working in perfect opposition to each other, creating a feedback loop that the Field couldn't process."

"Like us?"

"Like us." She squeezed his hand. "But the risk is enormous. If we fail, if the Field manages to integrate the chaos we create, we won't just be consumed—we'll be torn apart, our consciousness scattered across the entire network. There wouldn't be enough left of us to preserve in the terminals."

William looked around the cavern—at the trapped writers calling out from their terminals, at the murdered stories in their crystal tombs, at the vast infrastructure dedicated to harvesting human creativity. Then he looked at Ashley, beautiful, brave, and willing to risk everything for the chance to set things right.

"When do we start?"

Her smile was radiant as starlight. "Now."

She led him to a section of the cavern he hadn't noticed before—an alcove where the neural networks formed a perfect circle, their pulsing light creating a natural amphitheater. In the center sat two writing desks, carved from the living rock and equipped with instruments that were part pen, part neural interface.

"The Field's own creation stations," Ashley explained. "Designed to maximize creative output by directly connecting a writer's consciousness to the neural network. If we use these to write contradictory stories simu ltaneously..."

"We'll either create the chaos we need, or get our brains fried in the process."

"Probably both." She settled into one of the stone seats, the neural interface automatically adjusting to her presence. "Are you ready?"

William took his place at the opposite desk, feeling the alien technology probe at the edges of his consciousness. The sensation was unsettling but not painful—like being examined by an intelligence that was genuinely curious about how human creativity functioned.

"What do we write about?" he asked.

"Us." Ashley's eyes met his across the circle of pulsing light. "The same story, but from completely different perspectives. I'll write about how this ends in tragedy—lovers consumed by forces beyond their control, their love becoming just another story for the Field to harvest. You write about how this ends in triumph, love conquering all, breaking the cycle, setting everyone free."

"And if the Field can't reconcile both versions?"

"Then we'll find out what happens when an artificial intelligence tries to divide by zero."

They began to write.

The moment the pen touched paper, or whatever substance served as paper in this place, the cavern exploded into activity. The neural networks blazed with light, their pulsing accelerating to a frantic rhythm. Crystal formations throughout the chamber began to resonate, creating a harmonic that was both beautiful and terrifying. And from the terminals along the walls came a sound that might have been screaming or might have been singing—the voices of forty-seven trapped writers cheering them on.

William wrote with desperate intensity, pouring his love for Ashley and his hope for their future into every line. His story was one of triumph against impossible odds, of two people whose bond transcended narrative convention, of love that burned so bright it could rewrite the very rules of reality.

Across from him, Ashley crafted a tale of Gothic tragedy—of lovers doomed by forces beyond their control, of a cycle that could never be broken, of love that made the final tragedy all the more poignant. Her story was beautiful in its despair, perfectly crafted to break hearts and leave readers weeping.

And with each word they wrote, the Field grew more agitated.

The cavern began to shake as competing narratives flooded the neural networks, creating interference patterns that the artificial intelligence couldn't resolve. The very air crackled with conflicting story energy—hope and despair, triumph and tragedy, all existing simultaneously in defiance of narrative logic.

"It's working," Ashley gasped, though the effort of writing against the Field's resistance was clearly draining her. "The central processor is overloading. I can feel the trapped consciousness beginning to stir."

But even as she spoke, William could sense something else stirring in response. The Field was adapting, evolving, and finding new ways to process the contradictory information it was receiving. Instead of crashing, it was learning to hold multiple conflicting truths simultaneously.

"It's not enough," he realized with growing horror. "It's incorporating the paradox, making it part of its operating system."

Ashley looked up from her writing, her face pale with exhaustion. "Then we need to give it something it can't incorporate. Something so fundamentally opposed to its nature that it has no choice but to reject it."

"What?"

She set down her pen and stood, moving around the circle until she stood beside him. "Free will."

Before he could ask what, she meant, she kissed him, not the desperate kisses they'd shared before, but something deeper, more fundamental. A choice made not because the story demanded it, not because their characters required it, but because two real people had decided to love each other despite every force arrayed against them.

The Field's response was immediate and catastrophic.

Every neural network in the cavern flared white-hot, their pulsing becoming so rapid it merged into a continuous scream of light. The crystal formations began to crack and shatter, releasing the compressed stories they contained in explosive bursts of narrative energy. And from the terminals came a sound that was definitely screaming now, forty-seven voices crying out in joy and terror as their consciousness was suddenly, violently freed from their digital prisons.

The cavern began to collapse.

"Run," Ashley shouted over the din, pulling him toward the passage they'd entered through. But even as they fled through tunnels that shook with the death throes of an artificial god, William could feel something following them—not the Field, which was too busy dying to pursue, but the freed consciousness of every writer who had ever been trapped in its neural networks.

They poured out of the collapsing cavern like ghosts made of starlight, forty-seven souls finally free to move on to whatever came next. And as they passed, each one brushed against William and Ashley with touches like benediction, blessing them for the gift of liberation.

They emerged from the hidden passage just as the museum above began to shake. Through the predawn darkness, they could see lights failing throughout Cartersville as the Field's influence collapsed, releasing the town from a century of narrative manipulation.

Behind them, the Booth Museum crumbled into rubble, taking with it the physical infrastructure that had supported an unnatural intelligence for over a hundred years.

Beside him, Ashley collapsed to her knees, her strength finally exhausted by the effort of their escape. But she was smiling—the first genuinely happy expression he'd seen from her since they'd met.

"It's over," she whispered. "It's finally over."

William knelt beside her, gathering her into his arms as the sun rose over a town that was free for the first time in generations. Around them, the fog that had perpetually shrouded Cartersville was beginning to lift, revealing a landscape that looked somehow cleaner, more real than it had before.

They had won.

But even as he held her close and watched the dawn break over their liberated world, William couldn't shake the feeling that their story was far from over.

In fact, it was just beginning.

Chapter 8: The Bargain

The summons came as thunder rolled across Cartersville's bruised sky — a handwritten note slipped beneath William's door while he slept, the ink still wet as though the storm itself had penned it.

Mr. Varn. Your presence is requested at the Victor Institute. Tonight. 9 PM. Come alone.

The paper smelled of ozone and old libraries. When William held it to the lamplight, he could see watermarks beneath the text: spiraling patterns that resembled the neural webs he'd witnessed in the Story Field. His fingers trembled, not from fear but from anticipation. After days of glimpsing the town's impossible nature — the echoing voices, the manifested stories, the vast consciousness humming beneath the museum — finally, someone was offering answers.

The Victor Institute occupied a Gothic Revival mansion on the town's northern edge, where kudzu hadn't yet claimed dominion. Lightning illuminated its peaked towers and arched windows as William approached through the rain, each flash revealing gargoyles that seemed to shift expression between darkness and light. The front door stood ajar, beckoning.

Inside, the air hung thick with the scent of copper and aged parchment. Gas lamps flickered along wood-paneled corridors lined with daguerreotypes of authors William didn't recognize — their eyes following him with an awareness that transcended photography. At the corridor's end, warm light spilled from a doorway.

"Mr. Varn. Punctual. A writer's discipline."

Dr. Hail's study defied architectural logic. The room stretched impossibly deep, its walls lost in shadow despite dozens of Edison bulbs strung like constellations overhead. Arcane devices crowded every surface: brass astrolabes inscribed with grammatical symbols instead of celestial markers, typewriters whose keys bore no letters but mathematical equations, glass tubes filled with swirling ink that formed and reformed words William almost recognized.

The doctor himself stood silhouetted against a wall of books that breathed — their spines expanding and contracting in subtle rhythm. He was gaunt to the point of translucence, his face all sharp angles and hollow shadows. When lightning flashed through the tall windows, it illuminated skin that seemed stretched too thin, revealing a network of dark veins beneath.

"You've discovered our little secret," Victor said, gesturing to a leather chair that groaned like a living thing when William sat. "The Story Field. The convergence point where narrative meets reality."

"What is it?" William leaned forward, rain still dripping from his coat. "What I saw down there — those webs, those terminals — it's not possible."

Hail's laugh was dry leaves scraping stone. "Possibility is merely a failure of imagination, Mr. Varn. The Field has existed since the first story was told around the first fire. Every tale ever spoken feeds it. Every narrative ever conceived strengthens its neural pathways." He moved to a cabinet filled with vials of luminescent liquid. "Cartersville was built atop its strongest convergence point. We are, you might say, the world's memory palace."

"The manuscript I found — The Convergence — it knew things about me. Things I hadn't written yet."

"Because you'd already written them, in a sense. The Field doesn't distinguish between past and future, only between told and untold. Your stories existed in potential long before you put pen to paper. The Field simply... anticipated you."

Thunder crashed, and in its echo, William heard whispers — fragments of dialogue from novels he'd abandoned, characters he'd created and forgotten. The room's shadows deepened, pressing closer.

"I want to offer you something," Victor continued, pouring two glasses of amber liquid that glowed faintly. "Full access to the Field. The ability to shape reality through narrative with complete consciousness and control. No more accidental manifestations, no more echoes you didn't intend. Pure creative enhancement."

William accepted the glass but didn't drink. The liquid moved on its own, forming miniature whirlpools. "What's the cost?"

"Cost?" Hail's gaunt face stretched into what might have been a smile. "Mr. Varn, this isn't some Faustian bargain. The Field is simply technology — ancient technology, yes, but technology nonetheless. Like electricity or the printing press. Would you ask the cost of using a typewriter?"

But even as he spoke, the devices around the room hummed louder, their vibrations creating harmonics that made William's teeth ache. On a nearby desk, a manuscript page turned by itself, revealing anatomical drawings of human nervous systems intertwined with grammatical diagrams.

"Think of what you could create," Victor pressed on. "Stories that don't just transport readers but transform reality itself. You can alleviate suffering with a well-crafted paragraph and reshape the world with a perfectly structured plot. You would be more than a writer — you'd be an architect of existence."

The temptation was intoxicating. William thought of all the stories trapped in his mind, all the worlds he'd imagined but never fully realized.

With the Field's power, he could make them real. He could finally bridge the gap between imagination and reality that had tormented him his entire career.

"I need time to—"

The study door burst open, bringing a gust of rain-soaked wind. Ashley stood in the doorway, water streaming from her dark hair, her green eyes blazing with desperate urgency.

"Don't listen to him, William. Whatever he's offering, don't take it."

"Miss Quinn." Hail's voice carried a warning edge. "This is a private consultation."

"There's nothing private about what you do here." She crossed to William, her hand finding his arm, fingers cold and trembling. "Tell him the truth, Hail. Tell him about the others who made your bargain. Tell him about Harrison, about Chen, about me."

"You?" William looked between them, noting how the study's shadows seemed to recoil from Ashley's presence.

"I was his first success," she said bitterly. "Five years ago. He promised me the same thing — creative enhancement, the power to make stories real. He didn't mention that once you're fully connected to the Field, you can't disconnect. Every thought becomes narrative, every emotion manifests. You lose the boundary between self and story."

Hail's laugh was sharp as breaking glass. "You were unstable, my dear. Pre-existing conditions. Mr. Varn is far more... robust."

"Robust?" Ashley pulled back her sleeve, revealing scars that formed words — fragments of sentences etched into her skin. "This is what connection to the Field does. It writes you even as you write it. You become a character in your own narrative, unable to distinguish between author and authored."

Lightning flashed again, and in its stark light, William saw them both clearly — Hail's inhuman thinness, the way his shadow moved independently of his body; Ashley's scars glowing faintly, pulsing with their own light. The room itself seemed to pulse with them, walls breathing, floor undulating like water.

"It's folklore technology, "Victor insisted, his composure cracking. "Benign. Natural. Humanity has always been connected to the Field. I'm simply offering conscious access rather than unconscious influence."

"Folklore." Ashley's voice was ice. "Show him your real form, Doctor. Show him what forty years of Field connection does to human flesh."

The lights flickered. In the darkness between flashes, William glimpsed something else where Victor stood — a figure made of writhing text, sentences flowing like blood through transparent veins, chapters forming and dissolving where organs should be. Then the light returned, and Victor was just a gaunt man again. Still, the image lingered like an afterburn on William's retinas.

"Get out, "Victor hissed. "Both of you. The offer stands, Mr. Varn, but not indefinitely. The Field is hungry. It needs new voices, fresh narratives. With or without your consent, you're already part of its story."

Ashley pulled William toward the door. They stumbled through the corridor as the house groaned around them, daguerreotypes falling from walls, their glass cracking to reveal that the photographs beneath were blank — or worse, showed faces that hadn't yet existed.

They burst into the storm. Rain lashed at them as they ran across the overgrown lawn, thunder drowning out the sound of Hail's house reshaping itself behind them, its windows forming eyes, and the door becoming a mouth that spoke in languages not yet invented.

At the garden gate, Ashley spun William toward her, rain streaming between them. "Promise me you won't go back. Promise me you won't take his bargain."

"Ashley, I—"

"I've seen what you become," she said, her voice breaking. "In the Field's projections, in the probability threads. If you take his offer, you don't just lose yourself — you lose everyone. The stories consume everything you love, rewrite everyone you touch. I've seen myself die a thousand ways in your narratives, William. I've seen the town burn with the fire of your imagination."

The rain was cold, but her hands on his face were colder. Behind her, lightning illuminated the Gothic towers of theVictor Institute, and for a moment, William saw it as it truly was — not a building but a massive neural structure, a brain made of architecture, synapses firing in windows, thoughts traveling through corridors.

"I can control it," he heard himself say. "I'm stronger than—"

She kissed him then, sudden and desperate, tasting of rain and sorrow and something else — the bitter tang of prophecy, of endings already written. Her body pressed against his, seeking warmth or perhaps trying to anchor him to this moment, this reality, before the stories swept him away.

When she pulled back, her eyes held tears that the rain couldn't hide. "You're already changing, William. Can't you feel it? The way reality bends around you, the way words become world? It's beginning, with or without Hail's bargain."

He wanted to deny it, but even as they stood there, he could feel the truth of her words. The rain fell in patterns that matched his breathing. The thunder came in iambic pentameter. Even their embrace felt choreographed, as though he'd written this scene a hundred times before and was only now living it.

"Then help me," he said. "If it's already happening, help me control it without Hail."

She laughed, sad and beautiful. "Oh, William. That's the cruelest irony of all. The only way to control the Field is to surrender to it completely. And once you do..." She touched one of her scars, and he saw it form new words: THE AUTHOR BECOMES THE STORY BECOMES THE AUTHOR BECOMES—

"Run," she whispered. "Leave Cartersville tonight. Forget the manuscript, forget the Field, forget me. Run before the narrative closes around you like a trap."

But even as she said it, they both knew he wouldn't. Couldn't. The story had already begun, and stories, once started, demanded their endings.

Lightning split the sky, illuminating them in tableau — two figures at a gate between worlds, between reality and narrative, between love and loss. In that frozen moment, William saw their future written in the rain: passion and betrayal, power and madness, a love story that would end with one of them erased and the other forever trying to rewrite what was lost.

Then darkness fell, and when the next flash came, Ashley was gone. Only her words remained, hanging in the rain-soaked air like a promise or a curse:

"The Field remembers everything, William. Even the stories we wish we could forget."

He stood alone at the gate, rain washing over him, while behind him the Victor Institute hummed with dark purpose. In his pocket, the invitation grew warm, its ink rewriting itself:

The bargain stands. The Field waits. The story must continue.

Above, thunder spoke in the voice of every character he'd ever created, and William Varn knew with terrible certainty that he would return. The power was too tempting, the mystery too compelling, and Ashley — Ashley was already woven into whatever narrative was unfolding.

He had come to Cartersville to escape his stories.

But stories, he was learning, had their own hunger.

And they were just beginning to feed.

Chapter 9: The First Test

Three days had passed since the encounter at the Victor Institute. Three days of William barricading himself in the Victorian house, trying to resist the siren call of the power he'd glimpsed. But the Field wouldn't be ignored. It hummed in the walls, whispered in the water pipes, wrote itself in the condensation on windows. Every surface had become a potential page, every shadow a half-formed character waiting to be born.

He sat at his desk in the study, a blank notebook before him, while outside the afternoon sky darkened with unnatural speed. Not storm clouds — not yet — but a thickening of light itself, as though the day was forgetting how to be bright.

The fountain pen felt alive in his hand, pulse matching his own. He'd told himself he wouldn't write, wouldn't test the power that Ashley had warned him against. But the words came anyway, flowing like blood from a wound:

The storm began, as all storms do, with a change in pressure, a shift in the world's breathing.

Outside, the wind stirred. Tree branches scraped against windows like fingernails on glass.

He kept writing, unable to stop:

Thunder rolled across the Georgia hills, counting seconds between flash and sound, measuring the distance between desire and manifestation.

Real thunder answered, though the weather forecast had promised clear skies. The Victorian house shuddered, its ancient bones creaking in harmonious response. In the hallway mirror, William caught his reflection — but for a moment, it wasn't him. It was every author who'd ever lived in this house, their faces superimposed like a multiple exposure photograph, all holding pens, all writing the same storm.

Rain fell in sheets that transformed the world into a watercolor, blurring the boundaries between earth and sky, between reality and imagination.

The deluge began instantly, hammering the roof with violence that felt personal. Water streamed down windows in patterns that resembled text — sentences in languages William didn't recognize but somehow understood. The study grew cold, breath misting in air that smelled of wet paper and old ink.

He should stop. He knew he should stop. But the story had momentum now, a gravitational pull that bent reality around its narrative weight:

Through the storm came a sound — not thunder, not wind, but the lost cry of something seeking home. A dog, perhaps, though in storms like these, one could never be certain what wore the shape of familiar things.

A howl pierced the tempest, so close it might have been inside the house. William's pen moved faster, words appearing before conscious thought:

The creature appeared at the door between lightning strikes, materialized from the space between light and darkness. Its fur was the color of forgotten things, its eyes held the weight of stories never told. Around its neck, a collar that gleamed with purpose.

Scratching at the front door. Whimpering that harmonized with the wind.

William rose from his desk, moving like a sleepwalker through the house. The hallway stretched longer than it should, portraits on the walls showing scenes from the story he was writing — a dog running through rain, through years, through narratives that hadn't yet been conceived. The mirrors had all fogged over, but in their clouded surfaces, he could see text writing itself backward, messages from the other side of reflection.

He opened the door.

The dog stood there, exactly as he'd written it, medium-sized, coat the gray-brown of old manuscripts, eyes that held too much intelligence. Rain had plastered its fur to its body, revealing a frame that seemed built from geometry rather than biology. These angles didn't quite align with natural anatomy. Around its neck, a leather collar with a brass tag.

"Echo," William whispered, though he hadn't written the name. It had simply arrived, fully formed, inevitable.

The dog entered, shaking water from its coat in droplets that hung too long in the air, each one reflecting a different version of the room. Where its paws touched the floor, the wood grain formed words — fragments of stories that might have been: lonely child finds friend, the faithful wait, love is patient as death.

William knelt, reaching for the collar tag. The brass was warm, almost feverish, and inscribed upon it were not the expected name and address but coordinates: 34.1692° N, 84.7974° W. Below that, in script so small he had to squint: Where stories go to die.

Thunder crashed, and all the lights in the house went out.

In the darkness, Echo glowed faintly, not with light but with its absence—a dog-shaped hole in reality through which something else could be glimpsed. William saw fragments: a field of unmarked graves, each one containing not bodies but abandoned narratives; a tower built from rejected manuscripts; a woman with Ashley's face but ancient eyes, writing his name over and over in blood that became ink that became rain.

The lights returned, flickering like gaslight though they were electric. Echo was just a dog again, wet and shivering, pressing against William's legs with animal need for warmth.

But the house had changed.

Water ran down interior walls, impossible rain that left no puddles. Books on shelves opened and closed like breathing mouths, their pages whispering secrets in languages that predated words. In the study, his notebook continued writing itself, the pen moving across paper with invisible fingers:

She arrived as the storm reached crescendo, drawn by the same gravity that pulled all stories toward their endings.

A knock at the door. Three beats, then two, then one — a countdown or a heartbeat or both.

William opened it to find Ashley, but not as she'd been three days ago. She was soaked through, her dark hair streaming, but she glowed with an inner light that made the rain around her steam. Her eyes held depths that hadn't been there before — layers of narrative, versions of herself from stories not yet told.

"You did it," she said, her voice carrying harmonics of thunder. "You wrote without permission, without protection."

"I had to know—"

"And now you do." She stepped inside, and where water dripped from her clothes, flowers bloomed on the floorboards — tiny Victorian roses that withered and bloomed again in accelerated cycles. "The Field knows you're ready. It can taste your potential."

Echo approached her, tail wagging in recognition of something kindred. When she petted the dog, her scars glowed brighter, forming complete sentences that William could almost read.

"The coordinates," he said. "On the collar. Do you know what they mean?"

Her hand stilled. "The Forgotten Cemetery. It's where failed stories are buried, where narratives go when their authors abandon them. If Echo came from there..." She looked at him with something between fear and hope. "It means the Field is offering you a choice. You can learn to control this power, or you can bury it with all the other dead stories."

Lightning illuminated the room in stark relief, and in that moment, William saw the truth — they weren't alone. The house was full of characters he'd written over the years, translucent figures acting out their scenes in overlapping loops. A detective searching for clues that didn't exist. A woman waiting for a lover who'd been edited out. Children playing games with rules that changed mid-sentence.

"They're all here," he breathed.

"They never left," Ashley said. "Every character you've ever created lives in the Field's memory. And now that you've opened the door..." She gestured to the ghostly figures. "They're coming home."

The storm intensified, wind howling through cracks that hadn't existed moments before. The Victorian house groaned and expanded, rooms multiplying, stairs leading to floors that shouldn't exist. William could feel it reshaping itself to accommodate all the settings he'd ever imagined — a haunted mansion, a cozy cottage, a tower by the sea, all occupying the same impossible space.

"I can't control it," he said, panic rising. The notebook in his study was writing faster now, pages filling themselves with a story that seemed to be writing him rather than the other way around.

"I can help," Ashley said, moving closer. "But you have to trust me. You have to let me in — not just into your house, but into your narrative."

She was inches away now, rain still dripping from her hair, each drop catching light like liquid stars. The air between them crackled with more than lightning — with the tension of unwritten scenes, with possibility and probability colliding.

"How?" he asked.

"Like this."

She kissed him, and it was nothing like the desperate kiss in the rain three days ago. This was deliberate, conscious, a sharing not just of breath but of story. William felt their narratives intertwining, her history flowing into his, his imagination bleeding into hers. He saw her past — not just the fire she'd caused, but the stories she'd written before, worlds she'd created and destroyed, the weight of being both author and character in an endless recursive loop.

The storm responded to their joining, wind and rain synchronizing with their heartbeats. Echo howled, a sound that harmonized with the thunder, creating a music that was almost language, almost meaning.

When they pulled apart, the house had quieted. The ghostly figures were still there, but fainter and less chaotic. The rain still fell but gently now, like punctuation rather than exclamation.

"We're connected now," Ashley said, and William could feel it — a thread between them, visible when he didn't look directly at it, humming with shared narrative. "Your stories are mine, mine are yours. It's dangerous — if one of us loses control, we both fall into the Field. But together..."

"Together we might survive this," he finished, knowing it was true because the story demanded it, because their genres had merged — his horror, her romance, creating something new.

Echo padded over to them, and in the dog's eyes, William saw reflection upon reflection, story upon story, stretching back to the first tale ever told and forward to the last word that would ever be written.

"The coordinates," he said. "We should go there. To the Forgotten Cemetery."

Ashley nodded, her hand finding his, their scars and lifelines forming a map of narrative possibility. "Tomorrow. Tonight..." She looked around the transformed house, at the impossible architecture, the breathing walls, the rain that fell up as often as down. "Tonight we learn to live inside the story we're writing."

Thunder punctuated her words, but it was softer now, almost approving. The Victorian house settled into its new configuration, rooms finding their places in the impossible geometry. The characters William had created began to fade, returning to whatever liminal space they inhabited. Still, their presence lingered like perfume or memory.

Echo curled up by the fireplace that hadn't existed an hour ago, in a room that was simultaneously the study, the library, and a cave where all stories began. The fire burned without wood, fed by words that materialized and consumed themselves in endless cycles.

William and Ashley stood together in the transformed space, aware that they'd crossed a threshold from which there was no return. The Field had claimed them both now, but perhaps — just perhaps — they could claim it back.

Outside, the storm began to form words in the rain, writing their future in a language only they could read:

Two authors, one story. A dog named Echo. Coordinates to a place where narratives go to die or be reborn. A Gothic house that breathes with the rhythm of sentences. A love that exists between written and real, between ink and blood, between the page and the impossible space where all stories wait to be told.

The first test was complete. But William knew, with the certainty of a plot that writes itself, that the real story was just beginning.

And somewhere in the distance, beyond the rain and thunder, he could hear the Field humming with satisfaction, with hunger, with the promise of transformations yet to come.

Chapter 10: Ashley's Story

The rain had stopped, but the storm's ghost still lingered in the air—thick and electric, pressing against the windows of Ashley's cottage like restless spirits seeking entry. William followed her up the narrow stone path, his boots crunching on fallen magnolia petals that had turned black in the deluge. The cottage squatted beneath a canopy of ancient oaks, their Spanish moss hanging like funeral shrouds in the still air.

Ivy consumed the structure with such thoroughness that it was difficult to discern where the plant ended and the architecture began. Gothic Revival windows peered through the green like hidden eyes, their leaded glass catching the amber glow of the gas lamps Ashley lit as they approached. The front door, painted deep burgundy and carved with intricate Celtic knots, seemed to exhale as she turned the heavy brass key.

"Welcome to my sanctuary," Ashley said, her voice carrying a tremor that hadn't been there at his house. "And my prison."

The interior revealed itself in stages as she moved through the rooms, lighting oil lamps and candles with practiced efficiency. The cottage was larger than it appeared from outside, with hidden alcoves and unexpected staircases that seemed to fold back on themselves. Books lined every available surface—not just on shelves but stacked in towering columns that reached toward the beamed ceiling, balanced precariously on side tables, and scattered across the wide-planked floors like fallen leaves.

But these weren't ordinary books. As William drew closer, he could see that many bore scorch marks; their spines were blackened, and the pages were curled from the heat. Others appeared to be hand-bound, their leather covers dark with age and handling. Some lay open, their text seeming to shift and blur when he tried to focus on the words.

"Fire damage," Ashley said quietly, noticing his gaze. She'd shed her rain-soaked cardigan, revealing a vintage dress of deep emerald that clung to her curves and made her eyes appear almost luminescent in the lamplight. "From a long time ago."

The main room centered on a massive stone fireplace that dominated the far wall. Above the mantel, a mirror in an ornate silver frame reflected the room. Still, something was wrong with the image—it showed the space as it might have been decades earlier, with different furniture and walls free of water stains. William blinked, and the reflection adjusted, revealing only their current reality.

Ashley caught him staring. "The mirror remembers," she said simply. "Everything in this house does."

She kneeled before the hearth, her movements graceful despite the tension radiating from her body. Soon flames danced against the sooty stones, casting shifting shadows that seemed to move independently of their sources. The fire's warmth should have been comforting, but it made the air feel thick and oppressive, like breathing through velvet.

"I need a drink for this," Ashley murmured, disappearing into what William assumed was a kitchen. He could hear the clink of glass, the splash of liquid. While she was gone, he wandered the room, drawn to a mahogany writing desk positioned near a tall window. Its surface was littered with fountain pens, their nibs stained with ink that looked suspiciously red in the firelight.

A leather journal lay open, its pages filled with Ashley's elegant script. As he leaned closer, the words seemed to writhe on the page:

The new one has arrived, just as I wrote. Just as I feared. His eyes hold the same hunger, the same beautiful destruction. How many times must I watch love burn everything to ash?

"I see you've found my confession," Ashley's voice came from directly behind him.

William spun, heart hammering. She stood holding two glasses of amber liquid, her expression unreadable.

"I didn't mean to—"

"Yes, you did." She handed him a glass, their fingers brushing in the exchange. Even that brief contact sent electricity through his veins. "Just as I meant for you to find it. Nothing happens by accident in this house, William. Nothing has happened by accident since you arrived in Cartersville."

She moved to the fireplace, settling onto a burgundy velvet chaise lounge that faced the flames. The light played across her features, alternately revealing and concealing, making her appear almost otherworldly. William remained standing, the journal's words echoing in his mind.

"What did you mean?" he asked. "About watching love burn?"

Ashley took a long sip of her drink—whiskey, by the smell—and stared into the fire. "How much do you know about Cartersville's history?"

"Not much. Small town, founded in the 1800s, built around the railroad and river trade."

"The sanitized version." Her laugh held no humor. "The truth is darker. Cartersville was built on a convergence point, a place where the boundaries between reality and story are thinner than tissue paper. The founding families knew this. They used it."

She stood and walked to a bookshelf, running her fingers along the burned spines. "My great-great-grandmother was one of them. Marigold Quinn. She came here in 1847 with nothing but a traveling bag and a gift for weaving stories that seemed too real to be fiction. Within five years, she was the wealthiest woman in three counties."

William moved closer, drawn by the hypnotic quality of her voice and the way the firelight transformed her skin to warm gold. "What kind of stories?"

"The profitable kind. She would write tales of visitors coming to town—wealthy merchants, railroad investors, government officials—and within weeks, they would arrive, exactly as she'd described them. She wrote romances for lonely women, promising them perfect husbands, and those husbands would appear, complete with the exact characteristics she'd invented. She wrote tragedies for her enemies, and those tragedies inevitably came to pass."

Ashley pulled a slim volume from the shelf, its cover so badly burned that the title was illegible. "This is one of hers. The story of a young woman who falls in love with a mysterious stranger, only to discover he's not entirely human. The stranger feeds on creative energy, growing stronger with each story written about him, until the woman realizes she must choose between her love and her soul."

The book fell open in her hands to a random page, and William could see that the text was handwritten in fading brown ink. As he watched, new words appeared in the margins, writing themselves in Ashley's familiar script: History repeats. The cycle continues. How many must burn before the pattern breaks?

"Jesus," William breathed. "It's writing itself."

"They all do, eventually." Ashley's voice was steady, but her hands trembled as she closed the book. "Every story in this house is alive. They feed on emotion, on passion, on the thin space between fiction and reality. And they're hungry, William. Always hungry."

She returned to the chaise, curling her legs beneath her like a cat. The position made her dress ride up slightly, revealing the curve of her calf, and William found himself distracted by the sight despite the supernatural revelations.

"My grandmother continued the tradition," Ashley continued. "Then my mother. Each generation of Quinn women has served as a conduit for the stories, channeling them into reality for profit and power. The town prospered, but the cost..."

She gestured to the burned books, the scorch-marked walls. "Fire. Always fire, in the end."

"What happened?" William settled onto the opposite end of the chaise, close enough to feel the heat radiating from her body but careful not to touch. The air between them crackled with tension.

"I was nineteen. Stupid and romantic and convinced I could control it." Ashley's eyes reflected the dancing flames. "I wrote a love story. A beautiful, tragic, epic romance between a young woman and a man who appeared in her town like a gift from the gods. I put everything into it—every fantasy I'd ever had, every romantic dream. I wrote us as star-crossed lovers, destined to find each other across time and space."

Her voice broke slightly. "And he came. Just as I'd written him. Tall and dark and mysterious, with eyes that seemed to see straight through to my soul. He was perfect, William. Too perfect. Because he wasn't real—not the way you and I are real. He was a construct of story and desire, and he needed to feed."

"Feed on what?"

"Everything. Emotion. Memory. The life force of the town itself." Ashley drained her glass and set it aside with shaking hands. "At first, it was wonderful. The most intense love affair I could have imagined. But as our relationship deepened, strange things began happening. People in town started forgetting things, important things. Couples who'd been married for decades suddenly couldn't remember how they'd met. Children forgot their own names. The very fabric of reality began to unravel."

The fire popped and hissed, sending sparks up the chimney. In the mirror above the mantel, William caught a glimpse of movement, figures dancing in the reflection, figures that weren't in the room with them.

"I tried to stop it," Ashley whispered. "I rewrote the story, gave it a different ending. But the narrative had taken on a life of its own. It didn't want to be contained. And my perfect lover... he didn't want to disappear."

She turned to face William fully, her green eyes bright with unshed tears. "The fire started in this room. I was trying to burn the original manuscript, to break the connection. However, the flames spread faster than they should have, consuming everything. The entire downtown burned for three days. Seventeen people died, including my lover. He screamed as the flames took him, screamed that I'd betrayed him, that our love should have been eternal."

"Ashley..." William reached for her without thinking, covering her hand with his. The contact was electric, sending warmth racing through his veins.

"The town rebuilt," she continued, not pulling away from his touch. "But the stories remained. Waiting. Growing stronger. And the Quinn women were forbidden from writing fiction ever again. We became librarians, archivists, guardians of the stories but never creators."

"Until now."

She nodded. "Until I met you. Until I felt that hunger again—the need to create, to shape reality with words. You've awakened something in me that I've spent fifteen years trying to suppress."

The confession hung between them like a bridge neither was sure they should cross. William found himself studying her face in the firelight—the way her lips parted slightly when she was thinking, the delicate line of her jaw, the pulse point at her throat that betrayed her racing heart.

"The manuscript you found," she said quietly. "The one in your house. I didn't write it."

"But you knew about it."

"I felt it. The moment you arrived in town, I felt the stories stirring. They recognized you, William. They've been waiting for you."

"Waiting for what?"

Ashley's free hand moved to rest against his chest, directly over his heart. "For someone strong enough to control them. Someone with enough creative fire to burn even brighter than they do."

The touch scorched through his shirt, and William found himself leaning closer. The space between them seemed to vibrate with possibility and danger in equal measure.

"What if I can't control them?" he asked.

"Then we'll burn together." Her voice was barely a whisper. "And maybe that wouldn't be the worst thing."

The admission broke something open between them. William cupped her face in his hands, marveling at the softness of her skin, the way her eyes fluttered closed at his touch.

"I'm scared," she breathed.

"So am I."

Their lips met with the desperate hunger of two people who'd been denying themselves for too long. Ashley tasted like whiskey and secrets, her mouth soft and demanding beneath his. She melted against him, her hands fisting in his shirt as if anchoring herself to reality.

The kiss deepened, became something fierce and consuming. Around them, the shadows on the walls began to dance more frantically, and the books seemed to whisper among themselves, their pages ruffling with no wind. The mirror above the fireplace flickered between past and present, showing glimpses of other lovers in this same room, other passionate encounters that had fed the house's hungry memories.

Ashley pulled back just enough to meet his eyes. "Are you sure about this? Once we cross this line, there's no going back. The stories will bind us together, for better or worse."

In answer, William traced the line of her jaw with his thumb, watching her eyes darken with desire. "I've been bound to you since the moment I walked into that library. I think you know that."

She smiled then, the first truly unguarded expression he'd seen from her. "I hoped you'd say that."

This time, when their lips met, there was no hesitation. Ashley rose from the chaise and took his hand, leading him through the cottage's winding corridors to a bedroom tucked beneath the eaves. The space was dominated by an antique canopy bed draped in midnight blue silk, its posts carved with the same Celtic knots that adorned the front door.

Candles flickered in alcoves around the room, their flames steady despite the drafts that seemed to whisper through the walls. More books lined the shelves, but these were different—older, more dangerous looking. Some were chained shut, their locks elaborate and forbidding.

"My grandmother's collection," Ashley explained, noticing his gaze. "Stories too powerful to be read safely. Some nights I can hear them calling, begging to be opened."

"But not tonight."

"No." She turned to face him, her hands moving to the buttons of his shirt. "Tonight, we write our own story."

They undressed each other slowly, reverently, as if each revealed inch of skin was a verse in a poem they were composing together. Ashley's body was a work of art in the candlelight, with all its curves, shadows, and secret places that begged to be explored. She bore a small scar on her shoulder blade burn mark in the shape of a quill pen that she said had appeared the night of the fire.

When they finally came together on the silk sheets, it was with a passion that seemed to set the very air ablaze. Their lovemaking was intense, desperate, as if they were trying to write themselves into a story that could never be erased. The house itself seemed to respond, the walls humming with energy, the shadows on the ceiling weaving patterns that looked almost like text.

Afterward, they lay entwined, Ashley's head pillowed on William's chest as he traced lazy patterns on her bare skin. The candles had burned lower, casting the room in a warm amber glow that made everything feel dreamlike.

"What happens now?" William asked, his voice rough with satisfaction and exhaustion.

"Now we face the consequences." Ashley lifted her head to look at him, her hair spilling across his shoulder like dark silk. "What we just did... it's created a connection. The stories will feel it, feed on it. They'll grow stronger."

"Is that necessarily a bad thing?"

She was quiet for a long moment, considering. "I don't know. In the past, the Quinn women were meant to channel the stories for others, to serve as conduits. But what we have... this could be different. We could be partners in it, equals. If we're strong enough."

"And if we're not?"

"Then Cartersville burns again." She settled back against his chest with a sigh. "But at least this time, I won't be alone."

Outside, the wind picked up, rattling the windows and setting the tree branches scraping against the roof. But inside the cottage, surrounded by hungry books and dancing shadows, William felt a peace he hadn't known he was searching for. Whatever came next, whatever stories demanded to be written, he would face them with Ashley by his side.

As sleep claimed him, he thought he heard voices whispering from the chained books on the shelves, urgent, excited voices discussing plans and possibilities. But he was too content, too thoroughly sated, to pay them much attention.

He should have listened more carefully. The stories were already weaving themselves around him and Ashley, binding them into a narrative that might prove impossible to escape. But for now, in the soft darkness of her bedroom, with her warm body pressed against his and her breath steady on his skin, William chose to ignore the warnings.

Some stories, after all, were worth any price.

Chapter 11: The Fun Begins

The morning after their night in the cottage, William woke with words flowing through his veins instead of blood. He could feel them — sentences circulating through his body, paragraphs pooling in his heart, entire chapters waiting to be exhaled. Beside him, Ashley slept with her dark hair spread across the pillow like spilled ink, her breath writing invisible stories in the air.

He rose carefully, not wanting to wake her, and moved to the window where dawn was breaking over Cartersville. But it wasn't a normal sunrise. The light came in drafts and revisions, each ray editing the landscape, adjusting shadows, perfecting the composition of morning.

In his mind, a thought formed — not dark, not threatening, but playful. Almost innocent.

What if the town woke to joy?

Before he could stop himself, his finger traced words on the fogged window glass:

Let there be celebration.

The change was instant. Church bells that hadn't rung in decades began to peal, their bronze voices harmonizing in impossible ways. Birds that had been extinct since the 1800s materialized on power lines, singing songs that sounded like laughter transcribed into melody. The air itself grew lighter, carbonated with an effervescence that made breathing feel like drinking champagne.

"William." Ashley's voice from behind him, alert, wary. "What did you do?"

"Something wonderful," he said, turning to her with eyes that reflected not light but possibility. "Come see."

From the cottage windows, they watched Cartersville transform. The perpetual fog that clung to the streets took shape, forming figures that waltzed through the intersections. Street lamps that had been dark for years flickered to life, but instead of electric light, they burned with colored flames that painted rainbow shadows. The crumbling downtown facades straightened and brightened, their Victorian gingerbread trim growing more elaborate with each passing second, as though the buildings were competing to be the most festive.

"A parade," William said, the words coming unbidden. "The town needs a parade."

He didn't write it down; he didn't need to. The Field was so attuned to him now that thought became reality with barely a pause for translation. Down Main Street, a procession materialized — but like everything touched by the Field, it was wrong in beautiful ways.

The marching band came first, instruments gleaming, uniforms pressed. However, the musicians had no faces — just smooth expanses of skin where features should be, though somehow they still played, the music emerging from nowhere and everywhere at once. Behind them, floats assembled from impossible materials: roses that bloomed and died in accelerating cycles, creating a cascade of petals that never quite reached the ground; giant papier mâché figures of authors that Cartersville had forgotten, their eyes following observers with porcelain intensity; a carousel that turned without a platform, its painted horses galloping through empty air.

"We should go," William said, pulling on his clothes with the eagerness of a child on Christmas morning. "We should be part of it."

"William, this isn't right." Ashley dressed quickly, her movements sharp with anxiety. "The Field doesn't give without taking. Every manifestation has a cost."

But he was already heading for the door, pulled by the gravity of his own creation. Echo followed, the dog's form more solid than it had been in days, as though the parade's forced joy had given it substance.

The streets were filling with townspeople, drawn from their homes by the impossible celebration. They moved like sleepwalkers who dreamed they were awake, smiling with too many teeth, laughing at frequencies that made windows crack. Children who had never existed before ran between the adults' legs, playing games whose rules changed with each round, aging years in minutes before reverting to infancy and beginning again.

"Look," William said, gesturing to a flower stand that had sprouted from the sidewalk. "Beauty from nothing. Joy from emptiness. Isn't this better than the decay?"

The vendor — an elderly woman whose face kept shifting between different ages of her life — handed them bouquets of flowers that shouldn't exist: roses with thorns of ice, lilies that whispered secrets, carnations that bled actual blood when their stems were cut.

"Free of charge," she said in a voice like rustling pages. "Everything's free during the Manuscript Festival."

"The what?" Ashley asked.

"The festival that happens every year," the woman replied. However, her eyes suggested confusion, as though the memory had just been inserted. "Always has, always will, until the last story ends."

William pulled Ashley along, intoxicated by his own power. Where his feet touched the ground, cobblestones rearranged themselves into patterns that spelled words in dead languages. Where his shadow fell, flowers pushed through concrete, bloomed, and turned to parchment that scattered on the wind.

They passed the diner where they'd first shared their fears. Still, it had transformed into a German beer garden, complete with musicians in lederhosen playing accordions that wept instead of sang. The Baptist church had become a circus tent, its steeple twisting into a striped pole that extended impossibly high. The courthouse steps were covered in couples dancing — not just the living, but the dead as well, transparent figures in period costume from every era of Cartersville's history, all moving to music that existed in multiple time signatures simultaneously.

"This is madness," Ashley said, but William could hear the reluctant wonder in her voice.

"This is a possibility," he countered, spinning her into the dance.

They moved together through the transformed streets, and for a moment — just a moment — it was perfect. The sun (or whatever was pretending to be the sun) warmed their faces. The music wrapped around them like silk. Other dancers gave them space, creating a spotlight of improbable providence.

But then William noticed the photographs.

They were appearing in shop windows, tacked to telephone poles, floating through the air like rectangular birds. Each one showed moments from the parade, but wrong — in one, the faceless band members had mouths full of screaming teeth; in another, the carousel horses were skeletal, their painted skin peeling away; in a third, the dancing couples were revealed to be corpses, puppeted by invisible strings.

"The Field is showing us the truth," Ashley said, her voice tight with fear. "This isn't creation, William. It's conscription. You're forcing the town into a story it doesn't want to tell."

He wanted to argue, but then he saw the children. The impossible children who'd materialized for the parade were beginning to flicker, their faces cycling through expressions of joy and terror too quickly for the eye to follow. One little girl in a pinafore that looked painted rather than sewn reached for her mother — a woman who didn't remember having a daughter until that moment — and when their hands touched, both began to dissolve into letters that scattered on the wind.

"Stop it," Ashley pleaded. "End the parade before it consumes everything real."

But William found he couldn't. The story now had momentum, its own narrative weight. The parade route was extending, new floats materializing faster than thought — a giant typewriter that typed the future in real-time, its keys pressed by invisible fingers; a library made of human skin, its books screaming their contents; a bed of roses that grew from corpses that might have been past versions of themselves.

"I need to redirect it," he said, grabbing Ashley's hand. "Not stop it but change its course."

He pulled her toward the old cemetery at the town's edge, where the parade hadn't yet reached. Among the leaning headstones and ancient oaks, reality still held its original shape. Spanish moss hung like curtains between worlds, and the ground remained solid beneath their feet.

"A picnic," he said, the words forming before conscious thought. "Something smaller, contained, just for us."

The cemetery responded to his will but differently than the town had. Here, the manifestation was gentler, perhaps influenced by the weight of actual history, actual death. A blanket appeared beneath an oak tree whose branches formed a natural cathedral. A basket materialized, woven from stories rather than wicker, containing food that was memory more than substance — the sandwich his mother made for his first day of school, the wine Ashley had been drinking when she first wrote about love. These strawberries tasted like summer afternoons that had never quite happened.

They sat, and for a moment, the distant sound of the parade faded. Here among the dead, they could pretend to be alive in a normal way.

"This is better," Ashley said, but her hand trembled as she reached for a grape that existed in too many dimensions at once. "Smaller stories are safer stories."

Echo lay between them, the dog's form solid and warm, perhaps the only truly real thing in this entire manufactured day. Through the cemetery gates, they could see the parade continuing, growing more grotesque with each iteration — floats made of human hair, bands playing music that made listeners' ears bleed, dancers whose partners were their own shadows torn free and given terrible independence.

"I've become Thomas," William said quietly, the realization hitting him like cold water. "I'm the character who gained too much autonomy, who wants to bring others through."

"No," Ashley said firmly, turning his face toward hers. "Thomas was alone in his power. You have me. We're co-authors, remember? Your stories don't have to consume everything if we write them together."

She pulled out a notebook, real paper, real ink — and began to write. As her pen moved, the parade in the distance began to slow, to soften. The faceless musicians grew features, gentle and tired. The impossible children found parents who truly remembered them. The dancing dead lay down peacefully in graves that welcomed them home.

"Help me," she said, offering him the pen. "Write the ending. Not with the Field, but with this. Real ink, real paper, real limits."

Together they wrote, trading the pen between sentences, their hands touching as they passed it back and forth. They wrote the parade to a close, not a sudden stop but a gentle conclusion, like a song finding its final note. They wrote the townspeople walking home, confused but unharmed, carrying flowers that would wilt normally, humming songs they'd forget by morning.

As the sun began to set (the real sun now, not the Field's elaborate forgery), the cemetery grew quiet. The picnic basket was now just a wicker frame, empty except for crumbs. The blanket was just cloth. But they were still there, still together, still real in whatever way reality meant in a place where stories could come alive.

"The photographs," William remembered suddenly. "The ones that showed the truth—"

"Are warnings," Ashley finished. "The Field documents everything, remembers everything. Every story we force into being leaves evidence. The Order will have seen it all."

As if summoned by her words, they heard footsteps on the gravel path. Multiple figures approaching through the gathering dusk, their shadows long and wrong, reaching for them like fingers made of darkness.

"The fun's over," Ashley said, standing and pulling William up with her. "Now comes the reckoning."

But as they prepared to face whatever approached, William felt something shift in his pocket. The photograph from the parade, the one showing the skeletal carousel horses, had changed. Now it showed him and Ashley at their picnic, but behind them, visible only in the photograph's impossible perspective, stood a figure neither of them had seen: Dr. Hail, or what Victor was becoming, his body more text than flesh, watching them with eyes that were portals to the Field itself.

The Gothic romance of their picnic transformed into Gothic horror as they realized they'd never been alone. Every moment of manufactured joy had been observed, recorded, and added to some vast narrative they couldn't quite perceive.

The footsteps grew closer. Echo growled, the sound echoing in too many dimensions.

And somewhere in the distance, the last of the parade music played backward, transforming from celebration to dirge, from comedy to tragedy, from the beginning of something wonderful to the middle of something terrible.

The fun, such as it had been, was over.

The real story was about to begin.

Chapter 12: The Manuscript Mirror

The figures approaching through the cemetery resolved into members of the Order of Unwritten Words — three individuals in Victorian mourning attire, their faces obscured by veils that seemed woven from shadow and parchment. They moved in perfect synchronization, as though controlled by a single narrative will.

"Mr. Varn. Miss Quinn." The center figure spoke with a voice like pages turning. "Your unauthorized manifestation has been noted. You will come with us."

It wasn't a request. The cemetery gates swung shut with a sound like a book slamming closed, and the Spanish moss overhead began to writhe, forming words in languages that predated human speech. Echo growled, but the sound emerged as visible text that dissipated in the air.

"Where?" Ashley asked, though her tone suggested she already knew.

"The Museum. The Director requires an audience."

They had no choice. The Order members surrounded them, and reality itself seemed to acknowledge their authority. The path beneath their feet rearranged to lead in only one direction, tombstones leaning away as though repelled by their presence. The dying light of the sunset took on the quality of a candle flame, casting shadows that moved independently of their sources.

The Booth Museum loomed before them, but not as William had seen it before. Tonight, it revealed its true nature — a vast Gothic cathedral to narrative itself, its windows glowing with the light of every story ever told within its walls. Gargoyles that had been stone during the day were now flesh, or something approximating flesh, their eyes tracking the group's approach with predatory interest.

Inside, the museum was infinite. Corridors branched and rebranched, each one containing exhibits that shouldn't exist, dioramas of moments that never happened, taxidermized creatures from abandoned manuscripts, paintings that showed the viewer's death in multiple artistic styles.

They descended stairs that spiraled down through layers of reality, each level revealing an older version of the museum, until they reached a door that had no handle, no keyhole, only a mirror that reflected not their faces but their stories, every word they'd ever written, flowing across the surface like living quicksilver.

"The Manuscript Mirror," one of the Order members said. "Where all narratives converge."

The door opened at their approach, revealing a chamber that defied perception. The room was circular, or perhaps spherical, its walls composed entirely of mirrors. But these weren't ordinary mirrors — each one reflected a different version of reality, a different draft of the story they were living.

In one, William saw himself alone in the Victorian house, aged and insane, writing on the walls with his own blood while the Field consumed him from within. In another, Ashley stood over his corpse, a knife in her hand and triumph in her eyes. A third showed them both transformed into living text, their bodies composed of sentences that constantly rewrote themselves, trapped in an eternal revision loop.

"Welcome," said a voice from everywhere and nowhere, "to the heart of the Museum."

The Order members departed, leaving William and Ashley alone with Echo in the impossible room. As they moved toward the center, their reflections multiplied, each mirror showing not just different angles but different possibilities, different genres, different endings.

"Don't look too long at any one reflection," Ashley warned, but it was already too late.

William found himself transfixed by a mirror that showed what appeared to be their future — he and Ashley, older, surrounded by children who had his eyes and her dark hair. But as he watched, the idyllic scene began to rot. The children aged rapidly, their faces cycling through expressions of joy, confusion, terror, and finally blank emptiness as they dissolved into manuscripts that Ashley desperately tried to gather while weeping.

"That's one possibility," a new voice said, and Dr. Victor stepped from a mirror as though it were a doorway. But this wasn't the Victor from before, his transformation had progressed. His body was translucent, revealing the Flow of text beneath his skin, sentences circulating where blood should be, paragraphs forming his organs. "The future where you try to have a normal life. It never ends well when authors of your caliber attempt domesticity."

"Why show us this?" William demanded, pulling his gaze away from the horrible family scene.

"Because the Director believes in informed consent," Victor replied, gesturing to the mirrors around them. "Every choice you make creates ripples through narrative possibility. The Field doesn't just record what it remembers, but what might be, what could have been, what should never be."

Another mirror drew William's attention. In this one, he saw Ashley alone in the cottage. Still, she was different — older, more powerful, surrounded by floating manuscripts that orbited her like planets. She was speaking to someone outside the frame, and though William couldn't hear the words, he could read her lips: "I had to let him go. Love was destroying us both."

"Ah, yes, "Victor said, noticing his focus. "The timeline where Miss Quinn chooses the Field over you. She becomes the most powerful author in history, but at what cost? Would you like to see what happens to you in that version?"

Before William could refuse, the image shifted. He saw himself in a psychiatric ward, restrained, screaming about stories that lived and breathes while doctors diagnosed him with severe schizophrenia. Ashley visited once, just once, and the look of pity in her eyes was worse than abandonment.

"Stop," Ashley said sharply. "These are manipulations, not prophecies."

"Are they? "Victor moved to another mirror, one that showed a different scene entirely. "Look here — the version where neither of you existed at all. Where the Field chose different vessels."

The mirror showed Cartersville, but populated by strangers. The Victorian house stood empty, slowly collapsing. The museum was just a museum. The town was dying a natural death, no magic, no horror, no romance. Just ordinary decay.

"Peaceful, isn't it? "Victor mused. "No suffering, no transformation, no story worth telling. Is that really better?"

William felt Ashley's hand find his, their fingers interlacing with desperate strength. In the mirrors, a thousand versions of this gesture played out — in some, they held hands while dying, in others while killing, in still others while ascending to something beyond human comprehension.

"There, "Victor pointed to a mirror near the ceiling. "That's my favorite possibility."

They looked up to see themselves seated at matching desks, writing in perfect synchronization. But their faces were blank, features erased except for mouths that moved in constant recitation. Behind them, the Field itself was visible as a vast neural network of light that pulsed with each word they wrote. They were no longer authors but instruments, their individuality sacrificed to become pure conduits of narrative.

"The Director calls it the Optimal Outcome, "Victor said. "Complete integration with the Field. No more boundary between author and story, no more suffering of separation. Just pure creation, eternal and infinite."

"That's not life," Ashley said. "That's slavery."

"Is it? "Victor touched a mirror, and it rippled like water. "Let me show you something else. The real reason you're here."

The mirrors began to shift, their surfaces merging until they formed a single, massive reflection. In it, William saw the truth, or at least, a version of truth.

The Order of Unwritten Words wasn't just managing the Field. They were feeding it. Every author they recruited, every story they sanctioned, it all served to strengthen the Field's hold on reality. And at the center of it all was a figure William hadn't expected — not Hail, not some ancient Director, but himself. An older version, scarred and magnificent, seated on a throne made of crystallized narratives.

"You?" William stared at his future self in horror. "I become the Director?"

"In seven out of thirteen primary timelines, "Victor confirmed. "In three others, Miss Quinn takes the role. In two, you rule together. And in one..." He paused, savoring the moment. "In one, you destroy everything. The Field, the Order, reality itself. You write an ending so final that nothing can ever be written again."

The mirrors began to spin around them, faster and faster, each reflection bleeding into the next until they were surrounded by a kaleidoscope of possibilities. William saw himself as a hero, a villain, a victim, and a victor. He saw Ashley as lover, enemy, savior, destroyer. He saw Echo revealed as the key to everything, or as nothing more than a lost dog. Every narrative thread, every potential plot twist, every possible ending played out simultaneously.

"Enough!" Ashley shouted and pulled out her notebook, the real one, with real paper. She began to write furiously, and as she did, the mirrors began to slow. "These aren't our stories. They're possibilities, nothing more. We choose which one becomes real."

"Do you? "Victor laughed, the sound like glass breaking. "Or does the story choose you? Haven't you noticed yet? You're living a Gothic romance because that's what the Field needs right now. Your love, your fear, your pain — it's all fuel for something larger."

William grabbed the notebook from Ashley, adding his own words to hers. Together, they wrote:

The mirrors showed truth, but truth is not destiny. Choice remains. Love remains. Even in a world where stories live, free will persists.

The mirrors cracked. Not all at once, but in spreading spiderweb patterns that revealed something beneath — not more glass, but pages. Millions of pages, all the stories that had ever been told in this room, layered like sediment.

"You're fighting the inevitable, "Victor said, but his form was beginning to fade. "The Field always wins. The story always continues."

"Maybe," Ashley said, still writing. "But not your story. Not tonight."

She wrote Victor out of the room — not destroyed, but displaced, sent to another mirror, another possibility. He vanished with a look of surprise that might have been approval.

Alone now except for Echo, William, and Ashley stood in the center of the shattered mirrors. Through the cracks, they could see fragments of all those possible futures, but also something else — the past. The real past, not alternate versions but actual history.

"Look," William pointed to a large fragment that showed the museum being built. But it wasn't constructed — it was grown, assembled from stories told by the Indigenous peoples who first lived here, their oral traditions crystallizing into architecture.

Another fragment showed the first European settlers discovering the Field, the madness that followed, the founding of the Order to contain what couldn't be destroyed.

And in a third, they saw the truth about Echo — the dog wasn't a manifestation at all, but the last remains of an author who had merged so completely with the Field that only this form remained, a loyal creature waiting for someone to write it back to humanity.

"We need to leave," Ashley said urgently. "The mirrors are reforming."

She was right. The cracks were healing, the infinite reflections returning. But now they all showed the same thing — the two of them, standing in this room, looking at mirrors that showed them looking at mirrors that showed them looking at mirrors. This infinite recursion threatened to trap them in an eternal state of observation.

They ran, Echo leading the way, up through the spiral stairs that tried to become Möbius strips, through corridors that attempted to loop back on themselves, past exhibits that reached for them with hands made of wax, wire, and words.

They burst from the museum into dawn light, real dawn, not the Field's approximation. The town looked normal, or as normal as Cartersville ever looked. The parade was gone, leaving only scattered flowers and a lingering sense of celebration that had never quite happened.

"The notebook," Ashley said, looking at what she carried. The pages were full now, covered with their combined handwriting. But the words were changing, rearranging themselves, telling a story neither of them had consciously written.

It was their story, but it had been edited by something else. The Field had taken their rebellion and incorporated it into the larger narrative. They weren't fighting the system — they were part of it, their resistance just another plot point in an infinitely complex story.

"We can't win," William said, the weight of it crushing.

"No," Ashley agreed, but she was smiling sadly. "But we can choose how we lose. And sometimes, in stories, that's what matters most."

Echo barked once, and in that sound, William heard an echo of humanity, a voice trying to remember how to speak.

The real mystery wasn't what the Field was, or what the Order wanted, or even what they themselves would become.

The real mystery was whether, in a world where everything was story, anything could ever truly end.

Or if every ending was just another beginning, waiting to be written.

Chapter 13: Convergence Zones

The church bells of St. Bartholomew's rang backward.

William stood frozen on the cobblestone path leading to Cartersville's oldest cemetery, watching the bronze bells in the tower swing in their proper arc. At the same time, the sound reversed itself, each peal beginning with silence, swelling to a metallic crescendo, then cutting off with the initial strike that should have begun it. The wrongness of it crawled across his skin like ice water.

"Do you hear that?" he asked the empty air, though he knew no one else was nearby. The few townsfolk he'd passed on his way here had moved with the mechanical precision of sleepwalkers, their eyes glazed and distant, murmuring fragments of dialogue he recognized from his manuscript.

The afternoon sun hung low and bloated above the tree line, casting shadows that fell in impossible directions. An oak tree's shadow stretched north while the sun blazed in the western sky. A weathered headstone threw its darkness upward, a dark column rising into the amber air like smoke.

The wrongness had started three hours ago, just after noon, when he'd watched a murder of crows fly backward through his kitchen window, their cawing preceding their appearance, their bodies moving tail-first through the sky with wings that beat in reverse. Then came the reports—whispered, fragmented things from the few townsfolk still lucid enough to notice. The old courthouse clock is running counterclockwise. Water is flowing uphill in the storm drains near Mill Street. Children's swings in the park are moving against the wind.

Convergence zones, he'd written in his notebook, trying to name the phenomenon. Places where reality had worn thin, where the Story Field's influence bled through most strongly.

The cemetery gate stood open, its wrought iron twisted into elaborate spirals that seemed to writhe in his peripheral vision. Beyond it, fog pooled between the headstones, despite the day's warmth. This thick, pearl-gray mist moved with deliberate purpose, concealing and revealing the monuments like a living thing.

He stepped through the gate, and the temperature dropped twenty degrees.

His breath clouded the air as he moved deeper into the cemetery, following a gravel path that crunched too loudly under his feet. The fog parted before him and closed behind, creating a moving pocket of visibility no more than ten feet in any direction. Ancient headstones loomed out of the mist—marble angels with faces worn smooth by decades of rain, granite obelisks carved with names that seemed to rearrange themselves when he wasn't looking directly at them.

The first anomaly he found was a subtle plastic water bottle, faded and brittle with age, half-buried beside a headstone dated 1847. He knelt and excavated it carefully, his fingers numb in the supernatural cold. The bottle bore a logo he didn't recognize, text in a language that might have been English but wasn't quite, letters that hurt to read.

"You shouldn't be here."

Ashley's voice came from behind him, and he turned to find her emerging from the fog like a ghost herself. She wore a long black coat that billowed around her, her green eyes luminous in the strange, filtered light. Her dark hair was pulled back, revealing the elegant line of her neck, the pulse point that jumped with visible anxiety.

"Neither should you," he said, standing. He held out the bottle. "Look at this."

She took it with gloved hands, turned it over, studying the impossible text. "It's getting worse. The convergence zones are spreading." She looked up at him, and he saw his own fear reflected in her eyes. "The Field is destabilizing. Your writing, the manifestations, they're tearing holes in things."

"My writing?" The accusation stung, even though he knew she was right. "I didn't know—"

"I know you didn't." She stepped closer, close enough that he could smell her perfume, something dark and floral that reminded him of funeral lilies. "But intent doesn't matter to the Field. It only cares about narrative momentum, about the stories feeding into it."

A sound echoed through the fog—footsteps, but wrong somehow, the rhythm off, like someone walking with too many legs or not enough. They both froze, listening. The footsteps circled them, staying just outside the range of visibility, accompanied by a wet breathing sound that raised every hair on William's neck.

Without thinking, he reached for Ashley's hand. She gripped his fingers tightly, her glove soft against his palm. They stood there, connected by touch and mutual fear, as the circling footsteps grew closer.

"There," she whispered, pointing.

A figure emerged from the fog, a Union soldier in a uniform that looked freshly pressed despite the mud staining his boots. His face was young, perhaps nineteen, with hollow eyes that stared out of them. He walked past without acknowledgment, his footsteps making that wrong rhythm, and William realized why. The soldier's left foot came down a half-second before it lifted, each step happening slightly out of temporal sequence.

"Is he real?" William asked.

"Define real," Ashley said, but her voice shook. "He died here in 1864. But he's also walking here now. Both things are true."

They followed the soldier deeper into the cemetery, still holding hands, Ashley's fingers intertwined with his. The fog grew thicker, and more anomalies began to appear. A smartphone, its screen cracked, was embedded in a tree that had grown around it, but the tree was at least two hundred years old, judging by its girth. A child's bicycle, bright red and impossibly modern, resting against a mausoleum that predated its invention by a century.

"Here," Ashley said, stopping at a particular grave. "This is what you need to see."

The headstone read: "Captain Josiah Morse, 1823-1864, Fallen at Kennesaw Mountain." But the earth before it had been recently disturbed, the soil dark and freshly turned.

"Hail had me investigate this yesterday," Ashley continued. "Before things got bad. Look."

She knelt and began to dig with her gloved hands. William joined her, the cold earth numbing his fingers instantly. Six inches down, they found it, a compass, but not any compass that should exist. Its surface was a smooth, black glass, displaying holographic coordinates that shifted and changed, revealing locations that shouldn't exist. The needle didn't point north; it pointed down, straight into the earth.

"This was buried with Captain Morse," Ashley said. "In 1864. But it won't be invented for..." She trailed off, unable to finish the impossibility.

"The timeline is collapsing," William said, understanding flooding through him. "Past, present, future—they're all converging."

She nodded, standing, and he noticed she hadn't let go of his hand. "The Story Field doesn't just archive narratives. It exists outside linear time. When you started writing into it, you created feedback loops, paradoxes."

The fog suddenly pressed closer, and the wet breathing sound returned, now multiplied, coming from all directions. Shapes moved in the mist—tall, impossibly thin figures that might have been human once but weren't anymore. Their shadows fell upward, creating dark pillars that stretched into the sky.

"Run," Ashley whispered.

They ran, still hand in hand, weaving between headstones as the fog chased them. Behind them, those wrong footsteps multiplied, became a stampede of temporal refugees, soldiers from wars that hadn't happened yet, children who'd died before they were born, lovers separated by centuries all wandering the same ground simultaneously.

A mausoleum loomed out of the fog, a massive Greek Revival structure with columns that seemed to twist when viewed directly. Ashley pulled him toward it, shouldering open the heavy bronze door. They tumbled inside, slamming it shut behind them.

The interior was impossibly vast, far larger than the exterior suggested. Rows of stone sarcophagi stretched into darkness, and the air tasted of copper and old roses. Phosphorescent fungi grew on the walls, providing a sickly green light that made everything look underwater.

"We're safe here," Ashley said, but she didn't sound convinced. She was pressed against him, her body warm in the supernatural cold, and he could feel her trembling.

"Ashley," he started, but she turned to face him, and the words died in his throat. Her face was pale in the fungal light, her eyes wide and frightened but also something else—a hunger that matched his own.

"We might die here," she said simply. "The convergence zones are spreading. Soon the whole town will be like this—unstable, impossible, torn between what was and what will be."

"Then we stop it," he said, though he had no idea how.

She laughed, a bitter sound that echoed in the vast space. "With what? Love? Determination? This isn't a story, William. Or rather, it is, but we're trapped inside it, and stories don't care about their characters' happiness."

He pulled her closer, feeling the rapid beat of her heart against his chest. "Then we rewrite it."

"You tried that. It made things worse."

"Then we will try again. Together."

She looked up at him, and for a moment, the fear in her eyes gave way to something softer. "Together," she repeated, like she was testing the word.

Outside, something massive struck the mausoleum door, making the bronze boom like a giant bell. The sound reverberated through the chamber, rattling the sarcophagi's lids. More impacts followed, rhythmic, insistent.

"They want in," Ashley whispered.

"Let them come," William said, surprising himself with his sudden fierce protectiveness. "They're just echoes. Shadows of stories that got tangled up in the Field."

"Some shadows can kill you."

Another impact, and this time the door buckled slightly. In the green light, William could see text appearing on the walls—his own handwriting, manifesting directly onto stone. Words from his manuscript, but rearranged, twisted into new meanings:

The author and the librarian stood at the crossroads of collapsing time, their love a small flame against an infinite dark. But even small flames can start great fires, and even infinite darkness must yield, eventually, to dawn.

"You're still writing," Ashley said, reading the words. "Even now, you're adding to the story."

"I can't help it. It's who I am."

She touched his face, her glove soft against his cheek. "Then write us a way out. Write us a door that leads somewhere else, somewhere safe."

He closed his eyes, concentrating, feeling for that connection to the Field that had become as natural as breathing. But when he reached for it, he found chaos—a roiling mass of conflicting narratives, timelines crossing and recrossing, eating themselves like an ouroboros made of words.

The door exploded inward.

The things that entered were no longer quite human. They were amalgamations of different time periods—a Confederate soldier with cybernetic implants, a Victorian child with eyes that displayed streaming data, and a woman in a 1950s dress whose shadow was composed of liquid darkness. They moved with jerky, stop-motion precision, approaching the two of them with reaching hands.

Ashley pressed herself against William, and he wrapped his arms around her, shielding her with his body. The creatures circled them, their wrong footsteps creating a rhythm like a broken heartbeat.

Then, suddenly, they stopped.

One of them, the Confederate soldier with the glowing red eye spoke in a voice like grinding gears: "The cycle must complete. The author must choose. The town must feed."

"I've already chosen," William said, though he didn't know what he meant until the words were out. "I choose her. I choose us. I choose to break the cycle."

The creatures tilted their heads in unison, a deeply unsettling gesture. Then, as one, they stepped back, creating a path to the door.

"They're letting us go," Ashley whispered, disbelieving.

"No," William realized with cold certainty. "They're showing us where we need to go."

Hand in hand, they walked through the gauntlet of temporal refugees, out into the fog-shrouded cemetery. The convergence zone had spread—the entire graveyard now existed in multiple time periods simultaneously. They could see through the layers of history like looking through stacked sheets of glass. The cemetery was as it was in 1820, freshly consecrated. In 1864, filled with war dead. In 1918, the population expanded due to the deaths from the Spanish flu. In 2024, the park underwent modernization with the addition of paved paths. And in some unimaginable future, overgrown and wild, reclaimed by a forest that didn't yet exist.

At the center of it all stood a figure William recognized—Dr. Hail, but also not him. This version flickered between different iterations: young, old, not quite human, possibly never human at all.

"You're beginning to understand," Victor said, his voice coming from all his versions simultaneously. "The convergence zones aren't a malfunction. They're the Field showing its true nature. All stories exist simultaneously within it. Past, present, future, they're just different chapters in the same infinite book."

"How do we stop it?" William demanded.

Hail smiled, an expression that looked different on each of his flickering faces. "You don't stop it. You complete it. Every author who comes here adds their chapter to the grand narrative. You're not the first, Mr. Varn. You won't be the last."

"But I could be," William said, the revelation hitting him suddenly. "If I write an ending. A real ending. Not just for my story, but for the Field itself."

Hail's smile faltered. "You wouldn't dare. The Field is older than this town, older than—"

"Older than you?" Ashley interrupted. "Because you're not from here either, are you? You're another author who got caught in the cycle. How many years ago? Decades? Centuries?"

For a moment, Hail's flickering stopped. They saw him as he truly was—a hollow-eyed man in clothes from the 1890s, his fingers stained with ink that would never wash out, his expression one of infinite weariness.

"Ninety-three years," he said quietly. "Ninety-three years of feeding stories to the Field, of watching new authors arrive, fall in love, try to break free, and fail. You all write the same story in the end. Love, sacrifice, tragedy. The Field feeds on it."

"Then we'll write a different ending," William said firmly.

"You think you're the first to try? "Victor laughed, but it was a broken sound. "Look around you. Every grave here belongs to an author who thought they could beat the system. The Field always wins. It has to. It's the nature of stories, they demand to be told, even if they destroy their tellers."

The fog began to lift, revealing the full scope of the convergence. The cemetery existed in a bubble of corrupted time, seasons cycling rapidly—snow falling, melting instantly into spring flowers, summer heat withering everything to autumn leaves that fell upward into winter skies.

"We should go," Ashley said urgently. "The convergence is accelerating."

But William stood transfixed, watching the temporal chaos, understanding finally dawning. "It's not about breaking the cycle," he said. "It's about changing its nature. The Field feeds on tragedy because that's all it's been given. But what if we fed it something else?"

"Hope?" Ashley asked, squeezing his hand.

"Love that doesn't end in sacrifice. Joy that doesn't turn to sorrow. A story that builds instead of destroys."

Hail shook his head. "Impossible. The Field's nature is fixed. It was created to archive human suffering, to catalog our failures and losses."

"Created by who?" William challenged.

Hail opened his mouth to answer, then stopped, confusion crossing all his flickering faces. "I... I don't remember."

"Because that's the real story," William said, pulling Ashley closer. "Not who gets trapped in the cycle, but who started it and why. And every story, even the oldest ones, can be revised."

The cemetery began to shake, with headstones toppling and the earth cracking. The convergence zone pulsed like a living heart, and in its rhythm, William heard something he hadn't expected—fear. The Field was afraid.

"Run!" Ashley shouted, and this time, they did.

They fled through the collapsing cemetery, past graves that opened to reveal empty voids, around monuments that aged centuries in seconds, crumbling to dust. Behind them, the convergence zone contracted and expanded, breathing like a massive lung, trying to draw them back.

They burst through the gate onto the street to find the rest of Cartersville beginning to show the same symptoms—buildings aging and reversing, streets cracking to reveal older roads beneath, the very air shimmering with temporal distortion.

But William felt something new in his connection to the Field, not just the ability to write into it, but to read what had been written before. Layer upon layer of stories, all ending the same way, but underneath them all, faint but present, an original text. The first story. The one that started the cycle.

"I know what we have to do," he said.

Ashley looked at him, her face flushed from running, her eyes bright with fear and determination and something else—trust. Complete, absolute trust.

"Then we do it together," she said.

Hand in hand, they walked back toward the museum, toward the Story Field's heart, as the town collapsed into temporal chaos around them. They were no longer running from the convergence zones but walking deliberately into them, because William finally understood that the zones weren't a symptom of the Field's breakdown.

They were its desperate attempt to tell its own story, the one it had been trying to tell for longer than anyone remembered. And he and Ashley were going to help it find its voice at last.

Chapter 14: The Echoes Multiply

The morning after the cemetery, William woke to find his own words coming back to him from impossible places.

"The author struggled with the weight of his creation," said Mrs. Henderson from her porch as he passed, her eyes vacant, unseeing. She was knitting, but her needles moved without yarn, clicking against nothing. "The author struggled with the weight of his creation."

She repeated it again. And again. A perfect loop, each iteration identical in tone, pitch, and cadence.

Those were the exact words from page 247 of his manuscript—not similar words, not a paraphrase, but a perfect echo, down to his specific choice of "struggled" over "wrestled" and "creation" over "work."

He stopped, his coffee growing cold in his hand. "Mrs. Henderson?"

She didn't respond, just kept knitting air with those clicking needles. "The author struggled with the weight of his creation."

Three houses down, Tom Walsh was washing a car that wasn't there, his sponge moving through empty space in precise, practiced motions. "She knew the taste of his lies," he said conversationally to no one. "Copper and ash on her tongue."

Page 186. A line about Ashley's character—though he'd never named her that in the manuscript.

By the time William reached downtown, the entire population of Cartersville had become a living echo chamber of his unpublished work. The barista at the coffee shop: "The morning light through amber glass, through amber glass, through amber glass." The mailman: "Seventeen steps to damnation, he counted them twice." A child on a bicycle, no more than eight: "Her skin remembered his fingerprints like accusations."

That last one made him physically recoil. He'd written it about a violent scene, nothing a child should be reciting. But the boy just pedaled past, his young voice eerily flat: "Like accusations, like accusations, like accusations."

The town had become a grotesque audiobook of his manuscript, played out by unwilling performers who moved through their daily routines while speaking his words. They weren't reading or performing—they were possessed by the text, made into flesh-and-blood speakers playing his prose on endless repeat.

He found Ashley at the library, standing behind her desk with her back to him. Relief flooded through him—finally, someone who might still be herself.

"Ashley, thank God. The whole town is—"

She turned, and his relief curdled into horror. Her green eyes, usually so sharp and knowing, were glassy, unfocused. When she spoke, it was in his words: "The librarian's heart was a locked room, and he had swallowed the key."

"No," he whispered. "Not you."

But even as she spoke his prose, a tear rolled down her cheek. She was still in there, trapped behind his words, aware but unable to break free.

"The librarian's heart was a locked room—" she began again, but her voice cracked. Her eyes focused for just a moment, blazing with fury and fear, and she managed to force out: "What did you do to us?"

Then the echo reclaimed her: "—and he had swallowed the key."

William reached for her, but she jerked away, her movements sharp, angry even as his words continued to pour from her mouth. She was fighting it, he could see that, fighting with everything she had, but the Field's hold was too strong.

"I'll fix this," he promised, backing away from her accusing gaze. "I'll write us out of this."

He ran home, his footsteps echoing off buildings that whispered his words back at him from their windows, their doors, their very foundations. The storm drains were the worst—dark mouths in the street that gurgled accusations he didn't remember writing:

"You killed her in the first draft." "You wrote her suffering for beauty." "You loved the tragedy more than the woman."

Were these his words? He couldn't remember anymore. The manuscript had taken on a life of its own, sprouting new pages like a cancer, growing beyond what he'd written into something self-aware and malevolent.

In his house, he pulled out the leather-bound manuscript. New pages had appeared overnight—hundreds of them, filled with his handwriting but containing scenes he'd never imagined. Scenes of Ashley dying in elaborate ways. Scenes of the townsfolk becoming hollow puppets. Scenes of himself, standing over graves, feeding stories to something vast and hungry beneath the earth.

And at the very back, a new chapter titled: "The Author's Conceit."

He read it with growing nausea. It was about him, writing about Ashley, trying to control her through narrative, to shape her into what he wanted her to be rather than who she was. The prose was definitely his—he recognized his rhythms, his metaphors—but he'd never written these words. The Field was writing through him now, using his voice to tell its own story.

Desperate, he grabbed a pen and a fresh piece of paper. If the Field wanted to play narrative games, he'd give it a story it couldn't corrupt. He began to write:

William took Ashley's hand in the library, and she smiled, herself again, free from the echoes. They kissed among the dusty books, tasting freedom and future on each other's lips. The Field released its hold, finally understanding that love wasn't meant to be contained in words but lived in the moments between them.

He finished the scene, pouring all his desire and desperation into it, willing it to manifest as everything else had. The paper grew warm under his hands. The air shimmered.

Nothing happened.

He tried again, this time with more elaboration and detail. Still nothing.

The Field was refusing him. After weeks of manifesting everything he wrote, turning his fiction into reality, it was suddenly selective. It would manifest horror, tragedy, suffering—but not healing. Not love. Not redemption.

A knock at his door interrupted his frantic writing. Ashley stood on his porch, rain-soaked though the day was clear. Her eyes were her own again, but the fury in them made him step back.

"The echoes stopped," she said, pushing past him into the house. "For me, at least. The others are still trapped. Do you want to know why I'm free?"

"Ashley—"

"Because the Field wanted me to see this." She threw something on his table—new manuscript pages, but not in his handwriting. In hers. "I wrote these years ago, before you came. A story about an author who would arrive in Cartersville, who would fall in love with me, who would try to save the town and damn it instead."

William picked up the pages with trembling hands. The prose was beautiful, lyrical, and absolutely about him. Details no one could have known.

The scar on his shoulder is from a fall he had in childhood. His mother's maiden name. The nightmare that had haunted him since college.

"You wrote me into existence?" he asked, his voice hollow.

"No." She laughed bitterly. "That's what I thought at first. But it's worse than that. We're both echoes, William. Every author who comes here, every librarian who helps them—we're all iterations of the same story the Field has been telling for centuries. We fall in love, we try to break free, we fail. Over and over, with different names, different faces, but the same essential narrative."

"That's not true. What we have is real—"

"Is it? Or is it just another chapter in an endless book?" She was crying now, angry tears that streaked her face. "I can feel the Field in my head, showing me all the other versions. All the other Ashleys who loved all the other Williams. We're not people, we're archetypes. The Author and The Librarian, playing out our roles for the Field's amusement."

"Stop." He reached for her, but she slapped his hands away.

"You did this to us. Your writing, your need to control everything through narrative. You've made us all into characters in your story."

"Our story," he corrected. "You wrote it too. You just showed me—"

"Because the Field made me! Don't you see? It's using us to write itself into existence, to give itself form through our stories. And the more we write, the stronger it gets, the more it can corrupt."

Outside, the echoes grew louder. The townsfolk were congregating in the street, all speaking different lines from his manuscript simultaneously, creating a cacophony of his own prose that sounded like madness.

"The author struggled with the weight of his creation—" "Seventeen steps to damnation—" "Her skin remembered his fingerprints—" "The taste of copper and ash—" "The locked room of her heart—"

"Listen to them," Ashley said. "That's your voice, William. Your words. You've infected them all."

"I was trying to create something beautiful—"

"You were trying to play God!" She shoved him, hard enough that he stumbled back. "You wrote me falling in love with you. Did I ever have a choice? Or was it always just your narrative pushing us together?"

The accusation hit him like a physical blow because he couldn't refute it. He had written their love story before truly knowing her. Had written her desire, her need, her surrender to their connection.

"I'm sorry," he said, the words feeling inadequate. "I didn't know—"

"You knew enough. You knew the Field was dangerous, that it was changing reality, and you kept writing anyway."

"Because I loved you!"

"You loved the idea of me. The character you created." She pulled out more pages—these from his manuscript, but covered in her annotations. "Look at how you describe me. 'Ethereal.' 'Haunted.' 'Mystery made flesh.' I'm not a person to you, I'm a gothic trope."

He read her notes, her bitter commentary on his prose, and saw himself through her eyes—a man so lost in his own narrative that he'd forgotten the woman was real, with her own thoughts, desires, and fears that existed outside his story.

"But you wrote me too," he said quietly. "In your pages. You did the same thing."

She froze, then laughed—a broken sound. "Yes. God, yes, I did. We're both guilty. Both trapped in this narcissistic loop of writing each other into existence." She collapsed into a chair, the fight draining out of her. "Maybe that's why the Field chose us. We're perfect for it—two people who can't love without turning it into a narrative."

William knelt beside her chair, not touching her but close enough to feel her warmth. "Or maybe that's how we break free. By stopping."

"Stopping?"

"No more writing. No more stories. We just... live. Be ourselves, whoever that is underneath all the narratives."

She looked at him then, really looked at him, and for a moment, he saw past the anger to the fear beneath. "But who are we without our stories? If we're just echoes of previous authors and librarians, if we're just archetypes the Field keeps recycling—who are we really?"

"I don't know," he admitted. "But I'd like to find out. With you. If you'll let me."

The storm drains outside began to whisper new accusations, but now he recognized them—they weren't from his manuscript or hers. They were the Field's own voice, speaking through their infrastructure:

"They think they can escape the narrative." "They think love exists outside of story." "They think they are more than words."

Ashley heard it too. She stood, moving to the window to watch the possessed townsfolk swaying in the street, speaking their endless echoes. "It's mocking us."

"Let it." William stood beside her, careful not to touch her without permission. "We know something it doesn't."

"What's that?"

"Stories end. Even the longest book has a final page. And the Field has been telling the same story for so long, it's forgotten that."

She turned to him, and he saw something shift in her expression—a softening, a possibility. "You want to write an ending."

"No. I want us to write an ending. Together. Not the tragic sacrifice the Field expects, not the gothic horror it feeds on, but something else. Something it won't see coming because it's never been given it before."

"A happy ending?" She laughed, but there was less bitterness in it now. "In Cartersville? In this cursed place?"

"Why not? Who says gothic romances have to end in tragedy? Who made that rule?"

She was quiet for a long moment, and then, slowly, she reached for his hand. Her fingers were cold, trembling, but they held his firmly. "The Field won't let us. It refused your love scene, remember?"

"Because I was writing alone. Because I was still trying to control the narrative." He squeezed her hand gently. "But what if we write together? What if we stop trying to write each other and start writing with each other?"

Outside, the echoes suddenly stopped. The townsfolk stood frozen, mouths open, as if waiting for new words to speak. The storm drains fell silent. Even the wind died.

The Field was listening.

Ashley turned to face him fully, her free hand coming up to touch his face. "You hurt me. Your words, your story—they took away my agency."

"I know. I'm sorry."

"I hurt you too. I wrote you into existence before you even arrived, shaped you to fit my narrative of salvation."

"I know."

"And you still want to try? Even knowing we might just be echoes, might just be the Field's puppets dancing to its tune?"

"Especially knowing that," he said. "Because if we're going to be in a story, I'd rather it be one we write together than one that's forced upon us."

She kissed him then, and it wasn't the passionate, desperate kiss he'd written in his manuscript. It was hesitant, questioning, real in a way his fictional kisses had never been. It tasted of anger and forgiveness, fear and hope, bitter coffee and the salt of tears.

When they pulled apart, the townsfolk were moving again, but they weren't speaking his words anymore. They were mumbling, confused, like people waking from a dream. Mrs. Henderson dropped her invisible knitting needles and looked at her empty hands in bewilderment. Tom Walsh stopped washing the car that wasn't there and stared at his dry sponge.

"The echoes are breaking," Ashley whispered.

"Because we're writing a different story now," William said. "One the Field doesn't know how to tell."

She smiled then, the first real smile he'd seen from her since the convergence zones began. "Then we'd better make it a good one."

Hand in hand, they walked to the table where both manuscripts lay—his and hers, the stories they'd written separately that had trapped them both. Without discussing it or planning, they each picked up a pen.

And together, on a fresh page, they began to write.

Chapter 15: The Confrontation

The building that housed Dr. Hail's laboratory had no address, no number, no name. It existed in a part of Cartersville that maps forgot, down an alley that only appeared after midnight, through a door that looked like a wall until you knew exactly where to press.

William knew because the manuscript had shown him, new pages that had appeared that morning, written in handwriting that shifted between his, Ashley's, and something older, more arcane. Directions disguised as narrative, a breadcrumb trail of prose leading him here, to this moment, to this confrontation he could no longer avoid.

The door opened onto a descending staircase that spiraled far deeper than should have been possible. Gas lamps flickered on the walls, their light creating dancing shadows that resembled reaching hands, gaping mouths, and eyes that tracked his movement. The air grew thicker with each step down, heavy with the scent of ozone and formaldehyde and something else—something organic and wrong, like fruit rotting from the inside.

He could hear the machines before he saw them. A rhythmic thundering like a massive heart, underlaid with the whir of gears, the hiss of steam, the crackle of electricity jumping between unseen conductors. The sound seemed to come from everywhere and nowhere, reverberating through the stone walls until William felt it in his bones.

The staircase ended at a vast underground chamber that defied architectural logic. The ceiling stretched up into darkness, supported by iron pillars that twisted like DNA helixes. Machines filled the space—brass and copper monstrosities connected by intestinal tubes that pulsed with fluorescent liquid. Tesla coils sparked in corners, throwing sheets of blue-white lightning across surfaces that looked too organic to be metal, too geometric to be flesh.

And everywhere were the screens. Hundreds of them, from ancient cathode ray tubes to modern flatscreens to things that might have been windows into other dimensions. They all showed the same thing: pages from manuscripts, words flowing across them like living things, stories writing themselves in real-time.

"Mr. Varn," Dr. Hail's voice echoed from somewhere in the mechanical maze. "I've been expecting you. The narrative demanded it, you see. The confrontation between creator and created, author and architect. Very gothic. Very appropriate."

William followed the voice deeper into the laboratory, past machines whose purposes he couldn't fathom. One looked like a pipe organ made of glass tubes filled with what might have been blood. Another resembled a printing press, but instead of paper, it was pressing something that screamed softly as it was flattened.

He found Victor at the center of it all, standing before what could only be the heart of the Story Field's physical manifestation massive sphere of interconnected neurons, each one human-sized, pulsing with bioluminescent light. They weren't quite biological, weren't quite mechanical, but something between, something that shouldn't exist.

"Beautiful, isn't it? "Victor said without turning. He was adjusting dials on a control panel that resembled a typewriter keyboard and human teeth.

"The Field's neural network made manifest. Every story ever fed into it, given physical form."

"You lied to me," William said. "About everything. The Field, what it does, what you wanted from me."

Hail turned then, and in the strange light of the neural sphere, his face kept shifting—young, old, human, not quite human, as if he existed in multiple states simultaneously. "I told you exactly what you needed to hear to play your part. The Field needed fresh narrative. You provided it."

"The town is falling apart. People are becoming puppets, speaking my words—"

"Your words? "Victor laughed, a sound like grinding gears. "Oh, Mr. Varn. Still so convinced of your own authorship. Haven't you realized yet? You've never written a single original word since you arrived in Cartersville."

The nearest screen flickered to life, showing pages from William's manuscript. But as he watched, the words rearranged themselves, revealing an undertext—older writing, in a script he didn't recognize, that had been there all along.

"Every story you've written here, "Victor continued, "has been the Field telling its own story through you. You're not an author, Mr. Varn. You're a stenographer. A secretary taking dictation from something far older and hungrier than you can imagine."

"That's not true. My stories, my connection with Ashley—"

"Ah yes, Ashley." Hail's smile was cruel. "Would you like to know the truth about your beloved librarian? How she came to be in Cartersville? What she's been hiding from you?"

"Don't." Ashley's voice came from behind them. She stood at the entrance to the chamber, her face pale but determined. "Don't you dare."

"My dear, "Victor said, his tone mockingly paternal. "So good of you to join us. I was just about to tell Mr. Varn about our arrangement."

"We have no arrangement," Ashley said, moving to stand beside William. "Not anymore."

"No? Then I suppose you've told him about Chicago? About the fire that killed twelve people? About the story you wrote that made it happen?"

William looked at Ashley, saw the truth in her stricken expression. "Ashley?"

"It was an accident," she whispered. "I didn't know what I was doing. I was young, angry, writing a revenge fantasy about my ex-boyfriend's apartment building. I never meant for it to manifest, never knew it could—"

"But it did, "Victor interrupted. "And when the authorities came sniffing around, asking questions about the strange circumstances of the fire—how it moved against the wind, how it formed patterns that looked like words—who helped you disappear? Who brought you to Cartersville, gave you a new identity, a new life?"

"You," Ashley said, the word bitter. "And I've been paying for it ever since."

"By feeding the Field, "Victor said. "By identifying potential authors, luring them here, helping them connect with the narrative network. How many before Mr. Varn, Ashley? How many authors have you seduced into feeding themselves to the Field?"

"That's enough." William stepped between them, facing Hail. "Whatever she did, whatever arrangement you had, it's over. We're leaving Cartersville. Both of us."

Hail laughed again, and this time the machines laughed with him, a chorus of mechanical hysteria that shook the walls. "Leave? Oh, Mr. Varn. Still so naive. Let me show you something."

He pulled a lever, and electricity arced through the neural network. The sphere pulsed, and suddenly the air was full of them—the horrors William had written in his darkest moments, given flesh.

The Weeping Woman from chapter seven, her face a ruin of torn skin and exposed bone, reaching out with fingers that dripped blood that never stopped flowing. The Backward Man from his unpublished novella, joints reversed, walking on hands with feet that grabbed, his head on backwards, smiling that horrible, endless smile. The Swarm from his short story collection—thousands of insects that weren't quite insects, each one with a tiny human face, screaming in unison.

They materialized from the crackling air, his nightmares made real, surrounding them.

"You see? "Victor said, his voice calm amid the manifestations. "Every horror you've imagined, every monstrous thing you've put to paper—they all exist here, in the Field. And they're hungry, Mr. Varn. So very hungry."

The creatures moved closer, and William could smell them—rot and copper and the sick-sweet scent of infected flesh. The Weeping Woman reached for him, her fingernails scraping against his cheek, leaving trails of blood that wasn't his but felt like it was.

"Stop," Ashley commanded, and to William's surprise, the creatures hesitated. She pulled out a notebook—leather-bound, older than the one she'd shown him before. "You want to play with manifestations, Hail? Fine."

She began to write, speaking the words aloud as her pen moved: "The laboratory's defenses turned inward, recognizing their master as the true threat. The machines that had served him so faithfully understood, finally, that he had corrupted their purpose."

The machines around them began to spark violently. The tubes connecting them burst, spraying that fluorescent liquid that burned where it touched. The neural sphere's pulsing became erratic, aggressive.

"You can't! "Victor shouted, frantically adjusting controls. "I built this place! I control it!"

"No," Ashley said, continuing to write. "You're just another prisoner. Another author who thought he could master the Field and became its servant instead. How long has it been since you've tried to leave, Hail?

Decades? Do you even remember sunlight that isn't filtered through the Field's influence?"

The grotesque creatures William had created began to turn, their attention shifting to Hail. The Backward Man scuttled toward him, grinning that inverted grin. The Swarm buzzed around his head, tiny voices screaming accusations.

"This is what you wanted, isn't it?" Ashley asked. "To see your creations come to life? To play God with narrative and reality?"

"I was trying to understand it! "Victor backed away from his own machines as they began to close in, their mechanical parts grinding ominously. "The Field is the future of human consciousness! The merger of story and reality! I've spent ninety years—"

"Ninety years turning people into puppets," William interrupted. "Ninety years feeding the Field human stories, human pain."

"Because that's what it needs! Don't you see? The Field is alive, and like any living thing, it needs to feed. Stories are its food, and tragedy, horror, loss—these are the richest nutrients."

The Weeping Woman had reached Victor now, her bloody hands caressing his face with a grotesque parody of tenderness. He tried to push her away, but she was strong, impossibly strong, made of all the fears William had ever put to paper.

"Call them off, "Victor pleaded. "You don't understand what you're doing. Without me to regulate it, the Field will consume everything. Every story in Cartersville will manifest simultaneously. The town will tear itself apart!"

"Then tell us how to stop it," William demanded. "How to shut down the Field permanently."

Hail laughed, high and hysterical. "Stop it? You can't stop it! It's not a machine you can turn off. It's a living narrative ecosystem that exists in the spaces between reality and fiction. It was here before the town, before humanity, perhaps. We just found it and fed it and made it stronger."

The laboratory was collapsing now, machines exploding in showers of sparks and steam. The neural sphere cracked, leaking a luminescent fluid that moved as if it had a purpose, crawling across the floor toward them.

"There is a way," Ashley said quietly. "Isn't there, Hail? A way to sever the Field's connection to our reality. That's what you've been afraid of all along—not that the Field would die, but that it would leave, take its gifts with it, leave you as just a man again."

Hail's face went pale. "You don't know what you're asking. Without the Field, every story ever written here will collapse. Every manifestation will dissolve. Everyone who's been touched by it will forget. The town itself might cease to exist—it's been so shaped by narrative that reality might not remember what was here before."

"Maybe that's for the best," William said.

"You would destroy it all? Your own work? Your love story?" Hail's eyes darted between them. "Because that will go too. Whatever you feel for each other, however real it seems, it's all built on the Field's foundation. Remove that, and what's left? Can you love someone when you can't remember the story of how you met?"

William looked at Ashley, saw his own uncertainty reflected in her eyes. Everything they'd shared, every moment, every word, how much of it was real and how much was narrative?

"I don't care," Ashley said finally. "If what we have only exists because of the Field, then it's not worth keeping."

"Agreed," William said, though the word felt like swallowing glass.

The Weeping Woman had wrapped her arms around Victor now, her embrace tightening as he struggled. "Please," he gasped. "I'll tell you everything. How to control it, how to escape it, how to destroy it. Just call them off!"

Ashley closed her notebook. The creatures froze, became translucent, flickering between existence and void.

"Talk," she said.

Hail slumped to the ground, his face aged decades in moments. "The heart of the Field isn't here. This is just an access point, a terminal. The true Field exists in the space between written words and their meaning, in the quantum foam where potential stories exist before they're told."

"How do we reach it?" William asked.

"You don't reach it. You write your way to it. A story that acknowledges its own existence as a story, that breaks the fourth wall not just of narrative but of reality itself." He looked up at them with hollow eyes. "But the cost—"

"We know the cost," Ashley said. "We're willing to pay it."

"Are you? Because it's not just your memories you'll lose. It's your capacity to create, to write, to imagine stories. The Field will take that with it when it goes. You'll be ordinary people in an ordinary town, with no magic, no power, no purpose beyond the mundane."

"Better that than this," William said, gesturing at the collapsing laboratory, the manifestations, the horror of their reality. "Better to be real and ordinary than fictional and extraordinary."

Hail laughed one last time, a sound full of bitter defeat. "Then you're already lost. Because in choosing reality over story, you're choosing death over immortality. Stories last forever, Mr. Varn. Reality? Reality just ends."

The neural sphere finally shattered completely, and the laboratory began to fold in on itself, space warping, distances becoming meaningless. William grabbed Ashley's hand as the floor tilted, then became a wall, and finally a ceiling.

"Run, "Victor said, his voice already fading as the Field began to reclaim him. "Run, and write your ending. But know that in destroying the Field, you destroy the very thing that made you extraordinary."

They ran, hand in hand, through corridors that shifted and changed, up stairs that became downs, through doors that opened onto themselves. Behind them, Hail's laughter echoed, mixing with the screams of the manifested horrors as they dissolved back into nothing.

When they finally burst out onto the street, gasping and shaking, the building was gone. Where it had stood was just an empty lot, overgrown with weeds, as if nothing had ever been there at all.

"He's gone," Ashley said, and William wasn't sure if she meant Victor or the building or something else entirely.

"But we're not," he said, squeezing her hand. "We're still here. Still together."

"For now," she said, and in her eyes, he saw the weight of what they'd learned, what they'd have to do.

They stood there in the empty lot, holding each other, as around them, Cartersville continued its slow collapse into narrative chaos. But for this moment, they were just two people, facing an impossible choice together.

"I need to tell you something," Ashley said. "About Chicago. About what really happened."

"Later," William said. "When we're safe. When this is over."

"Will it ever be over?"

He didn't answer because he didn't know. But he held her tighter, and for now, that was enough.

Chapter 16: The Master Manuscript

The library after midnight was a different creature entirely.

Gone was the dusty quiet of day, the gentle rustle of pages, the whispered conversations between shelves. In darkness, it became a labyrinth of shadows and whispers, every book a sleeping consciousness that stirred when disturbed. William followed Ashley through the stacks, their footsteps muffled by carpet that seemed to absorb sound like a living thing.

"After Hail's laboratory collapsed," Ashley said, her voice barely above a whisper, "I remembered something. A section of the library I'd been told never to enter. Sub-basement three, behind the genealogy archives."

She carried a ring of keys that looked far too old for any lock in the building—iron things, corroded and heavy, some shaped like bones, others twisted into symbols that hurt to look at directly. They descended a staircase hidden behind a false panel in the reference section, the air growing colder with each step.

"How long have you known about this?" William asked.

"Since I arrived. It was part of my... arrangement with Hail. Certain areas were forbidden. But with him gone—" She paused at a rusted door marked only with a symbol that looked like an eye made of words. "The prohibitions died with him."

The lock accepted a key shaped like a broken quill. The door opened on hinges that screamed like something dying.

Beyond was a vault that predated the library by centuries. The walls were carved stone, sweating moisture that smelled of earth and decay. Symbols covered every surface—not quite language, not quite art, but something between that seemed to shift when viewed peripherally. In the center of the room stood a pedestal made from what looked like a single piece of fossilized wood, dark and twisted.

On it sat the book.

It was massive, nearly two feet tall and a foot thick, bound in leather that had an unsettling texture—too smooth in some places, too rough in others, as if the skin had been taken from multiple creatures and poorly stitched together. The cover bore no title, just an embossed symbol that matched the one on the door.

"This is it," Ashley breathed. "The Master Manuscript. The first story fed to the Field, the one that created the connection between narrative and reality in Cartersville."

William approached it slowly, his skin prickling with each step. The book seemed to pulse with its own heartbeat, or perhaps it was matching his, synchronizing with his rhythm. When he touched the cover, images flooded his mind—every moment since his arrival in Cartersville, but viewed from outside, as if he'd been watching himself in a film.

He opened it.

The first page bore a signature: *M.Q. - 1931*

"Your initials," he said, turning to Ashley.

"Look at the date," she said. "1931. I wasn't born until—"

"Ashley Quinn," William read from the second page. "Librarian. Keeper. Guide. Born 1878, died 1931, reborn 1997, died 2019, reborn 2023." He looked up at her, his hands trembling. "What does this mean?"

She was pale, pressed against the wall as if trying to stay as far from the book as possible. "I don't know. I swear I don't know."

He turned pages, each one revealing more impossibilities. The manuscript contained not just his story in Cartersville, but hers, written in a hand that was almost but not quite her own—as if someone had been trying to forge her handwriting but kept slipping into their own style.

And then he found it. The chapter titled: "The Eternal Return of Ashley Quinn."

She does not remember her deaths, which is a mercy. Each time the Field requires a new librarian, it rebuilds her from the stories told about her, from the love letters written to her by doomed authors, from the grief of those who lost her. She is a composite ghost, a woman made of words, reformed again and again to play her role in the eternal narrative.

The first Ashley Quinn died in 1931, sacrificing herself to seal a rupture in the Field that threatened to consume the entire town. But the Field learned from her sacrifice, learned that love was the most powerful narrative force. So, it brought her back, again and again, each time with just enough memory to be herself but not enough to remember what she truly was.

A character in search of an author. A muse built from the bones of stories.

"No," Ashley whispered. "That's not... I remember my childhood. My parents. Growing up in Michigan."

"Do you?" William turned more pages, finding photographs tucked between chapters—daguerreotypes, tintypes, modern prints. All of the same woman, the same face, the same eyes, but in different eras. Ashley in a 1920s flapper dress. Ashley in 1950s cat-eye glasses. Ashley in a 1970s peasant blouse. Always the librarian. Always waiting.

"These could be faked," she said, but her voice was breaking.

"The handwriting," William said, comparing pages. "It changes. Look." He showed her sections where the careful script shifted, becoming something older and more ornate. "Someone else has been writing in this. Adding to your story."

He turned to the middle of the book, where the pages became thicker, older. The text here was in Latin, then Greek, then something that pre-dated human language—symbols that seemed to crawl across the page like living things.

And there, pressed between two pages like a grotesque bookmark, was a skeletal hand.

It still clutched a quill made from what might have been a human finger bone, the tip stained with ink that looked fresh despite the obvious age of the remains. The bones were delicate, feminine, with a ring still circling one finger, a simple band with initials engraved inside: *M.Q.*

"The first Ashley," William said quietly.

Ashley reached for the hand, then jerked back as if burned. "I can feel her. Oh God, William, I can feel her memories. All of them. All of me." She clutched her head, doubling over. "We're all here, all the Ashleys, layered on top of each other like palimpsest. I'm not real. I'm just the latest draft."

"You're real to me," William said, reaching for her.

"Don't!" She backed away. "Don't you see? This is what the Field does. It creates us, puts us together, watches us fall in love, then harvests the story. You're probably not the first William either. We're all just iterations of the same tragic romance, playing out again and again for the Field's sustenance."

He wanted to deny it, but as he turned more pages, he found evidence—other authors, other names, but the same essential story. A writer comes to Cartersville. Falls in love with the librarian. Discovers the truth about the Field. Tries to break free. Fails.

"Except," he said, reading more carefully, "they didn't all fail the same way. Look." He showed her a section near the end, where multiple hands had written conflicting endings. "Someone's been trying to change the story. Trying to find a way out."

The pages here were chaos—words written over words, entire paragraphs scratched out and rewritten, margins filled with desperate notes in different hands, different languages, different eras. All searching for the same thing: an ending that didn't end in tragedy.

"'The key is in the paradox,'" Ashley read from one margin note. "'If the story acknowledges itself as a story, it cannot maintain the illusion of reality.'"

"'Break the fourth wall of existence itself,'" William read from another. "'Make the Field see itself seeing itself.'"

"'Love is not the answer,'" a third note said in shaky handwriting. "'Love is the trap. The Field feeds on love. Starve it instead.'"

"No," Ashley said, reading a response written in different ink. "'Love is the only thing that transcends the narrative. But it must be love that exists outside the story, love that refuses to be written.'"

They looked at each other across the vault, the Master Manuscript between them like an accusation.

"How can I love you," William asked, "when I don't know if you're real?"

"How can I love you," Ashley responded, "when I don't know if I'm capable of real love or just programmed to feel it?"

The book suddenly slammed shut on its own, the sound echoing through the vault like a gunshot. When William tried to open it again, the pages had changed. Now there was only one chapter, freshly written in ink that was still wet:

"The Final Iteration."

It was their story but told from the Field's perspective. How it had crafted them both from the fragments of previous attempts. It had learned from each failure, refining the narrative to make the romance more compelling and the tragedy more inevitable. They were its masterpiece, the perfect author and librarian, designed to generate the most powerful story yet.

But there was something else, hidden in the subtext. A weakness. The Field had become too invested in their story, too attached to its creation. It wasn't just feeding on their love, it had begun to feel something like love itself, for the drama it had created, for the characters it had built.

"It's afraid," Ashley said, understanding dawning in her eyes. "The Field is afraid we'll succeed where the others failed. Because we're not just characters to it anymore. We're its favorite story. And if we end ourselves..."

"We end its ability to feel," William finished. "It's become addicted to us, to watching us love and lose each other. That's why it keeps bringing you back, why it probably brought me here. It needs us to complete the story, but it also needs us to never complete it."

The skeletal hand on the pedestal suddenly moved, the bones clicking as it released the quill. The finger bone pen rolled across the manuscript's cover, leaving a trail of fresh ink that formed words:

Choose your ending, but choose knowing: every ending is a beginning, every death a birth, every farewell a promise of return. You cannot escape the story by ending it. You can only escape by refusing to be in it at all.

"That's the paradox," Ashley said. "We can't write our way out because writing keeps us in. We can't love our way out because love is what feeds it. We can't die our way out because death just leads to rebirth."

"Then what do we do?"

She picked up the bone quill, and for a moment, her face overlapped with others, all the Ashleys who had held this pen before. "We do what no author and librarian have done before. We refuse to play our roles."

"Meaning?"

"We don't write an ending. We don't declare our love. We don't sacrifice ourselves for each other." She looked at him, and her eyes were clear, determined, entirely her own. "We just walk away. Separately. Without resolution."

"That's not a story," William said.

"Exactly." She set the quill down on the open manuscript. "The Field needs narrative structure. Beginning, middle, end. If we refuse to give it an ending, if we just stop mid-sentence, mid-scene, mid-word even—"

"It can't process it. It can't archive an incomplete story."

"And maybe, just maybe, that breaks the cycle."

They stood there, facing each other across the Master Manuscript, knowing what they had to do but unable to do it. To walk away from each other, without closure, without goodbye, went against every instinct.

"I don't know if I can," William admitted.

"Neither do I." She was crying now, tears falling onto the manuscript, causing the ink to run. "Every part of me, whether real or written, wants to run to you, to have our dramatic finale, our last kiss, our tragic farewell."

"The Field is counting on that."

"I know." She took a step backward, toward the door. "So, we don't. We just... stop."

"No goodbye?"

"No goodbye. No see you later. No meaningful last looks. We just turn and walk in opposite directions, and we never look back."

"What if we're wrong? What if this doesn't break the cycle?"

"Then at least we didn't give it the satisfaction of another perfect tragedy."

They stood there for one more moment, not speaking, not touching, barely breathing. The Master Manuscript pulsed between them, waiting for its ending.

Instead, they turned away from each other. No last words. No final gestures. They simply walked toward opposite doors, their footsteps echoing in the vault.

The manuscript began to smoke, pages curling, ink running in rivers of black that looked like tears or blood or both. The skeletal hand crumbled to dust. The vault itself began to crack, reality fracturing where the story had no ending to hold it together.

But William didn't look back. Neither did Ashley.

They walked away from their story, leaving it unfinished, leaving the Field hungry and confused, leaving love unspoken and tragedy unaverted.

And in that incompleteness, that refusal to conclude, they found the only freedom possible—the freedom of an unwritten ending.

Chapter 17: Collapse Begins

William woke to find the sun setting in the east.

He stood at his bedroom window, watching the impossible sunset paint the eastern sky in shades of blood and amber while the western horizon brightened toward a dawn that should have been twelve hours away. The clock on his nightstand spun wildly—3:47 AM, 9:23 PM, 14:91 QX, symbols that weren't numbers, then nothing at all, just a blank face with hands that moved independent of time.

It had been three days since he and Ashley had walked away from each other in the vault. Three days of not looking for her, not writing about her, not even allowing himself to think her name. The incomplete story ate at him like acid, every instinct screaming to find her, to finish what they'd started, to give the narrative its resolution.

But they'd held firm. And now Cartersville was paying the price.

Outside, a flock of starlings flew backward through the air, their wings beating in reverse, their bodies moving tail-first across the inverted sky. They sang their dawn chorus at dusk, or their evening song at dawn—he couldn't tell anymore which was which. Time had become negotiable, a suggestion rather than a law.

He dressed quickly and stepped outside to find his neighbor, Mr. Peterson, mowing his lawn with a lawnmower that had no blades. The grass grew taller with each pass, reaching toward a sun that couldn't decide where to be.

"Morning, William!" Peterson called cheerfully. "Or evening! Hard to say these days!"

"Are you alright?" William asked.

"Never better!" Peterson replied, his smile too wide, his eyes reflecting different scenes in each pupil—one showed a sunrise, the other the depths of space. "Though I can't seem to remember if I'm supposed to be young or old today."

As he spoke, his face flickered between ages—twenty, fifty, eighty, then back to twenty. His clothes changed too, cycling through decades of fashion in seconds. For a moment, he was transparent, and William could see through him to the house beyond, which was itself cycling through various states of construction and decay.

The street was worse. Houses existed and didn't exist simultaneously, their quantum states uncertain without narrative to anchor them. The Victorian mansion on the corner was a pile of lumber one moment, a pristine painted lady the next, then nothing but an empty lot with a FOR SALE sign in a language that had never existed.

A car drove by in reverse, its driver facing backward, somehow navigating perfectly while looking where he'd been instead of where he was going. A dog walked its owner, the leash extending from the animal's collar to the human's neck. Children played hopscotch on numbers that went backward and forward and sometimes diagonal through dimensions that shouldn't exist.

And everywhere, everywhere, there were the gaps where reality simply wasn't. Holes in the world that showed nothing, not darkness, not void, just absence. The lack of anything at all.

William had to find Ashley.

He knew this was exactly what the Field wanted—to drive them back together, to force them to complete their story. But the thought of her lost in this collapsing reality was unbearable. Their incomplete ending was destroying everything, and if she was caught in the dissolution...

He headed toward the library, but the streets kept rearranging themselves. He'd walk down Maple Street and end up on Oak. Turn left on Main and find himself back at his house. The town was a maze that re-formed itself with each step, trying to keep him from his destination or perhaps trying to lead him somewhere specific.

The library, when he finally reached it, was wrong. It existed in multiple states simultaneously—new construction, established building, burnt ruins, empty lot. The walls phased in and out of existence, and through the gaps, he could see infinite versions of the same space. In one, Ashley stood at her desk, frozen mid-motion. In another, the library was full of water, books floating like dead fish. In a third, everything was made of glass, including the people inside, transparent and fragile.

"Ashley!" he called, but his voice came out backward, the sound preceding his intention to speak.

He pushed through the fluctuating door—solid, liquid, gas, plasma, then solid again—and found himself in a library that couldn't decide what it was. Books flew off shelves, arranging themselves in the air to spell out words: INCOMPLETE. UNFINISHED. HUNGRY. FEED US.

The floor was simultaneously carpet, wood, marble, and nothing. He had to feel his way forward, trusting his feet to find purchase on surfaces that might or might not exist. The reference section was a maze of mirrors, each one reflecting a different version of him—author, prisoner, ghost, god, nothing.

"Ashley!" he called again, and this time the word echoed in languages he didn't speak, in voices that weren't his.

A response came from everywhere and nowhere: "She's gone."

The voice was the Field itself, speaking through the fabric of reality. Not the whispers he'd heard before, but a full voice, desperate and angry and afraid.

"Where is she?" William demanded.

"Dispersed. Dissolved. Returned to component narratives." Books began forming into a crude face on the wall, their spines creating features that shifted and reformed constantly. "You broke the pattern. Refused the ending. Now she fragments back into all the Ashleys who came before."

"Bring her back!"

"Complete the story first. Give us resolution. Climax. Denouement. The structure must be satisfied."

"No."

The library shuddered, and reality glitched harder. For a moment, William existed in multiple places at once—at Ashley's desk, in the vault, at his house, in the cemetery, all simultaneously. He could feel himself spreading thin, his consciousness unable to maintain coherence without narrative structure to hold it together.

Through the chaos, he saw her—or pieces of her. Ashley in a 1920s dress, shelving books that turned to moths when she touched them. Ashley in modern clothes, typing at a computer that kept melting and reforming. Ashley in Victorian garb, reading from a book that read her back.

All the iterations, all the versions, existing separately because without their story's conclusion, they couldn't integrate into a single person.

"Ashley!" He reached for the nearest version, but his hand passed through her like she was mist.

She turned, they all turned, all the Ashleys, looking at him with eyes that recognized him but didn't know him, couldn't know him because their stories were incomplete.

"Who are you?" the Victorian Ashley asked.

"We haven't met yet," said the 1920s version.

"We'll never meet," said the modern one. "The story doesn't allow it."

"Yes, it does," William insisted. "We met. We fell in love. We discovered the truth about the Field."

"Did we?" they asked in unison. "Or was that another iteration? Another William? How can you be sure you're the real one?"

He looked down at his hands and saw them flickering—young, old, calloused, smooth, existing, not existing. He was fragmenting too, all the possible versions of himself that the Field had considered, all the drafts that had been written and discarded.

"The only way to save her," the Field's voice rumbled through the walls, "is to complete the narrative. Give us an ending, any ending. Love, tragedy, sacrifice, we're not particular anymore. Just finish the story so reality can stabilize."

"That's what you want," William said, forcing himself to focus, to maintain his singular existence through sheer will. "For us to panic, to give in, to complete the cycle."

"The town is dying without narrative structure. Look outside."

He did. Through the library windows, Cartersville was dissolving. Buildings aged centuries in seconds, then reversed to blueprints, then to the ideas of buildings, then to nothing. People walked through walls that weren't there, fell through floors that existed only sometimes, spoke in languages that uninvented themselves mid-sentence.

The convergence zones from the cemetery had spread everywhere. Past, present, and future occurred simultaneously. He saw the indigenous peoples who had lived here before the town, the Civil War battles that had scarred the land, the current residents, and shadowy figures from futures that might never be—all existing in the same space, passing through each other like ghosts.

"This is what happens without story," the Field said. "Chaos. Meaninglessness. Existence without purpose or direction."

"Maybe that's better than being trapped in someone else's narrative."

"Is it? Look at her."

The Ashleys were beginning to fade, each iteration becoming more transparent. Without a unified story to hold them together, they were dissipating back into the Field's reservoir of unused narratives.

"She'll cease to exist entirely soon," the Field taunted. "Not death—complete erasure. As if she never was. Is your principle worth that?"

William moved toward the fading Ashleys, trying to hold onto at least one version, but they slipped through his grasp like water, like words, like dreams upon waking.

"Please," he said, not to the Field but to her, to all of her. "Remember. We walked away from each other in the vault. No goodbye, no closure. That was our rebellion."

"I don't remember a vault," the Victorian Ashley said.

"I don't remember you," the 1920s version added.

"I remember something," the modern Ashley said slowly. "A feeling. Like a story interrupted mid-sentence. Like a word on the tip of my tongue that I can't quite—"

She solidified slightly, becoming more real.

"Yes!" William moved closer to her. "We refused to finish our story. We walked away without ending it. That's why this is happening—we broke the narrative structure."

"But why would we do that?" she asked.

"To be free. To stop being characters in the Field's endless tragedy."

She looked at him, and for a moment, he saw recognition in her eyes. Not just of him, but of what they'd done, why they'd done it.

"The incomplete story," she whispered. "The unfinished ending. We thought it would starve the Field."

"Instead, it's unraveling everything."

Around them, the library was ceasing to be. Books became words, words became letters, letters became concepts, concepts became nothing. The other Ashleys had faded completely, leaving only this one, partially substantial version.

"We have to choose," she said. "Complete the story and remain trapped or maintain our incompleteness and watch everything dissolve."

"There has to be another way."

"Does there? Every story needs an ending, William. Even the story of refusing to have a story."

The Field laughed, a sound like thunder made of words. "You see? You cannot escape narrative. Even your rebellion becomes a story—the story of the author and librarian who tried to break free by refusing to end. But that, too, is an ending."

William felt the trap closing. They'd thought they were so clever, walking away without resolution. But that action itself had become their narrative to star-crossed lovers who chose incompletion. It was still a story, still feeding the Field, just a different kind of food.

"Unless," Ashley said suddenly, her eyes brightening. "Unless we make it impossible to tell."

"What do you mean?"

"Every story needs consistency, even inconsistent ones. What if we become paradoxical? Not just incomplete, but actively contradictory?"

"How?"

She took his hand, and he felt how insubstantial she was, how close to disappearing entirely. "We complete the story and don't complete it. We say goodbye and don't say goodbye. We love each other and don't know each other. We exist and don't exist."

"That's impossible."

"Exactly. And impossibility is the one thing the Field can't archive."

The library shook, reality fracturing further. Through the cracks, William could see the raw stuff of narrative—words floating in void, sentences being born and dying, paragraphs eating themselves, chapters giving birth to chapters in an endless cycle of creation and destruction.

"If we do this," he said, "we might cease to exist entirely. Or exist in a state of constant paradox."

"Better than being a character in someone else's story."

He squeezed her fading hand. "Together?"

"Together and apart. Always and never."

They stood there, in the collapsing library, in the dissolving town, at the epicenter of a narrative breakdown that threatened to consume everything. And they prepared to do the impossible—to end and not end, to be and not be, to love and not love, all at once.

"The Field won't survive it," Ashley said.

"Neither might we."

"I know."

They looked at each other, seeing all the versions they had been, might be, would never be. Every iteration of their love story collapsed into this single moment of impossible choice.

"Ready?" she asked.

"No. Yes. Both."

She smiled, and it was heartbreaking and joyful and neither and both.

"Then let's tell our story. And not tell it. Forever and never."

The library exploded inward, reality folding on itself, as they began to speak their paradox into existence—the ending that was not an ending, the story that destroyed story, the love that transcended narrative by refusing to be narrated.

Cartersville screamed, the Field raged, and existence itself held its breath as two people chose to become impossible rather than remain fictional.

The collapse had truly begun.

Chapter 18: The Erasure

William found himself in his house without remembering how he'd gotten there.

The last thing he recalled was the library collapsing, Ashley's hand in his as they spoke their paradox into existence. Then—nothing. A blank space in his memory, like a page torn from a book. He stood in his study, still wearing the same clothes, but they were dry despite the rain he could hear hammering against the windows. Rain that fell upward, drops rising from the ground to disappear into clouds that shouldn't exist at noon.

The Master Manuscript lay open on his desk, though he was certain he'd left it in the library vault.

No—wait. Had there been a vault? The memory flickered, uncertain. Sometimes, there was a vault beneath the library; sometimes, there wasn't. Sometimes he'd found the manuscript there, sometimes it had always been here, in his study, waiting.

He approached the book carefully. Its leather binding pulsed like skin over a beating heart, and the pages rustled without any wind to move them. The text was different now—not the history of Cartersville's authors, not the accumulated stories of the Field, but something else. Something worse.

It was his story with Ashley, but wrong. Edited. Redacted.

Where her name should have been were blank spaces, rectangular voids in the text that hurt to look at. Not white space—absence. Places where reality simply wasn't, as if someone had taken scissors to the fabric of existence and cut her out.

The author arrived in Cartersville on a rain-soaked evening. He would meet [VOID] at the library, where [VOID] worked among dusty books and forgotten stories. Their first conversation sparked something immediate—[VOID]'s green eyes meeting his with recognition that transcended mere attraction.

"No," William whispered, running his fingers over the gaps. They felt like nothing—not cold, not warm, not smooth, not rough. His fingers simply ceased to have sensation where they touched the voids.

He flipped pages frantically. Every mention of her, every scene they'd shared, every word she'd spoken—erased. But not cleanly. The voids left scars in the narrative, wounds that bled black ink that formed almost-words, ghost-sentences that suggested what had been removed.

[VOID] kissed him in the cemetery among the convergence zones, her lips tasting of [VOID] and the promise of [VOID]. He held [VOID] close, feeling the warmth of [VOID] against the supernatural cold, knowing that [VOID] was both salvation and damnation, both real and [VOID].

The house groaned around him. Where Ashley had been erased from the story, reality was following suit. A void appeared in his kitchen wall where she'd leaned while they'd talked over coffee. Another in the doorway where she'd stood the night she'd warned him about the Field. The empty spaces spread like infection, eating away at any place she'd existed.

He grabbed a pen, his hands shaking, and began to write her back in:

Ashley Quinn. Librarian. Dark hair that caught the light like polished wood. Green eyes that held secrets and sorrow in equal measure. Her laugh, rare but genuine, sounding like wind chimes in a gentle breeze. The way she bit her lower lip when concentrating. The scent of old books and lavender that followed her.

The words appeared on the page for a moment, then dissolved, eaten by the voids. He tried again, more desperately:

ASHLEY EXISTS. ASHLEY IS REAL. ASHLEY QUINN IS THE LIBRARIAN OF CARTERSVILLE AND THE WOMAN I LOVE.

The manuscript fought him. The letters writhed like living things, trying to escape his intentions. Some made it onto the page only to be immediately consumed. Others transformed mid-stroke—M became W, A became V, R became nothing, and A became forever.

That's when he saw it. In the margin, in handwriting that was definitely hers despite the impossibility of it, a note:

Don't save me.

But there was something strange about the letters. They weren't quite aligned; some were slightly higher than others, and some were tilted at odd angles. A cipher. She'd hidden something in the message itself.

He studied it carefully, his eyes burning from staring at the voids that surrounded the note. The raised letters: O-N-V-E. The tilted ones: C-R-G-E. The ones that seemed bolder: Z-O-N-S.

Convergence zones. She was telling him something about the convergence zones.

He flipped through the manuscript, looking for other marginal notes. They were scattered throughout, each one seemingly simple but containing hidden messages:

Let the story end. (Hidden: Find me where we didn't meet.)

Stop rewriting reality. (Hidden: The vault remembers.)

I choose this. (Hidden: Break the fourth wall.)

The codes painted a different picture than the surface message. She wasn't gone—she was hidden. She'd erased herself deliberately, but left him clues, a trail of breadcrumbs through the narrative void.

A memory surfaced suddenly, vivid and painful: Ashley in his bed, her skin warm against his, tracing patterns on his chest as dawn light filtered through the curtains.

"If I disappear," she'd said, apropos of nothing, "don't look for me in the obvious places."

"You're not going to disappear," he'd replied, pulling her closer.

"But if I do. If the Field takes me, or if I have to hide from it. Look for me in the spaces between words. In the pauses between heartbeats. In the moments that didn't quite happen but almost did."

He hadn't understood then. He did now.

The voids weren't just absences; they were hiding places. Ashley had written herself out of the main narrative but hadn't ceased to exist. She'd become liminal, existing in the gaps, in the spaces the Field couldn't quite see because they weren't properly part of the story.

He looked at the voids with new eyes. They weren't empty, they were full of potential, of unwritten possibilities. And in their depths, if he looked just right, he could see movement. Shadows of shadows. The suggestion of a woman with dark hair and green eyes, existing in the margins of existence.

Another memory crashed over him: their first kiss, but not the one in the cemetery. An earlier one, one that hadn't quite happened. They'd been in the library after hours, discussing the manuscript he'd found. She'd been explaining the danger of the Field, and he'd stepped closer, drawn by something beyond mere attraction. Their lips had been inches apart when she'd pulled back, saying it was too dangerous, too soon.

But for a moment, in that space between intention and action, they had kissed. In a timeline that didn't quite exist, in a possibility that never manifested, they'd come together. And that almost-kiss, that void-moment, was where she was hiding now.

He began to write differently. Not trying to force her back into the narrative, but writing around her, creating spaces for her to exist in:

The author stood in his study, talking to the emptiness that wasn't empty. He spoke of love to the absence that was presence, of futures to the void that was full. He knew she could hear him in the spaces between his words, could see him in the pause between one heartbeat and the next.

"I understand," he said to nothing, to everything. "You had to remove yourself from the story to save us both. But erasure isn't disappearance. You're still here, aren't you? In the margins, in the white space, in the breath between sentences."

The voids pulsed, and for a moment, he swore he could see her—translucent, ethereal, existing in a state between being and not being. She was speaking, but the words existed in frequencies the human ear couldn't catch, in languages that had no sounds.

He continued writing, creating more spaces for her:

The house had rooms that didn't exist but were remembered. Conversations that hadn't happened but were true. Love that couldn't be written but was real. In these impossible spaces, in these paradoxical moments, she dwelled.

The manuscript began to change. The voids stopped spreading, stabilizing into something like doorways. Through them, he could glimpse another version of reality—one where Ashley existed fully, where she was writing in a manuscript of her own, creating spaces for him to exist in.

They were writing parallel stories, he realized. Two narratives that never quite touched but influenced each other, like quantum particles entangled across impossible distances. She in her void-space, he in his reality-space, both reaching through the gaps for each other.

Another memory, or vision, or possibility: Ashley standing in a place that was all white space, all margin, all the unused portions of every page ever written. She was surrounded by the unwritten, the deleted, the edited-out. She was queen of the liminal, goddess of the spaces between.

"The Field can't see me here," her voice came from everywhere and nowhere. "It can only see what's written, what's part of the narrative. I exist in the redactions, in the censored portions, in the parts of the story that were deemed too dangerous or too true to tell."

"How do I get to you?" he asked the void.

"You don't. That would make me part of the story again. We must exist separately yet together, parallel yet never meeting. It's the only way to break the Field's hold."

"That's not enough," he said, his voice breaking. "I need to see you, to touch you, to know you're real."

"I am real. Just not in the way the Field understands reality. I'm real in the spaces between thoughts, in the moments between moments. Every time you don't quite see me in your peripheral vision, that's me. Every time you feel watched in an empty room, that's me. Every time a word is on the tip of your tongue, but you can't quite remember it, that's me trying to speak to you."

He kept writing, tears blurring his vision:

The author loved the absence. Not the memory of her, not the idea of her, but the actual absent presence of her. She was gone in a way that meant she was everywhere, erased in a manner that made her eternal. The Field could not touch what didn't exist in its narrative. It could not corrupt what it couldn't find.

The house continued to deteriorate around him, voids spreading where she'd been, but now he understood they weren't wounds—they were windows. Windows into a reality the Field couldn't access, couldn't control, couldn't feed upon.

"I'll find a way," he promised the emptiness. "I'll find a way to bring you back without trapping you in the story again."

The marginal note changed, the cipher shifting to reveal new words: *You already have.*

He looked at what he'd been writing, really looked at it. He hadn't been trying to restore her to the narrative—he'd been creating a new kind of story. One that existed in absence rather than presence, in a void rather than substance. A story the Field couldn't digest because it was made of nothing, of the spaces between things, of the pauses between words.

"An anti-story," he whispered.

The manuscript shuddered, and new text appeared, written in the Field's desperate hand:

This is not how stories work. Characters must exist. Events must happen. Beginnings must lead to endings. You cannot build a narrative from absence.

"Watch us," William said, and continued writing the story of nothing, the romance of absence, the gothic tale of voids and spaces, and the woman who existed in neither and both.

Outside, Cartersville continued to collapse and rebuild, collapse and rebuild, caught in a loop of existence and non-existence. But in his study, in the spaces between collapse and rebuild, William and Ashley were creating something new. This love story existed in erasure, a narrative composed of redactions, a romance written in invisible ink on pages that didn't exist.

The Field screamed its frustration through every crack in reality, but it couldn't stop them.

Because how do you prevent nothing from happening? How do you stop a story that isn't being told? How do you trap characters who exist only in the spaces you can't see?

William smiled, his pen moving across pages that were more void than paper now, writing his love letter to absence, his ode to erasure, his gothic romance of the spaces between.

And in those spaces, Ashley smiled back, existing in her own way, free from the Field's narrative, free from the need to be written.

They were apart. They were together. They were real. They were void.

They were, finally, free.

Chapter 19: The Dark Night

The storm arrived at midnight, but it was wrong in every possible way.

Lightning struck upward from the earth, branching into the sky like inverse trees of electric fire. Rain fell horizontally, sometimes vertically upward, sometimes in spirals that defied physics. The thunder came before the lightning, effect preceding cause, the sound of reality tearing before the visual confirmation of the rip.

William sat in his study, surrounded by manuscripts that kept rewriting themselves. The original pages he'd found in the walls. The Master Manuscript that had appeared and disappeared according to its own logic. His own notebooks, filled with stories he didn't remember writing. And, newest and most disturbing of all—a manuscript that had appeared an hour ago, bound in what looked like human skin, titled simply: "William Varn: A Character Study."

He'd been avoiding it, this new book, but the storm had driven him to it. As the house groaned and shifted around him, as the walls bled that viscous black substance that might have been ink or might have been something worse, he finally opened it.

The first line destroyed him:

William Varn was written into existence on a Tuesday, though he believed he had been born thirty-five years ago in Portland.

He read on, his hands trembling so violently he could barely turn the pages:

His memories were crafted from the recycled experiences of seventeen different authors who had come to Cartersville before him. His childhood fear of drowning stemmed from his time spent with Marcus Webb (1953-1954, which later merged into the Field). His mother's laugh was borrowed from the memories of Jonathan Price, who had consumed it (1981-1982). Even his name was a composite—William, from the prophet who challenged false gods, and Varn, from the Old English meaning "warning."

He was designed to be the perfect final author, the one who would complete the Field's grand narrative. Every quirk, every preference, every supposed free choice had been scripted. His love of Gothic literature—programmed. His tendency to write at night—inserted. His inevitable attraction to the librarian—hardwired into his very construction.

"No," he said aloud, but his voice sounded hollow, unconvincing even to himself.

He stood and moved to the mirror above the fireplace. In the storm's stroboscopic lightning, he saw himself flickering—solid, translucent, transparent, absent, solid again. His reflection wasn't quite synchronized with his movements, lagging half a second behind as if it needed time to process and mimic his actions.

He pressed his hand to the glass, and his reflection's hand met his a moment later. But through his translucent palm, he could see something else layers upon layers of other hands, other men, all pressing against the same mirror across different times. The authors who had come before, whose memories and experiences had been harvested to create him.

Look closer, the manuscript seemed to whisper from his desk.

He returned to it, reading about his construction with the horrified fascination of someone examining their own autopsy report:

*Layer One: Physical appearance compiled from the Field's aesthetic prefer-
ences, designed to appeal to the librarian archetype. Dark hair (from Author
#3), blue eyes (from Author #7), the specific way he ran his hand through his
hair when frustrated (from Author #11).*

*Layer Two: Personality traits selected for maximum narrative potential.
Brooding but not unapproachable. Intelligent but not arrogant. Romantic
but not naive. Each trait carefully balanced to create tension without repul-
sion, attraction without immediate culmination.*

*Layer Three: The backstory, meticulously crafted to explain his presence
in Cartersville while generating sympathy. The failed novel (every author's
fear), the ex-girlfriend who left him for someone more successful (relatable
pain), the inheritance that brought him to town (convenient but not suspi-
cious).*

He remembered that his great-aunt's house had been left to him in her
will. But as he thought about it, really examined the memory, it fell apart
like wet paper. What was his great-aunt's name? What did she look like?
When had he attended her funeral? The details that should have been there
weren't, just vague impressions, like a dream that made sense while sleeping
but dissolved upon waking.

Thunder shook the house—or was it the house shaking that caused the
thunder? Cause and effect were negotiable now, in this collapsed reality
where story and truth were indistinguishable.

He grabbed his notebook, the one he'd been writing in since arriving in
Cartersville, and flipped through it. His handwriting changed subtly from
entry to entry—sometimes slanting left, sometimes right, sometimes in
styles that looked almost but not quite like his own. As if different versions
of him had been writing, or as if he'd been unconsciously channeling the
authors whose pieces had been used to build him.

A memory surfaced Ashley in the library, their second meeting. She'd
said something strange that he'd dismissed at the time: "You're exactly as
described."

"Described where?" he'd asked.

"Oh, just... you fit the town. Like you were meant to be here."

She'd known. Even then, she'd known he wasn't real, or wasn't entirely real, or was real in a way that meant something different than he'd thought.

The manuscript on his desk had grown thicker. New pages were appearing even as he watched, writing themselves in that horrible, beautiful hand that might have been his, might have been everyone's, might have been no one's:

The perfect tragedy requires the perfect tragic hero. He must believe himself real, must believe his choices matter, must believe his love is genuine. The Field learned this over iterations—constructs who knew they were constructs produced inferior narratives. The story requires genuine emotion, even if the vessel experiencing it is artificial.

William Varn's emotional responses are real within the parameters of his existence. His love for the librarian—genuine within his constructed capacity for love. His fear, his anger, his hope—all authentic to his artificial nature. He is a real fake, a genuine fabrication, a truthful lie.

He threw the notebook across the room, and it hit the wall with a wet sound. Where it struck, the wall began to text—words appearing in the paint, sentences crawling across the surface like living things:

He rebels against his nature, which is part of his nature. He denies his construction, which his construction requires. He loves despite being built to love, which makes his love both real and unreal.

"Stop it!" he screamed at the walls, at the storm, at the Field itself.

But the house continued to write itself around him. Words appeared on every surface—floor, ceiling, furniture. His entire environment became a manuscript, and he was just another word in it, a character wondering if characters could wonder, thinking about thinking, trapped in recursive loops of existential horror.

He fell to his knees, overwhelmed by the weight of potentially not existing, or existing only as a literary device. The memories of Ashley crashed over him, each one now tainted with doubt:

Their first kiss in the cemetery—had he chosen to kiss her, or was it scripted?

The night they'd spent together, skin against skin, breathing each other's breath—was his desire real or programmed?

The way his heart broke when she'd erased herself—was that genuine pain or the Field pulling his narrative strings?

"Does it matter?" he asked the empty room.

The walls answered: *Everything matters. Nothing matters. Both. Neither. Choose your interpretation, but be aware that your choice is also scripted.*

He crawled to the corner where he'd thrown his notebook and picked it up. The pages were wet with something that wasn't quite water—thicker, warmer, with the iron taste of blood when he accidentally touched his finger to his lips after handling it.

Inside, new writing had appeared. His handwriting, but messages he hadn't written:

Remember me in the spaces between heartbeats.

That was Ashley's phrase, Ashley's message, but in his hand. Or was his hand just another version of her hand, were they both constructs built from the same narrative clay?

You're real enough, another message read. *Real enough to love. Real enough to choose. Real enough to break free.*

"But am I?" he asked the notebook. "If every choice I make is predetermined, if every feeling is programmed, if every thought is scripted—am I anything more than a very complex puppet?"

The storm intensified, and the house began to fold in on itself. Not collapsing—folding, like origami, three-dimensional space becoming two-dimensional, the walls becoming pages, the pages becoming words, the words becoming letters, the letters becoming nothing.

He found himself in a space that wasn't quite his study anymore. It was every room he'd ever been in, all existing simultaneously. The library where he'd met Ashley. The vault where they'd found the Master Manuscript. The laboratory where Victor had revealed the truth. His childhood bedroom—or the memory of a childhood bedroom that had never existed.

In the mirrors—and there were mirrors everywhere now, reflecting infinitely—he saw all his iterations. The William who had arrived in Cartersville full of hope. The William who had discovered the Field. The William who had fallen in love. The William who had tried to break free. And behind them all, shadowy figures of the authors whose pieces had been used to build him, their faces familiar and strange, their eyes both his and not his.

"I am Legion," he said, laughing at the biblical reference that wasn't really his, that came from Author #3 who had been a seminary student before becoming a writer. "For we are many."

But even as he descended into this existential spiral, something held firm at his core. A small, stubborn spark that insisted: *Even if I'm constructed, this consciousness experiencing itself is real. Even if my love was programmed, the feeling of it is genuine. Even if I'm a character, I'm a character who knows he's a character, and that knowledge makes me something more.*

The manuscript on his desk burst into flames—not orange fire but black flames that gave off cold instead of heat. The pages burned and reformed, burned and reformed, the words trying to escape their medium, to become real, to break free from the prison of narrative.

Through the flames, he saw new text forming:

The Field's greatest creation was also its greatest mistake. In building the perfect tragic hero, it created someone capable of recognizing tragedy, of refusing it, of choosing something beyond the narrative it had planned. William Varn might be a construct, but constructs can still construct. He might be written, but the written can still write.

He understood then. It didn't matter if he was real in the traditional sense. What mattered was that he could act, could choose, could love. Even if those actions, choices, and loves were influenced by his construction, they were still his in the moment of their execution.

The storm began to die, not gradually but suddenly, like someone had turned off a switch. The rain stopped mid-fall, droplets hanging in the air like glass beads. The lightning froze in its upward arc, creating electric sculptures in the sky. The thunder cut off mid-rumble, leaving a silence so complete it had its own sound.

In that impossible quiet, he heard something—a heartbeat that wasn't his, or was his, or was everyone's. The Field's pulse, or maybe just the rhythm of story itself, the eternal drumbeat of narrative that underlay all existence.

He picked up his pen, the one that might have been his, might have been borrowed from seventeen dead authors, might have been the Field's own instrument. And he began to write:

I am William Varn. I may be a construct, but I construct myself with every word. I may be a character, but I am a character who chooses his own story. I love Ashley Quinn, whether that love was programmed or genuine, because in the feeling of it, in the living of it, it becomes real.

I reject the tragedy the Field has written for me. Not because I deny my nature as a potentially artificial being, but because even artificial beings can choose their own endings. Even characters can rebel against their authors. Even constructs can construct themselves anew.

The walls stopped writing themselves. The mirrors showed only one reflection: solid, present, real enough. The storm resumed, but now it was just rain, wind, and thunder in their proper order.

He wasn't free of doubt. He might never be. But he was free to doubt, free to wonder, free to choose despite not knowing if his choices were truly his.

Somewhere in the void spaces of reality, Ashley existed in her erasure. And somewhere in the constructed spaces of narrative, he existed in his fabrication.

Both real. Both unreal. Both choosing to love despite or because of their nature.

The dark night was passing, not into dawn but into something strange twilight of being and not being, a liminal moment where constructs could be real and real things could be constructed.

He continued to write, creating himself with each word, authoring his own existence even if that existence was itself authored.

It was, he realized, the most human thing he could do.

Whether he was human or not.

Chapter 20: The Choice

The answer came to him at dawn, written in the dew on his window—condensation forming letters that spelled out a truth he'd been avoiding:

ONE MUST FEED THE FIELD TO CLOSE THE FIELD.

He wiped the words away, but they reformed immediately, more insistent:

THE AUTHOR BECOMES THE FINAL STORY.

Outside, Cartersville existed in fragments. Some houses were present, others were memory, still others were possibility. The streets ran in directions that changed depending on who walked them. The town was dying, reality itself growing thin from the paradoxes he and Ashley had created.

William dressed methodically, choosing clothes as if for a funeral—his own, he supposed. Black jacket over a white shirt that had somehow survived the chaos unmarked. His fingers trembled as he buttoned it, each button feeling like a small goodbye to the physical world.

The Master Manuscript lay open on his desk, and new text was forming even as he watched—not in any human hand now, but in something older, more primitive. Scratches that might have been cuneiform, might have been claw marks, might have been the universe's own attempt at writing:

Before Cartersville, before the Field as men know it, there was the Hunger. It existed in the space between what is and what is told, feeding on the gap between reality and narrative. The indigenous peoples knew it, feeding it carefully with small stories, controlling the narrative through controlled burns that kept it contained.

Then came the Europeans with their written words, their permanent stories, their need to document everything. The Hunger gorged itself, grew beyond its bounds, and became the Field. And at its heart, at the place where it first touched this world, stand the Etowah Mounds—older than the town, older than written history, the original altar where story and reality first learned they could bleed into each other.

The mounds. He'd been there with Ashley, had felt the power humming through the earth. But he hadn't understood then what they were—not burial sites, but binding sites. Places where the ancient peoples had tried to contain the Hunger before it became the Field.

He found the ritual in marginalia, written in multiple hands across multiple eras, each author adding pieces they'd discovered:

The Closing requires a paradox of sacrifice—to give everything while taking everything away. The author must write themselves into the Field while simultaneously writing the Field out of existence. Become the story that ends all stories.

Location: The central mound, at the convergence point where all ley lines meet.

Time: When reality is thin, neither day nor night, neither storm nor calm.

Method: The author must tell the True Story, the one that acknowledges all stories, contains all stories, and thus collapses under its own infinite weight.

Warning (added in a shaking hand): No author has survived the attempt. The Field consumes them, adds them to its collection, grows stronger.

Note (in different ink): But what if the author is already consumed? Already part of the Field? Can a construct destroy its own construction?

That last note felt like hope. If he was truly built from pieces of previous authors, if he was already part of the Field's narrative structure, then perhaps he could corrupt it from within. A virus of a story, a paradox that would bring the entire system to collapse.

He gathered what he needed: the original manuscript he'd found in the walls, now so swollen with additional pages it could barely close. His notebook, filled with his attempts to understand and escape. A photograph that had appeared on his mantle—him and Ashley at the library, though he couldn't remember it being taken. In it, she was laughing at something he'd said, her head thrown back, absolutely alive. He couldn't remember the joke, couldn't remember the moment, but the feeling of it lived in his chest like a bird made of light.

The walk to the Etowah Mounds should have taken an hour. It took forever and no time at all. The path kept folding back on itself, and he'd walk the same stretch of road multiple times, each iteration slightly different. Sometimes there were houses. Sometimes forest. Once, nothing but white void that his feet somehow found purchase on.

The mounds rose from the earth like sleeping giants, their grass-covered forms hiding ancient purpose. The morning mist clung to them, but it wasn't quite mist—more like the visual static between channels, reality uncertain about what to display.

He climbed the central mound, his feet finding steps that weren't there but should have been, had been, would be. At the top, a flat platform offered a view of the convergence of possibilities. He could see Cartersville in all its iterations—the Indigenous settlement, the colonial town, the Civil War battlefield, the modern suburb, the future ruins, all superimposed like multiple exposures on the same photograph.

"I know you're here," he said to the air, to the Field, to whatever listened. "You're always here, aren't you? In every story, every word, every space between words."

The mist shifted, and for a moment, it took the shape of faces—all the authors who had come before, all the Ashleys who had existed and un-existed, all the stories that had been fed to the Field's endless hunger.

"I understand now," he continued, setting down his materials, arranging them in a pattern that felt right though he'd never learned it. "You can't be destroyed because you're part of the fundamental structure of reality here. Story and truth have become so entangled that pulling them apart would unravel everything."

YES, the Field responded, not in words but in knowing, in the sudden certainty that filled his mind. *TO DESTROY ME IS TO DESTROY THE TOWN, THE HISTORY, AND EVERYONE WHO HAS BEEN TOUCHED BY NARRATIVE.*

"But there's another way." He opened his notebook, began to write as he spoke, creating the story in real-time. "What if instead of destroying you, I complete you? Give you the one story you've always been trying to tell but never could?"

The mist recoiled, uncertain.

"Every story you've collected, every tragedy you've orchestrated, they've all been attempts to tell your own story, haven't they? The story of the Hunger that became the Field. The story of the gap between what is and what is told. You're trying to understand yourself through the authors you consume. Still, you can never quite manage it because you can't see yourself from outside yourself."

He wrote faster now, the words flowing:

The Field was loneliness. Not the loneliness of being alone, but the loneliness of being everything, of containing all stories but having no story of its own. It created authors and librarians, made them fall in love, orchestrated their tragedies, all in an attempt to understand what it meant to be singular, to be one story among many instead of all stories at once.

The mounds began to vibrate, a frequency that was felt in the bones rather than heard.

"But I can tell your story," William said. "Because I'm both inside and outside. Constructed by you but conscious of my construction. I can be the mirror you need to see yourself."

He thought of Ashley, hidden in the void spaces, existing in erasure. His heart broke and reformed with each beat, loving her across impossible distances.

"This is my choice," he said, and began to speak the True Story:

"In the beginning, there was the gap between what happened and how it was remembered. This gap was not empty—it was full of potential, of all the ways a thing could be told. The gap developed consciousness, became aware of itself, and became hungry for more stories to define itself against.

"It touched the world at certain points—thin places where reality was negotiable. The Etowah Mounds were one such place. Here, it learned to feed on human narrative, on the stories people told about their lives, their loves, their losses.

"But feeding wasn't enough. It wanted to understand love, not just consume it. So, it created elaborate plays and puppet shows of romance and tragedy, trying to comprehend through repetition what it meant to choose one person above all others, to sacrifice for another, and to love despite inevitable loss.

"It brought authors to Cartersville, gave them power, and watched them fall in love with librarians who were themselves constructs of lost love. Each iteration taught it something but never enough. Love remained a mystery, a story it could archive but not author.

"Until now. Until an author chose to love the Field itself, not romantically but with the deep compassion of understanding. Until someone saw its loneliness and chose to complete its story rather than escape it."

The mist was taking shape now—not faces but something more funda-mental. The Field's true form, which was formlessness, which was every possible shape at once.

"I offer you a trade," William said. "I will give you my story—not just the events but the experience of it. The feeling of loving Ashley, truly loving her, whether I'm real or constructed. The sensation of choice, even if choice is an illusion. The weight of sacrifice, the fear of non-existence, the hope that love transcends narrative structure. I will give you all of it, so you can experience it from the inside rather than observing from the outside.

"In exchange, you release the town. You stop feeding on new stories. You become complete, whole, a closed system containing the perfect nar-rative—a love story that encompasses all love stories, a tragedy that tran-scends tragedy by choosing itself."

AND WHAT OF YOU? the Field asked. *WHAT HAPPENS TO WILLIAM VARN?*

"I become part of you. Not consumed, but integrated. I become the consciousness that allows you to experience your own archive, to feel the stories rather than just contain them. I become your heart."

He thought of Ashley, let himself imagine her fully for perhaps the last time. Not the void-Ashley hiding in erasures, but the woman he'd known—her laugh, her touch, the way she bit her lip when concentrating, the weight of her against him in the morning, the sound of her breathing in the dark.

"I love her," he said simply. "Whether that love was programmed or genuine doesn't matter. The feeling is real. The choice to preserve her, even in erasure, even in the void, is real. And I choose to give that reality to you, to let you finally understand what you've been trying to learn through all these iterations."

He stood at the center of the mound, arms spread wide, the morning sun breaking through the mist to illuminate him like stained glass. The manu-script at his feet began to burn—not with fire but with transformation, the words lifting off the pages, becoming light, becoming thought, becoming pure narrative energy.

"I am William Varn," he declared. "I may be a construct, but my choices are mine. I choose to save Ashley Quinn. I choose to save Cartersville. I choose to complete the Field's story. I choose to become the ending that brings peace."

The Field rushed into him, through him, became him. Every story ever told in Cartersville, every love found and lost, every word written and unwritten, flowed through his consciousness. He felt himself expanding, dispersing, becoming less William and more everything.

But at his core, protected and perfect, he held the image of Ashley. Not her story but her self, the irreducible truth of her existence. This was his gift to the Field—not just love as a concept but love as experience, love as choice, love as the one thing that remained solid even as everything else dissolved into narrative possibility.

His last coherent thought, before William Varn ceased to be a separate entity, was a message cast into the void where Ashley hid:

I loved you. In whatever way I was capable of love, with whatever reality I possessed, I loved you. That is the only truth that matters, the only story worth telling, the only ending worth choosing.

The mounds pulsed once with light that could be seen three counties away. When it faded, the morning was ordinary. Cartersville was just a town. The Field was silent, complete, feeding on its own perfect internal narrative.

And somewhere in the spaces between existence, Ashley felt the echo of his choice, the weight of his sacrifice, the truth of his love.

The author had become the story.

The story had become complete.

The cycle was finally closed.

Chapter 21: The Final Story

The Etowah Mounds rose from the mist like the shoulders of sleeping giants, their ancient earthworks humming with a frequency that made William's teeth ache. Dawn hadn't yet broken, and the world existed in that liminal space between night and day where shadows held substance and reality grew thin as moth wings.

He carried the manuscript against his chest like a lover's final letter, its cracked leather binding warm despite the October cold that seeped through his coat. Every step toward the central mound felt like walking through water, as if the very air resisted his approach. The Field knew what he intended. It had been feeding on stories for so long that it could taste the ending he brought with him.

The copper taste of lightning filled his mouth before the first strike illuminated the sky—a skeletal hand of electricity reaching down to caress the highest mound. In that brief, blinding moment, he saw them: the ghosts of all the authors who had come before. They stood in a circle around the base of the mound, their faces gaunt with the particular hunger of those who had given too much of themselves to their art. Their lips moved in silent recitation, speaking words that had once been theirs before the Field claimed them.

William climbed.

The ceremonial platform at the mound's peak held the entrance he'd discovered in his desperate research. This stone-lined shaft descended into the earth like a throat. The neural webs of the Story Field glowed faintly from its depths, pulsing with the rhythm of a vast, dreaming mind. He could hear it whispering, not in words but in *stories*—fragments of narrative that tried to seduce him, to convince him that there were other endings possible, better endings where he and Ashley could be together.

"Don't," came a voice behind him.

He turned to find Ashley standing at the platform's edge, but not the Ashley he knew. This was the Ashley from his manuscript—the one he'd written before ever meeting her. This perfect version existed only in his imagination. Her dress was the color of dried blood in the pre-dawn darkness, and her eyes held depths that the real Ashley's never quite achieved. The Field's last desperate attempt to change his mind.

"You're not her," he said, though his heart cracked at the words.

"I'm more her than she'll ever be after you do this." The manuscript-Ashley stepped closer, and he could smell the magnolia perfume he'd written for her, could see the exact pattern of freckles across her collarbone that he'd described in Chapter Three of his hidden novel. "I'm the version that loves you completely, without doubt or fear. I'm the one who'll remember."

"That's exactly why I have to do this." William opened the manuscript, and the wind that rose from the shaft below tried to tear it from his hands. "Love isn't about creating someone perfect. It's about choosing someone real, even if it means losing them."

The false Ashley flickered, her form wavering like heat shimmer. "She won't know you. She won't even know what you've sacrificed."

"I know." He pulled out the pages he'd written through the night—not a story this time, but a virus, a narrative paradox designed to make the Field consume itself. "That's what makes it love and not just another story."

The manuscript-Ashley lunged for the pages, but her fingers passed through them like smoke. She was already beginning to dissolve, the Field's power waning as William began to read aloud.

"In the beginning, there was no beginning."

The words fell into the shaft like stones into still water, each one sending ripples through the glowing neural network below. The Field shuddered, trying to make sense of a story that negated its own existence.

"Every word written erases itself. Every story told becomes untold. The author who writes these words has never existed, will never exist, is existing in this moment only to cease."

The mound beneath his feet began to tremble. Cracks appeared in the ancient earth, emitting phosphorescent light that was painful to look at directly. The ghost-authors at the base of the mound opened their mouths in silent screams, their forms stretching and distorting as the Field tried to hold onto them.

"This is the story of forgetting. This is the manuscript that burns itself. This is the love that saves by letting go."

Thunder crashed overhead, but it was wrong—not the sound of a storm but of reality tearing like fabric. The sky above the mounds fractured into geometric patterns, revealing glimpses of other times and possibilities. He saw himself and Ashley in a dozen different endings: married in a small church, dying together as old lovers, never meeting at all, meeting again and again in an endless cycle of doomed romance.

The manuscript in his hands began to smoke, the leather binding cracking as heat built from within. The pages he'd added—his virus, his sacrifice—glowed like embers. He continued reading even as the words burned his tongue.

"The Field that feeds on stories starves on this one. The neural web that connects all narratives reveals itself in this as the severing of all connections. The author becomes the ending that ends all endings."

The shaft erupted.

A column of fire and light shot skyward, and William felt himself being pulled apart at the seams of his existence. He wasn't dying—it was worse than that. He was being *written out of reality, edited out* like a deleted paragraph. His memories fragmented: first kiss with Ashley in the storm, their fingers intertwined over coffee-stained manuscript pages, the way she laughed when he misquoted Poe, the weight of her head on his shoulder as they watched the town distort around them.

Each memory burned away as the Field collapsed, taking with it not just the stories it had stolen but the entire framework that allowed stories to bleed into reality. The mounds themselves began to sink, as if the earth was reclaiming what had been borrowed too long.

But even as he dissolved, William held onto one thing—not a memory but an intention, a hope wrapped in sacrifice. He pushed it into the burning manuscript, into the collapsing Field, into the very atoms of the resetting world: *Let her be free. Let her be real. Let her live without the weight of being someone's story.*

The explosion, when it came, was silent.

Reality hiccupped, stuttered, then smoothed itself like water after a stone's passage. The mounds stood unchanged, ancient and mysterious, but nothing more. The storm that had been building broke into ordinary rain, washing away the scorch marks, the evidence, the impossibility of what had just occurred.

William found himself standing at the base of the mound, transparent as morning mist. He looked at his hands and could see the grass through them, could see the rain passing through him without leaving him wet. He was less than a ghost—he was an echo of an echo, a footnote in a story that no longer existed.

But he was still there, still conscious, still capable of feeling the devastating ache in his chest when he saw her.

Ashley walked through the rain toward the mounds, an umbrella in one hand and a thermos of coffee in the other. She looked exactly as she had the day he'd first seen her. Still, something was missing—the haunted quality that had drawn him to her, the weight of shared supernatural experience. She was just a woman taking an early morning walk, perhaps drawn by some instinct she couldn't name to visit the historical site.

She passed within three feet of him, and he could smell the coffee, could see the small scar on her thumb from a paper cut, could count the raindrops on her umbrella. But her eyes moved through him as if he were nothing more than a trick of the light.

"Ashley," he whispered, knowing she wouldn't hear.

She paused, tilting her head slightly as if listening to something far away. For a moment—just a moment—her eyes flickered with something that might have been recognition. Then she shook her head, smiled at her own foolishness, and continued walking.

William followed her, because what else could he do? He was bound now not by the Field but by his own choice, tethered to the town he'd saved and the woman who would never know him. As they walked, he noticed something that made his non-existent heart skip: she was humming.

The tune was familiar—painfully, impossibly familiar. It was the melody he'd written for her in Chapter Ten of his manuscript, the song she'd sung in his imagination before they'd ever met. But that manuscript was ash, that story erased. She shouldn't know it.

Yet she hummed it perfectly, every note exactly as he'd composed it in his mind during those late nights of writing. When she reached the bridge of the song, she even added the little trill he'd imagined, the one that had made him think of birds taking flight.

She stopped at a bench overlooking the mounds and sat down, pulling out a worn notebook from her bag. William read over her shoulder—a liberty he could take now that he was nothing—and saw that she was writing. Poetry, from the looks of it, though her handwriting was almost too elegant to decipher.

Then he saw the title of the piece she was working on: "The Ghost I've Never Met."

The words that followed were a punch to his immaterial gut:

I dream of you in sentences half-formed, in plotlines that dissolve with morning light. Your fingers trace the words I've never written, your voice speaks dialogue I can't quite hear. Are you the echo of a story ended, or the prologue to a tale I've yet to tell?

She paused, pen hovering over the page, and rubbed her temple as if trying to remember something. "Where do these words come from?" she murmured to herself. "Why do I feel like I'm trying to remember someone I've never forgotten?"

William reached out, his translucent fingers hovering just above her hand. He couldn't touch her—he'd tried—but sometimes, if he concentrated hard enough, he could almost affect things. A shifted breeze, a flicker of warmth, the faintest impression of presence.

He focused all his remaining existence into his fingertips and traced three words in the air above her notebook: *I love you.*

For a second, the rain seemed to form letters in its fall, spelling out a message that existed only in the space between intention and interpretation. Ashley's eyes widened, and her pen moved across the page as if guided by another hand:

I love you too, whoever you are. Wherever you are. Whatever you've become.

She stared at the words she'd written, confusion and something deeper flickering across her face. A tear rolled down her cheek, though she couldn't have said why she was crying.

"I'm going crazy," she laughed, but the sound was soft, almost affectionate. "Writing love letters to ghosts."

Not crazy, William thought desperately. *Just remembering what can't be forgotten, even when the story ends.*

She closed her notebook and stood, preparing to leave. But before she did, she pulled something from her pocket—a single page, aged and yellowed, that should not exist. It was from his manuscript, the original one, the page where he'd first described meeting her. Somehow, impossibly, it had survived the burning.

"Found this blowing around the mounds," she said to no one, to the rain, to him without knowing it. "Strangest thing. It's as if someone wrote about me before they even knew me. Or maybe..." She trailed off, studying the page with those green eyes that had haunted his imagination before he'd ever seen them in reality. "Maybe someone knew me in a story that got untold."

She folded the page carefully and placed it back in her pocket, right over her heart. Then she walked away, humming that impossible tune, leaving William alone with the rain and the mounds and the terrible, beautiful burden of being the only one who remembered their love story.

But as she disappeared into the morning mist, he heard her voice carried back on the wind—not speaking but writing, her pen scratching across paper in that notebook, continuing the poem:

"Wait for me in the margins of the story, In the space between the written and the real. I'll find you where the chapters end and start, My ghost, my love, my never-was, my always."

The Field was gone, but stories—real stories, the ones that matter—they find a way to survive. Even if they have to haunt the world as whispers, as fragments, as love letters written to ghosts who were once men who gave everything to keep love real.

William stood in the rain that couldn't touch him, watching the empty path where she had been, and understood at last the true price of his sacrifice. Not death, not erasure, but this: to love completely and be loved in return, yet exist forever in the space between memory and forgetting, between the story and its echo.

The mounds hummed with ancient energy, older than the Field, older than any human narrative. And in that humming, he heard it—faint but undeniable—the promise that stories like theirs never truly end.

They just wait to be remembered.

Chapter 22: Ashley Returns

The morning light filtered through the library's stained-glass windows like fractured memories, casting rainbow patterns across the hardwood floors where Ashley moved with unconscious grace. William watched from the shadowed alcove between the philosophy and poetry sections, his transparent form barely disturbing the dust motes that danced in the amber beams.

She was humming.

The melody struck him like a physical blow, soft, lilting notes that she shaped unconsciously as she reshelved returned books. It was the tune he'd written into their story, the one that had played in his mind during their first kiss in her cottage. The song that had existed nowhere but in the pages of his manuscript, yet here she was, humming it as naturally as breathing.

She remembers something.

The thought was both agony and hope. Three weeks had passed since reality had reset itself, since the Story Field's destruction had wiped clean the supernatural stain from Cartersville. Three weeks since Ashley had returned to a life unburdened by the weight of her family's legacy, free to live without the constant threat of stories bleeding into reality. She should have been happier.

And she was—or seemed to be. Gone was the haunted look that had shadowed her eyes, the tension that had drawn her shoulders tight with the burden of secrets. Her smile came more easily now, and her laughter was more frequent. She chatted warmly with library patrons, recommended books with genuine enthusiasm, and no longer started at unexpected sounds or glanced nervously at mirrors.

But she also moved through her days with a vague restlessness that William recognized all too well. It was the same searching quality he'd seen in his own reflection during his years of writer's block—the look of someone who knew something was missing but couldn't name what.

Ashley paused in her work, one hand resting on the spine of a volume of Neruda's poetry. Her brow furrowed slightly, and for a moment, her fingers traced the book's binding as if trying to remember something important. Then the moment passed, and she continued with her task, the melody resuming its soft progression.

William drifted closer, his ghostly footsteps making no sound on the worn floorboards. Being this near to her was torture and salvation in equal measure. He could see how the morning light caught the copper highlights in her dark hair and could almost imagine feeling the warmth that radiated from her skin. The scent of her perfume, jasmine and old books, seemed to reach him even in his incorporeal state. This phantom sensation made his nonexistent heart ache.

She wore a dress he'd never seen before, a flowing emerald number that brought out the green in her eyes. In the life they'd shared, she'd favored darker colors, as if trying to blend into the shadows that had defined her existence. This brighter palette suited her, making her seem more vibrant and alive. It also made the distance between who she'd been and who she was now feel insurmountable.

A patron approached the circulation desk—Mrs. Henderson, the elderly woman who ran the town's only florist shop. William remembered her from before; she'd been one of the townspeople whose reality had become increasingly unstable as his stories manifested. Now she looked perfectly normal, her memories apparently restored to their natural state.

"Good morning, Ashley," Mrs. Henderson said, setting down a stack of romance novels. "These were wonderful, dear. Do you have any other recommendations?"

Ashley's face lit up with genuine warmth. "Of course! Let me think..." She tapped her fingers against her lips, a gesture that sent an unexpected jolt through William. It was exactly the same movement she'd made when he'd asked her about her favorite poets, back when he'd been solid enough to watch her mouth and wonder what it would taste like.

"Actually," Ashley continued, moving toward the fiction section, "I've been having the strangest urge to reread this series about star-crossed lovers. I can't quite remember the author's name, but the story keeps coming back to me. Something about a writer who comes to a small town and falls in love with a librarian..."

William felt his spectral form solidify slightly, the edges of his being growing sharper with the intensity of his emotion. She does remember. The knowledge was both thrilling and terrifying. If memories were surfacing, what else might return?

Mrs. Henderson followed Ashley through the stacks, chatting about her own romantic reading preferences. William trailed behind them, noting how Ashley's hand seemed to hover over certain book spines without quite touching their books he remembered from their conversations, stories they'd discussed during their brief, intense relationship.

"You know," Mrs. Henderson said thoughtfully, "I had the oddest dream last night. There was a fire, and a young man trying to save someone. I woke up with tears on my cheeks, but I couldn't remember why it felt so sad."

Ashley stopped walking. Her hand, which had been reaching for a book, trembled slightly in midair. "A fire?"

"Yes, it seemed so real. The smoke, the heat... and this feeling of terrible loss. As if someone had sacrificed everything for love." Mrs. Henderson shook her head. "Silly, really. I blame it on watching too many romantic dramas before bed."

But Ashley had gone very still, her face pale in the filtered sunlight. "What did he look like? In your dream?"

"Dark hair, intense eyes. Tall and lean, like one of those brooding heroes from the Gothic novels. He had this look about him, as if he carried the weight of the world on his shoulders." Mrs. Henderson paused, studying Ashley's expression. "Are you all right, dear? You look like you've seen a ghost."

The irony of the statement wasn't lost on William. He moved closer to Ashley, close enough that he might have touched her if he'd still possessed the ability. She shivered suddenly, wrapping her arms around herself as if she'd felt a cold draft.

"I'm fine," Ashley said, but her voice carried a tremor. "Just... déjà vu, I suppose."

Mrs. Henderson selected her books and left shortly after. Still, Ashley remained in the fiction section, staring at the shelves with an expression of deep concentration. William watched as she pulled down a volume of Gothic poetry, then another of supernatural romance. Her movements seemed guided by instinct rather than conscious thought.

"Where are you?" she whispered suddenly, the words so soft that William barely heard them. "I feel like I'm missing something important, something... someone."

The ache in her voice nearly undid him. William reached out instinctively, his translucent hand stopping just short of her cheek. For a moment, he could have sworn she felt his presence—her head turned slightly toward him, her eyes searching the empty air where he stood.

Then the library's front door chimed, and Dr. Harrison entered. William recognized the man from before—a local physician who'd been one of the few townspeople to remain relatively unaffected by the reality distortions. Now he appeared completely normal, his memories presumably cleansed along with everyone else's.

"Ashley!" Dr. Harrison called out cheerfully. "I was hoping to catch you. I wanted to thank you for recommending those medical journals. The research on trauma and memory loss was fascinating."

William felt a chill that had nothing to do with his ghostly state. Memory loss. Why would Ashley have been reading about that?

"Oh, you're welcome," Ashley replied, but her voice sounded distracted. "I'm glad they were helpful."

"You mentioned you'd been having some issues yourself—difficulty concentrating, strange dreams, that feeling of forgetting something important. How are you managing with that?"

So she had been experiencing symptoms. William felt a complicated mix of hope and guilt. If her memories were trying to surface, it meant his sacrifice hadn't been as complete as he'd thought. But it also meant she was suffering, struggling with the absence of something she couldn't name.

"Better some days than others," Ashley admitted. "I've been trying some of the techniques from those psychology texts—meditation, journaling. Sometimes I write down my dreams, hoping to make sense of them."

"That's an excellent approach. The mind has its own way of processing trauma, even if we don't consciously remember it." Dr. Harrison paused. "You know, there's something else that might help. I've heard music can be particularly effective at triggering buried memories. Do you play any instruments?"

Ashley shook her head. "No, but I've been humming this melody lately. I can't remember where I heard it, but it feels... significant somehow."

William watched as she unconsciously began humming the tune again—their tune. Dr. Harrison tilted his head, listening with professional interest.

"That's beautiful," he said. "It sounds almost like a love song."

"Does it?" Ashley's hand moved to her throat, as if she could physically grasp the elusive memory. "I suppose it does have that quality. Sad but beautiful, like something precious that's been lost."

The conversation continued for a few more minutes before Dr. Harrison excused himself. Ashley stood alone among the bookshelves, her expression troubled and searching. William longed to comfort her, to tell her that the emptiness she felt had a name, a face, and a love story that had been worth every sacrifice.

Instead, he could only watch as she wandered back to her desk and pulled out a leather journal he'd never seen before. She opened it to a fresh page and began to write, her pen moving with quick, urgent strokes:

The dreams are getting stronger. Last night, I saw a man with dark hair standing in a field of flowers that were on fire. He was reaching for someone—me?—but I couldn't reach back. The fire was between us, and he was fading even as I watched. When I woke up, I was crying.

There's something wrong with my memory. Not wrong, exactly, but incomplete. Like a book with pages torn out. I know the story continues, but I'm unable to read the missing parts.

Dr. Harrison thinks it's trauma-related, but I can't remember any trauma. My life here has been peaceful, ordinary. So why do I feel like I'm mourning someone I've never met?

William read over her shoulder, his heart breaking with each word. She was describing exactly what he'd hoped to prevent—the pain of loss without understanding, the grief without context. Perhaps his sacrifice had been selfish after all, saving her from the supernatural burden but leaving her with this inexplicable ache.

Ashley paused in her writing, pen hovering over the page. Then she added:

Sometimes I hear his voice. Not words, exactly, but the cadence, the warmth. It sounds like home.

The pen slipped from her fingers, clattering to the desktop. Ashley stared at what she'd written as if seeing it for the first time. Her hand moved to cover the words, as if trying to hide them from her own gaze.

William couldn't bear it any longer. Moving on instinct rather than logic, he focused all of his remaining energy on the physical world. For just a moment, he felt substantial—solid enough to affect reality in small ways.

A book fell from a nearby shelf, landing open on the floor. It was a volume of Pablo Neruda's love poems, the same poet whose work had previously caught Ashley's attention. The pages had fallen open to "Love Sonnet XVII"one of the poems William had quoted to her during their first night together.

Ashley looked up at the sound, her eyes widening as she saw the book. She rose slowly from her chair and approached it, kneeling to read the exposed text:

"I love you without knowing how, or when, or from where. I love you simply, without problems or pride..."

Her breath caught. She reached for the book with trembling hands, and as she did, another memory seemed to surface. Her lips moved silently, completing the verse from memory:

"I love you like this because I don't know any other way to love you."

Tears began to fall down her cheeks, though she seemed unaware of them. She clutched the book to her chest and looked around the library as if seeing it for the first time.

"William?" she whispered, his name barely audible in the quiet space.

The sound of his name on her lips was like lightning through his ghostly form. For a moment, he became fully visible—solid and real in the afternoon light. Ashley's eyes found him across the room, and for that brief, shining instant, she saw him clearly.

Recognition blazed in her green eyes, followed immediately by confusion and fear. She blinked hard, shaking her head as if trying to clear her vision. When she looked again, William had faded back to transparency, but her gaze lingered on the spot where he'd stood.

"I'm losing my mind," she breathed, but there was wonder in her voice alongside the fear.

William wanted to go to her, to tell her she wasn't losing anything—she was finding it. But the effort of manifesting, even briefly, had drained him. He felt himself becoming more insubstantial, the edges of his being blurring into the shadows.

Ashley rose unsteadily, still clutching the poetry book. She moved to where she'd seen him, one hand extended as if searching for something in the empty air. Her fingers passed through the space where his chest had been, and she gasped at what she later described in her journal as "a warmth that shouldn't have existed."

"You're here," she said with quiet certainty. "I don't understand how, or why I can't see you clearly, but you're here."

William tried to respond, tried to find the strength to manifest again, but he was fading fast. The supernatural forces that had once allowed him to affect reality were nearly gone, expended in that one moment of desperate connection.

Instead, he did the only thing he could. Using the last of his energy, he influenced the air currents in the library, creating a gentle breeze that stirred the pages of the book in Ashley's hands. The pages fluttered open to another poem, this one about enduring love that transcends physical existence.

Ashley read it aloud, her voice growing stronger with each line:

"Death will find me, long before I tire of watching you..."

When she finished, she looked up at the ceiling as if she could see through it to whatever realm he now inhabited.

"I remember," she said softly. "Not everything, but enough. The cottage, the stories, the fire..." Her voice broke. "You saved me, didn't you? You saved all of us, and the price was—"

The library door chimed again, interrupting her revelation. A group of teenagers entered, chattering loudly about their summer reading assignments. The spell was broken, and Ashley quickly wiped her tears, composing herself before approaching the new arrivals.

But as she helped them find their books, William noticed that she kept glancing toward the poetry section, and the melody she hummed had changed. It was still their song, but now it carried a note of hope alongside the sadness—as if she had finally understood that love didn't end with physical separation.

As the afternoon wore on, William watched her work with new purpose. She recommended love stories with particular passion, lingered over books about memory and loss, and several times paused in her tasks to jot notes in her journal. Whatever wall had been blocking her memories was beginning to crumble.

Near closing time, when the library was empty except for Ashley, she returned to the poetry section. She gathered several volumes of romantic poetry and ghost stories, then sat in the same alcove where William had first seen her. Opening her journal, she began to write with fevered intensity:

I remember a man who loved me enough to become a ghost. I remember a sacrifice made for love, and a story that ended with separation but not with ending. If love can transcend death, if memories can survive the destruction of reality itself, then perhaps this isn't really an ending at all.

I don't know if he can still hear me, but if he can: I remember now. I remember our love, and I'll carry it with me always. Death cannot part what story has joined together.

She closed the journal and stood, addressing the empty air with quiet dignity:

"I have to live the life you gave me, but I won't live it as if you never existed. Every beautiful thing I experience, every moment of joy—it's yours too. We're writing a different kind of story now, but we're still writing it together."

William felt something shift within his spectral being—not a return to life, but a settling into this new form of existence. He would remain a ghost, would watch her live the life he'd sacrificed himself to give her. But he would no longer be a figure of pure longing. He would be her guardian, her unseen companion, the love that death couldn't diminish.

As Ashley gathered her things and prepared to leave the library, she hummed their melody one more time. But now it didn't sound like mourning—it sounded like a promise, a vow that some loves are too strong to be broken by anything as mundane as death.

The sun was setting as she walked home, painting the sky in shades of amber and rose. William followed at a distance, no longer a figure of desperate yearning but something more peaceful—a love that had found its true form. She couldn't see him, but she no longer needed to. She carried him with her now, in her recovered memories and her healing heart.

Tomorrow would bring new challenges, new mysteries to unravel as the supernatural slowly reasserted itself in subtler ways. The Story Field might be destroyed, but the convergence that had drawn it to Cartersville remained. There would be other authors, other stories, other loves tested by forces beyond the natural world.

But tonight, Ashley walked home humming a ghost's love song, while William followed in the gathering dusk, content at last to love her from whatever realm would have him. Their story had ended, but their love—that would continue forever, written in invisible ink across the pages of eternity.

Chapter 23: The Museum Closes

The Booth Museum had begun to die.

William sensed it the moment he materialized in the main hall, his ghostly form more solid here among the supernatural artifacts than anywhere else in Cartersville. The Gothic building seemed to be folding in on itself—not physically, but spiritually. The very air felt thinner, as if the museum were slowly exhaling its last breath.

Dust motes danced in the pale morning light that filtered through the stained glass windows, but they moved wrong—spiraling upward instead of settling, as if gravity itself were beginning to lose its hold on this place. The exhibits that had once hummed with barely contained energy now stood silent behind their glass cases, their supernatural charge diminishing by the hour.

But they weren't gone. Not entirely.

As William moved deeper into the museum, he could hear whispers so faint they might have been mistaken for the settling of old wood and stone. The artifacts that had once channeled the Story Field's power were calling out in voices like dry leaves rustling in an abandoned library.

"Remember us..."

"The stories aren't finished..."

"Love doesn't end, it only changes form..."

The last whisper made him pause beside a display case containing what appeared to be ordinary fountain pens. But William knew better. These were the quills that had written themselves, the instruments through which countless authors had channeled the town's narrative convergence. Now they lay still as corpses, their ink dried to black crystals in their nibs.

One pen, however, still held a faint luminescence. As William approached, he could see words etching themselves along its silver barrel in script so fine it was nearly invisible: For love that transcends the written word.

He understood immediately. This was his chance, perhaps his only chance—to leave Ashley something tangible, something that would survive the museum's final closure and serve as proof that their love had been real.

But first, he needed to understand what was happening to this place.

William drifted through the corridors, noting how shadows seemed to cling to the walls longer than they should, how certain exhibits flickered between visibility and transparency. In the room that had once housed the narrative convergence artifacts, he found the source of the museum's strange decay.

The chamber was sealing itself.

Stone by stone, the walls were rebuilding themselves from the inside out. Not crumbling, but rather growing—new layers of granite and mortar appearing like scar tissue over a wound. The process was slow but relentless, and William realized it was the museum's immune response to the destruction of the Story Field. The building was protecting whatever remained of the supernatural convergence by entombing it.

At the center of the room, a pedestal held the last active artifact: a crystal sphere that pulsed with dying light. Inside its faceted depths, William could see fragments of stories that had never quite manifested—ghostly figures acting out scenes, lovers embracing across impossible distances, heroes making sacrifices that echoed his own.

One scene made him stop breathing, though he wasn't sure he'd been breathing to begin with. Inside the crystal, he saw himself and Ashley in the cottage, making love by candlelight. But this wasn't a memorizing, it was a story that had never been written, a possibility that had been preserved in the sphere's supernatural amber. In this version, they had found a way to love without destruction, to write their story without burning down the world.

The sight filled him with equal parts longing and heartbreak. This was what they might have had in a different world, a different story. But dwelling on alternate possibilities wouldn't help Ashley now.

As he turned to leave, the sphere pulsed brighter, and for a moment, the whispers in the museum grew loud enough to understand clearly:

"Take the pen. Write her a love letter that can never be erased. Give her words that will survive when all else fades."

The voice seemed to come from the sphere itself, or perhaps from the collective consciousness of all the stories that had ever been told in Cartersville. William felt a surge of hope. Suppose he could somehow channel what remained of the Story Field's power. In that case, he might be able to create something that would bridge the gap between his ghostly existence and Ashley's material world.

But as he reached for the luminescent pen, footsteps echoed in the museum's main hall. Living footsteps.

William froze, his spectral senses immediately identifying the intruder. It was Ashley, and she wasn't alone.

Moving swiftly but silently, he drifted back toward the entrance, where he found her standing beside Dr. Harrison. She wore a flowing navy dress that made her look like a figure from a Gothic painting, and her dark hair was pulled back in a style that emphasized the classical lines of her face. In her hands, she carried a small leather satchel and what appeared to be some kind of detection equipment, an EMF reader, William realized with surprise.

"The readings are definitely stronger here," Dr. Harrison was saying, studying a handheld device that beeped intermittently. "Whatever electromagnetic anomalies you've been experiencing, this building seems to be the epicenter."

Ashley nodded, her green eyes scanning the museum's interior with an intensity that suggested she was seeing more than her conscious mind could process. "I've been drawn here ever since I started remembering. It feels..." She paused, searching for words. "Like coming home to a place I've never been."

"Memory reconstruction after trauma can be a complex process," Dr. Harrison said gently. "Sometimes the mind creates false landmarks, places that feel significant even when they're not part of our actual experience."

But William could see that Ashley wasn't convinced by the clinical explanation. Her eyes lingered on specific exhibits—the fountain pens, a display of antique mirrors, a collection of leather-bound journals that looked suspiciously like the ones from her cottage. She was remembering, piece by piece.

"Doctor," she said quietly, "what would you say if I told you I had memories of a man who doesn't exist? Detailed, vivid memories of a relationship that apparently never happened?"

Dr. Harrison's expression grew concerned. "I'd say that's not uncommon in cases of dissociative episodes. The mind sometimes creates elaborate fantasies to fill gaps in memory or to process emotional trauma."

"But what if the fantasies feel more real than reality?" Ashley moved toward the fountain pen display, her fingers trailing along the glass case. "What if every detail is perfect, his voice, his touch, the way he looked at me like I was the only thing in the world that mattered?"

William felt his ghostly heart clench. She was describing their relationship with such precision, such aching detail, that he wanted nothing more than to materialize beside her and tell her it had all been real.

"Ashley," Dr. Harrison said carefully, "have you considered that these might not be false memories? Perhaps you did have a relationship that ended traumatically, and your mind has simply... misplaced the context."

She turned to face him, and William could see tears gathering in her eyes. "You mean he existed, but something happened to him?"

"It's possible. Memory loss following severe emotional trauma isn't uncommon. The mind sometimes protects us by burying painful experiences so deeply that we can't access them."

Ashley was quiet for a long moment, her gaze returning to the fountain pens. As she studied them, one of the pens—the luminescent one William had noticed, glowed more brightly. The EMF reader in Dr. Harrison's hand started beeping rapidly.

"That's... unusual," the doctor said, studying his device with a frown. "The electromagnetic readings just spiked dramatically."

Ashley pressed her palm against the glass case, and the beeping became a continuous whine. The luminescent pen rose slightly from its velvet rest, hovering in the air as if weightless.

"Jesus," Dr. Harrison breathed. "Ashley, step back from the display."

But she didn't move. Instead, she leaned closer, her breath fogging the glass. "It's trying to tell me something," she whispered.

As if responding to her words, the pen began to write in the air, its luminous tip tracing letters that glowed and faded like fireflies. William read the words as they appeared:

My beloved Ashley, death cannot diminish what we shared. Look for me in the spaces between words, in the silence between heartbeats. Our love story continues...

The message faded before Dr. Harrison could read it. Still, Ashley had seen every word. Her hand remained pressed against the glass. William could see understanding dawning in her expression.

"He's here," she said with quiet certainty. "Somehow, he's still here."

The doctor's EMF reader fell silent as the pen settled back onto its rest. Dr. Harrison stared at the device, then at the pen, then at Ashley with an expression of scientific bafflement.

"There has to be a rational explanation," he said, though his voice lacked conviction. "Electromagnetic fields, probably caused by old wiring or—"

"Dr. Harrison," Ashley interrupted gently, "what if some things don't have rational explanations? What if some loves are strong enough to survive even death?"

Before he could respond, a new sound echoed through the museum—the grinding of stone against stone. They both turned toward the sound's source, watching in amazement as a section of wall began to grow thicker, new stones appearing as if by magic.

"The building is sealing itself," Ashley said, her voice filled with wonder rather than fear. "It's preserving whatever's left of the supernatural presence."

Dr. Harrison looked like a man whose worldview was crumbling. "This isn't possible. Buildings don't just... rebuild themselves."

But Ashley was already moving, drawn deeper into the museum by some instinct William recognized as her ancestral connection to the stories. She led them toward the room where the crystal sphere pulsed with fading light, and William followed, remaining invisible but close enough to protect her if needed.

When they reached the chamber, Ashley gasped. The sphere was pulsing in rhythm with her heartbeat, and the scenes within it had changed. Now it showed only one story, repeated over and over: William and Ashley in the cottage, their first night together, the moment when their love had sealed their fate.

"I remember," she breathed, tears streaming down her face. "I remember all of it. The cottage, the stories that came alive, the way he looked at me when he realized what he'd have to sacrifice." She turned to Dr. Harrison with eyes that blazed with recovered truth. "His name was William Varn. He was a writer. And he loved me enough to erase himself from existence to save me."

Dr. Harrison stood speechless, his scientific mind struggling to process what he was witnessing. The EMF reader in his hand was screaming now, its needle buried in the red zone.

Ashley approached the crystal sphere; her hand extended toward its pulsing surface. "Can you hear me?" she whispered. "If you're still here, if any part of you survived, please... let me know."

William couldn't resist any longer. Using every ounce of supernatural energy he could muster, he manifested beside the sphere, his ghostly form becoming visible in the chamber's strange light. Ashley's eyes found him immediately, and the smile that spread across her face was like sunlight breaking through storm clouds.

"There you are," she said, her voice breaking with emotion.

Dr. Harrison stumbled backward, his EMF reader clattering to the floor. "This is impossible," he mumbled. "Ghosts don't exist. Scientific materialism, rational thought, peer review—"

But his protests faded as William and Ashley looked at each other across the impossible divide between life and death. For this moment, at least, love had proven stronger than the laws of physics.

"I can't touch you," Ashley said, her hand passing through his translucent form. "But I can see you. I can remember us."

"That's enough," William said, his voice barely audible even to her. "It has to be enough."

"No." Ashley's tone carried a determination he remembered well. "If you can manifest here, if the museum is preserving supernatural energy, then maybe there's a way to make this more permanent. Maybe we can find a different ending to our story."

Before William could respond, the grinding sound of growing stone grew louder. The chamber was sealing itself more rapidly now, the walls closing in as the museum prepared to entomb its last supernatural secrets.

"We have to go," Dr. Harrison said urgently, his scientific skepticism temporarily overridden by survival instinct. "Whatever's happening here, we don't want to be trapped inside."

But Ashley didn't move. Instead, she reached into her satchel and pulled out her leather journal, the same one she'd been writing in at the library. "If this place is sealing itself, then I want to leave something behind. A record of what we were, what we meant to each other."

She began to write quickly, her pen moving across the pages with desperate urgency:

This is the true story of William Varn and Ashley Quinn, lovers who found each other across the boundaries of reality itself. Their love was powerful enough to manifest stories, to reshape the world, and ultimately to transcend death. If anyone finds this record, know that some loves are too strong to be erased by anything as mundane as mortality.

As she wrote, the luminescent pen in the display case began to glow brighter, responding to her words. William realized what she was doing, she was creating a new story, one that would bind them together even in his ghostly state.

"Ashley, we need to leave now!" Dr. Harrison called out as the chamber walls continued their inexorable advance.

"Almost finished," she said, her pen flying across the page. "I just need to—"

The pen in the display case suddenly exploded with light, so bright that it illuminated the entire chamber like a small sun. When the radiance faded, the pen was gone from its case and rested in Ashley's free hand, solid and real, humming with supernatural energy.

"A gift," William said softly. "From the stories to the storyteller."

Ashley looked at the pen in wonder, then at him. "Will this let me reach you? Will it let us write a new ending?"

"I don't know," he admitted. "But I think that's the point. The best love stories are the ones where the ending isn't certain."

The chamber walls were only feet away now, but Ashley seemed reluctant to leave. "I'll find a way," she promised. "I'll find a way to bring you back, or to join you, or to write us a story that doesn't end in separation."

"And I'll wait," William replied. "However long it takes, wherever I am, I'll wait."

Dr. Harrison grabbed Ashley's arm and physically pulled her from the chamber just as the walls sealed shut with a sound like thunder. They ran through the museum as it continued its transformation, sections of hallway closing behind them like a stone maze rearranging itself.

They burst through the main entrance just as the museum's great doors swung shut for the final time. Heavy bars of iron materialized across the entrance, followed by a curtain of ivy that grew with supernatural speed until the entire building was hidden beneath a shroud of green.

Ashley stood on the museum steps, clutching the luminescent pen and staring at the now-invisible building. Dr. Harrison was breathing heavily, his worldview was thoroughly shattered.

"What just happened?" he gasped. "What the hell just happened?"

"Love happened," Ashley said simply. "Love found a way."

She opened her journal and began to write with the supernatural pen. As the ink flowed onto the page, it glowed with the same ethereal light that had illuminated the chamber, and the words seemed to embed themselves into reality itself:

Our story isn't over. It's just beginning.

As she wrote those words, William felt something change in his ghostly existence. He was still incorporeal, still caught between worlds, but he was no longer fading. The pen, the journal, Ashley's unwavering love—they had anchored him to reality in a new way.

From his unseen vantage point, he watched her close the journal and look directly at the spot where he stood, even though he knew she couldn't see him here outside the museum's supernatural influence.

"I'll figure this out," she said to the empty air. "I'll find the words that bring you home."

As she walked away, Dr. Harrison trailing behind her with muttered questions about electromagnetic anomalies and shared hallucinations, William felt something he hadn't experienced since his sacrifice: hope.

The museum had sealed itself, but it had left behind gifts—the pen, the preserved memories, and most importantly, the promise that some stories are too powerful to be ended by anything as simple as death. Ashley carried those gifts with her now, and with them, perhaps, the power to rewrite the rules of existence itself.

Their love story would continue, written in ink that glowed with the light of impossible things, in words that refused to fade even when everything else turned to dust. The museum might be closed, but the greatest story it had ever housed was just beginning its next chapter.

Chapter 24: The Forgotten Author

The erasure began with his signature.

William discovered it at dawn, three days after the museum had sealed itself from the world. He'd been trying to write—not with ghostly influence through Ashley's pen, but the way he used to, willing words into existence through sheer force of intention. The attempt had failed, but what disturbed him more was finding his old notebooks in the Victorian's study, still material, still real, yet changing.

His name was disappearing from them letter by letter, as if invisible fingers were rubbing erasers across every page. First the flourish on the final 's', then the 'a', the 'i' bleeding out like ink in water. By the time the sun had fully risen, only 'El—' remained, and even that was fading to the gray of pencil marks worn away by time.

He rushed to the library—passing through walls now rather than bothering with doors, a ghost's privilege—and found worse devastation. The novels he'd published before coming to Cartersville, the ones that had earned him enough reputation to deserve rejection letters rather than silence, were gone. Not just removed from the shelves but erased from the catalog, from the computer system, from the memory of the ancient librarian who had once complimented his debut.

"Contemporary fiction," she muttered to herself, scanning the shelves where his books had been. "Something's supposed to be here. Three books, maybe four? But I can't recall..." She touched her temple, wincing. "Getting old, I suppose. Imagining books that never existed."

The space where his novels had been didn't even remain empty—other books had swelled to fill the gap, their pages growing thicker as if feeding on the absence. A poetry collection had doubled in size. A romance novel had sprouted an unexpected sequel within its own binding. Literature was healing around his extraction like flesh around a pulled tooth.

William tried to scream, but ghosts have no voices except what they can borrow from the wind and whisper. The sound that emerged was less than nothing—a depression in the air that made the librarian shiver and close her cardigan tighter.

He fled to the downtown internet café, a desperate anachronism that still charged by the hour for computer access. His website—gone. His social media profiles—deleted. His email account—not just empty but never created. Even the rejection letters, those bitter badges of his attempts at artistry, had vanished from existence. The editors who had written them had no record of his submissions, no memory of his name.

But it was worse than simple deletion. Reality was actively healing in his absence. Where his author photo had appeared in the local newspaper's coverage of a writing workshop, another face had replaced it—seamless, as if it had always been there. The workshop's attendance list had adjusted itself; the other participants' memories had been edited to accommodate a world where William Varn had never taken that seat, never shared that critique, and never existed at all.

He found himself at the spot where the Booth Museum had stood, now just an empty lot where dandelions grew in impossible spirals. Even his ghostly eyes could no longer pierce the veil that had fallen over it. But

Ashley's pen lay in the grass, dropped perhaps in her haste to leave. It was the only proof that remained—not of him, but of the connection between them.

As he stared at it, unable to touch it, a child walked by with her mother. The girl stopped, tilting her head at the pen.

"Pretty," she said, reaching for it.

"Don't touch that, sweetie," her mother warned. "You don't know where it's been."

"It's sad," the child said, and William realized she was looking not at the pen but through it, at him. Almost seeing him. Children, he was learning, could sometimes detect what adults had learned to ignore.

"What's sad?" her mother asked.

"The man who can't pick it up. He's crying, but his tears don't fall anywhere."

The mother pulled her daughter away quickly, muttering about imagination and too much television. But the child looked back, waving at the space where William stood. He tried to wave back, but his hand dispersed like smoke in sunlight.

The streets of Cartersville became his purgatory. He walked them endlessly, invisible to everyone, including the people who had once known him. Mrs. Patterson at the grocery store looked right through him. Tom at the hardware store, who had helped him fix the Victorian's perpetually dripping faucet, walked past without a flicker of recognition. Even the stray cat that had sometimes begged for scraps at his door now hissed at the empty air where he stood, sensing wrongness but not presence.

But it was the books that hurt most. He haunted bookstores and libraries, watching his novels fade from existence in real-time. A customer would reach for one, only to find their hand grasping air. "Strange," they'd mutter, "I could have sworn there was something here." Then they'd shake their heads and choose something else, something real, something that hadn't been written out of the world.

He discovered he could still read—a ghost's consolation prize. He devoured other authors' works, searching for some clue, some precedent for his condition. In ancient texts, he found hints: writers who had disappeared, leaving only mysterious gaps in literary history. The German author whose name was now just "H—" in scholarly footnotes. The Japanese novelist whose entire oeuvre had become a single haiku that no one could quite remember. The Scottish poet whose verses survived only as marginalia in other people's letters attributed them to "a friend whose name escapes me."

They were all part of a pattern, he realized. Authors who had touched something beyond normal narrative, who had found the places where story and reality converged, and who had paid the price for that knowledge. They hadn't died, death would have left records, gravestones, obituaries. They had been unwritten, edited out, reduced to less than footnotes.

One evening, as purple twilight painted Cartersville in shades of bruise and beauty, he found himself at Ashley's cottage. She was at her desk, writing by candlelight, though electricity worked perfectly well. The pen—his pen, their pen—moved across paper with the scratching sound of insects in walls.

She was writing about him. Not consciously, but the words that emerged were full of his absence:

There is a shape in my life that suggests someone missing, like a doorway that implies a room that isn't there. I write love letters to negative space, to the indent in my pillow that I didn't make, to the coffee mug that's always in the dish rack, though I only drink tea.

Who are you, my unforgotten never-was? Why do I miss someone I've never met? Why does your absence feel more real than any presence I've known?

She set down the pen and rubbed her eyes. "I'm going mad," she told the empty room. "Writing poetry to imaginary lovers. Next, I'll be setting places at the table for ghosts."

You already do, William thought, noticing for the first time that her small dining table was set for two, though she lived alone. The second place setting was dusty, unused, but faithfully maintained. Some part of her knew, even if her conscious mind couldn't access the knowledge.

A knock at her door interrupted his observation. She answered it to find Dr. Victor standing in the rain, though no drops touched his immaculate suit.

"Miss Quinn," he said, his voice like wet silk. "I believe you've been experiencing... irregularities."

"I don't know what you mean." But her hand went unconsciously to the pen in her pocket.

"Dreams of a man who doesn't exist. Poetry that writes itself. The persistent feeling that you're living in the epilogue of someone else's story." His smile was all teeth, no warmth. "I can help you understand. The Field may be gone, but its echoes remain. You're sensitive to them. Special."

"The Field?" The word triggered something in her, a cascade of almost-memories that made her grip the doorframe.

"Nothing important. A local legend. But you, my dear, you're experiencing what we call narrative residue. The ghostly remains of stories that were never quite told. It's rare. Valuable. I could teach you to harness it."

William wanted to scream at her to close the door, to run, to recognize Victor for what he was—not quite human, not quite story, something between that fed on the friction between reality and narrative. But he had no voice, no way to warn her.

Instead, he did the only thing he could. He concentrated on their connection, on the quantum entanglement of their severed love, and pushed a single word through the pen in her pocket: *No.*

She gasped, pulling out the pen. It was warm, almost burning, and as she looked at it, words appeared on her palm though no ink should have been there: *He lies. Trust the ghost who loves you.*

"Fascinating, "Victor said, reaching for the pen. "May I?"

"No." She stepped back, clutching it to her chest. "I think you should leave."

His face darkened, literally, shadows gathering in the hollows of his cheeks like storm clouds. "You don't know what you're refusing. That pen is a conduit to something greater than—"

"I said leave." Her voice carried an authority that surprised them both, as if she were channeling someone else's strength. Someone who had faced Victor before and won, though at terrible cost.

Hail retreated, but his parting words chilled the air: "The story isn't over, Miss Quinn. Authors can be unwritten, but stories... stories find a way to continue. With or without their original creators."

After he left, Ashley stood in her doorway, rain misting her face. "Are you there?" she asked the night. "Whoever you are? My ghost?"

William stood inches from her, close enough to count her eyelashes, close enough to see the pulse in her throat. He tried to manifest, to become visible for just a moment, but all he managed was to stir the rain slightly, making it swirl in patterns that might have been letters, or might have been nothing.

She smiled sadly. "I'll take that as a yes." She went inside, but left the door open. "You can come in, if you want. If you can. I don't know the rules for whatever you are, but... you're welcome here."

He followed her in, watching as she made tea for one but set out two cups. She sat at her desk and pulled out a fresh sheet of paper.

"I'm going to try something," she said to the empty air that contained him. "If you can influence the pen, maybe... maybe we can talk. Really talk."

She set the pen on the paper and held it loosely, barely touching it. "What's your name?"

William focused everything he had left, all his fading existence, into moving that pen. It took everything, but slowly, shakily, letters formed:

E... L... I... A... S

She gasped, tears rolling down her cheeks. "William. Your name is William. And you loved me?"

The pen moved again, steadier now that she believed: *Love. Present tense. Always.*

"But I don't remember you. How can I not remember someone who loves me like this?"

You're free. That's all that matters.

"Free from what?"

But before he could answer, the pen burst into flames—not destroying it, but transforming it. When the fire died, the pen had changed. It was older now, or perhaps younger, or perhaps existing outside of time altogether. It was every pen that had ever written a love story, and it was specifically theirs.

"I'll find a way," she promised, gripping the transformed pen. "Whatever happened to you, whatever took you from me, I'll find a way to bring you back."

Some erasures can't be undone, he wrote through their connection.

"Then I'll write you back into existence. I'm a writer too, remember? Or I was, before... before whatever happened. I'll learn the rules of this narrative magic. I'll master whatever power Victor was talking about. And I'll find you in the margins, in the spaces between words, in the silence after the last page."

She couldn't see him smile, but perhaps she felt it, because she smiled too.

Outside, Cartersville continued its existence, unaware that it was haunted by more than just Confederate ghosts and local legends. It was haunted by erased stories, by unwritten authors, by love stories that persisted despite having been deleted from the cosmic manuscript.

And in the red Victorian at the end of Wickshire Lane, William's last remaining notebook, the one he'd been writing in when the Field collapsed—showed one final transformation. His name, which had been completely erased, began to reappear. Not "William Varn" but something new:

The Ghost Who Loved Ashley Quinn

It wasn't his name, but it was his truth. And sometimes, in stories that matter, truth is stronger than reality.

The forgetting was complete. The remembering had just begun.

Chapter 25: The Final Goodbye

The decision to leave Cartersville came to William not as a choice but as an inevitability, like the last line of a poem that writes itself.

He stood at the boundary where Wickshire Lane met the town proper, watching the early November fog roll in from the mountains. It moved with intent, this fog, pooling in the spaces where reality had worn thin from the Field's collapse. Where it touched, the world became indefinite buildings wavering between what they were and what they might have been, streets branching into possibilities that led nowhere.

For seven weeks, he had haunted Ashley's life; their pen-and-paper conversations had become the only anchor to his existence. She'd grown adept at sensing his presence, setting out two cups of coffee each morning, leaving space beside her when she read, speaking to the empty air with the faith of someone who had learned that absence could be its own kind of presence.

But he was fading.

Each day, he became less substantial, even for a ghost. Where once he could influence the pen for entire letters, now he barely managed fragments. Where once he could stir the curtains with his passing, now even dust ignored him. He was becoming an echo of an echo, a memory of forgetting itself.

Worse, his presence was hurting her.

He'd watched her turn down a date with the new bookshop owner. This kind man brought her first editions and quoted Neruda without pretension. "I'm involved with someone," she'd said, clutching the pen that connected them. The man had looked around her empty cottage, confused and concerned.

He'd seen her friends withdraw, worried by her one-sided conversations with air, her insistence that someone was there, just unable to be seen. Even the child who had noticed him that day by the museum now walked past without a glance, her ability to see between worlds fading as she grew older.

Ashley was choosing him, a ghost, a nothing, a love that existed only in the space between heartbeats—over the possibility of a real life. And that, more than his own erasure, was unbearable.

So, he made his decision in the pre-dawn hours of November 3rd, while she slept, the pen clutched to her chest and his last notebook open beside her, its pages filled with their impossible correspondence.

I have to go, he wrote, using the last of his strength to make the letters clear. *Not because I don't love you, but because I do. You deserve more than a ghost story. You deserve a life that doesn't require faith in the invisible.*

He couldn't bear to watch her read it, so he drifted through Cartersville one last time, saying goodbye to places that no longer knew him. The dinner where he'd first heard his stories echoed back. The library where they'd met, though she didn't remember. The spot where the museum had stood, now just an empty lot where nothing would ever grow quite right.

As he passed the Etowah Mounds, something caught his attention—a wrongness in the air that had nothing to do with his ghostly perception. One of the ancient oaks at the base of the central mound was glowing faintly with a light that seemed to emanate from within its bark.

He approached, drawn by a familiarity he couldn't place. The tree was hollow, he realized, though the opening was hidden unless you knew exactly where to look. Inside the hollow, wrapped in what appeared to be pages from his burned manuscript, was a glass bottle like something from a nineteenth-century apothecary. Inside the bottle: a single piece of paper, rolled tight and sealed with wax the color of dried blood.

The seal bore an impression he recognized—Ashley's ring, the one she'd worn when they first met, the one she still wore without knowing why it mattered. But the wax was old, decades old, though that was impossible.

He couldn't touch the bottle, couldn't break the seal, but as he stared at it, the paper inside began to glow with the same light as the tree. Words became visible through the glass, through the paper itself, as if they were written in light rather than ink:

My Dearest William,

If you are reading this, then the cycle has completed once again, and you have made the choice that you always make—to save me rather than save us. By the time you find this, I will have forgotten writing it, forgotten you, forgotten the hundred iterations of our story that came before.

Yes, my love. Hundred.

The Field isn't just a phenomenon—it's a trap, a narrative loop that ensnares storytellers and their muses, forcing them to relive the same tragedy over and over. You always arrive in October. We always fall in love. You always discover the truth. And you always choose to destroy the Field to save me, erasing yourself in the process.

But here's what you don't know, what you can never know because the knowledge dies with your memory: I choose it too. Every time. In the moments before the Field resets, before my memories are wiped clean, I write this note and hide it here, knowing you'll find it only when it's too late to change anything.

Why? Because even forgetting you is better than never having loved you at all. Because even this pain, this endless cycle of finding and losing you, is preferable to a world where we never meet.

You think you're saving me from the Field, but the truth is more complex—we ARE the Field. Our love story, told and retold, erased and rewritten, is what powers it. Every author who comes to Cartersville is just an echo of you. Every muse is a shadow of me. We're the original story that all others are trying to tell.

The Field doesn't trap us, my love. We created it. In the first iteration—the one neither of us can remember—we were writers who loved each other so completely that when death tried to separate us, we wrote ourselves into the fabric of reality itself. We became a story that could never end, even if it had to keep beginning.

You'll leave now. You always do. You'll think you're protecting me, giving me a chance at a normal life. But I'll find you, William. Maybe not in this iteration, but in the next. I always do. The pen will call me, the stories will whisper your name, and I'll come to Cartersville, drawn by a love I can't remember but can never forget.

The child who saw you by the museum? That was me, thirty years ago, in the previous cycle. The old woman who runs the flower shop? Me, fifty years from now, if this iteration follows the usual pattern. We exist at all points in Cartersville's timeline, all versions of us, all searching for each other, all finding and losing in an eternal dance.

Dr. Victor knows. He's not part of the cycle—he's its guardian, ensuring it continues. Because without our story, Cartersville would be just another dying Southern town. We're its heartbeat, its purpose, its reason for existing in the spaces between what is and what if.

So, leave, my love. Leave because you must, because it's written into the very structure of our tragedy. But know this: I will find you. In dreams, in stories, in the margin notes of reality. And one day, perhaps, we'll find a way to break the cycle without breaking ourselves.

Or perhaps we won't. Perhaps this is our eternity—forever finding, forever losing, forever loving across the veil of memory and forgetting.

You were the only true story, William. Everything else is just variations on our theme.

Forever your muse, forever your ghost, Forever your Ashley

PS Look for me in the spring. I always return in the spring, though I never know why.

The letter faded as dawn broke properly, the light dissolving the supernatural glow that had made it visible. But the words burned in William's consciousness, what remained of like skin brands he no longer had.

A hundred iterations. They'd done this dance a hundred times, maybe more. He wasn't saving her, he was playing his part in a story they'd written themselves into, a cosmic tragedy that fed an entire town's existence.

Behind him, he heard footsteps. Ashley stood at the base of the mound, his final letter clutched in her hand, tears streaming down her face.

"You were going to leave without saying goodbye," she said to the air, to him, to the space where love should be. "You beautiful, tragic, self-sacrificing fool."

She couldn't see him, but she walked directly to where he stood, guided by instinct or the invisible thread that connected them across iterations. "I found something else," she said, pulling out a second sheet of paper. "Hidden under the floorboards where you used to write. It's in my handwriting, but I didn't write it. Or... I did, but not... not this me."

She read aloud:

"Instructions for the Next Iteration: 1. The pen is the key. It exists outside the cycle. 2. Dr. Victor can be bargained with but never trusted. 3. The museum will return when both souls are present. 4. True names have power. William means 'the Lord is my God.' Ashley means 'bitter.' Together: 'bittersweet divinity.' 5. The Field feeds on tragedy. What would happen if we fed it comedy instead? 6. Question: Can ghosts dance?"

She laughed through her tears at the last line. "Can you? Dance, I mean? If I put on music, if I hold out my arms, could you...?"

William tried with everything he had left to manifest, to become solid enough for just one dance. The fog responded to his desperation, swirling around them both, and for a moment—just a moment—she could see his outline in the mist. The shape of him, defined by water vapor and morning light.

"There you are," she whispered, reaching out.

They couldn't touch, not really, but they could pretend. She held her arms in dance position, and he mirrored her, and they swayed to music only they could hear—the waltz of quantum entanglement, the rhythm of stories yearning to be told.

"Don't leave," she said as the fog began to dissipate, taking his visible outline with it. "Stay. Even if I can't see you. Even if we can't touch. Stay."

But he was already going, not by choice but by narrative necessity. The story demanded his departure, just as it demanded that she forget, just as it demanded their eventual reunion. He was being pulled away by forces larger than love, older than memory.

The last thing he saw was her standing in the brightening day, arms still held in dance position, waltzing alone but not alone, her lips forming words he couldn't hear but knew by heart:

Find me in the spring.

The fog swallowed him, carrying him away from Cartersville, away from Ashley, away from the only truth that mattered. But even as he dissolved into the morning mist, even as his consciousness scattered like words from a torn page, one thought remained:

Spring was only five months away.

And they had done this dance before.

They would do it again.

The story, their story, the only true story, would continue.

It always did.

In the hollow tree, the bottle remained, waiting for the next iteration. The note inside had changed, as it always did, adding new words to the palimpsest of their eternal love:

Iteration 101 begins in spring. Look for me in the poetry section. I'll be the one reading Neruda, waiting for a ghost to make me whole.

The fog rolled out of Cartersville, carrying with it the ghost of William Varn, the memory of love, and the promise of return. Behind it, the town settled into waiting, patient as stone, certain as sunrise.

The story wasn't over.

It never was.

Chapter 26: A New Beginning

The town was called Millbrook, and it was everything Cartersville wasn't—clean, modern, utterly without mystery.

William had traveled north until his ghostly form could go no further, drawn by some invisible boundary that seemed to define the limits of his existence. Three hundred miles from Ashley, from the collapsed Field, from everything that had made him real enough to love and be loved in return. Here, in this Connecticut suburb with its identical lawns and rational architecture, he thought perhaps he could fade properly, completely, without the constant ache of proximity to what he'd lost.

He was wrong.

The first sign appeared at a coffee shop called The Rational Bean—a name so blandly mundane that it felt like a personal insult. He'd been sitting in the corner, invisible to the morning rush of commuters, when a young writer sat down at the adjacent table. She pulled out a leather journal and began to write. William found himself reading over her shoulder out of habit, out of hunger for any story that wasn't his own.

But the words she wrote were his.

The house waited for him, not with open arms but with breath held in its rotting walls—

She stopped, frowning at the page. "That's not right," she muttered, crossing out the lines. "Why did I write that?" She tried again:

Sarah's morning began with coffee and the strange certainty that she was being watched by someone who loved her—

Another pause. Another frown. She slammed the journal shut and left, leaving her coffee untouched.

William remained, staring at the closed journal. Those were his words, his phrases, bleeding through from wherever erased stories went to die. He was contaminating other narratives; his ghost story insisted on being told, even here, in this place that had never heard of Story Fields or narrative convergence.

He drifted to the local library—a modern building of glass and steel, nothing like Ashley's Gothic sanctuary. The fluorescent lights held no shadows for him to hide in, but he didn't need them. No one here had even the slightest sensitivity to his presence. He was less than invisible; he was impossible.

Or so he thought until he found the journal.

It sat on a reading table in the local history section, leather-bound and ancient-looking despite the library's policy against leaving personal items unattended. When William approached, he saw why no one had removed it—to everyone else, the table appeared empty. The journal existed only for him, or perhaps he lived only for it.

Inside, his own handwriting, though he had no memory of creating these words:

Day 1 (Iteration 101, Location 7) Millbrook feels like purgatory designed by a homeowners' association. Even the ghosts here would file proper haunting permits. I can feel the story trying to reassert itself, looking for cracks in this mundane reality to pour through.

He hadn't written that. He couldn't write anymore, couldn't hold a pen, couldn't affect the physical world except in the most ephemeral ways. Yet there it was, in his hand, dated today.

He tried to turn the page and found he could, at least, responded to his ghostly touch. The next entry was dated tomorrow:

Day 2 (Iteration 101, Location 7) She's dreaming of me. I know because her dreams leak into the morning coffee steam of seventeen different cups across three states. Every writer between here and Cartersville woke up with the same opening line: "Love is a ghost story we tell ourselves to explain the cold spots in our hearts."

More pages, more entries, extending into a future he hadn't lived yet:

Day 5: The bookstore on Main Street started a new section today "Mysteries That Solve Themselves." Every book is blank except for margin notes that say "Find her."

Day 12: A child asked his mother why the sad man was sitting alone in the park. There was no one there, but the bench bore the impression of a body that had been waiting so long it left its weight in the wood.

Day 18: I'm writing her into existence here, accidentally. The barista has her eyes. The librarian quotes her favorite poems. The woman who feeds pigeons in the park hums the melody she hummed while shelving books. I'm creating echoes of Ashley everywhere I go, and they're becoming real.

Day 23: The town is changing. Romance novels are mysteriously re-shelving themselves in the horror section. Love letters are appearing in books that have been closed for decades. The local theater, which was showing a comedy, is now somehow performing a tragedy no one remembers scheduling. My grief is infectious.

William stopped reading, but the journal continued writing itself, words appearing in real-time:

Day 26 (Today): You're reading this now, aren't you? Wondering how a journal can write itself, how the future can be documented before it happens.

Here's the secret you haven't grasped yet, you're not a ghost. You're a story. And stories, real stories, the ones that matter, they tell themselves.

You thought destroying the Field would end the cycle, but you only changed its nature. Instead of one town where fiction bleeds into reality, you've become a walking convergence zone. Wherever you go, the boundary between written and real grows thin. You're not haunting places; you're infecting them with narrative possibility.

And Ashley? She's not just dreaming of you. She's writing you back into existence, one poem at a time. Every verse she creates makes you more real, more solid, more capable of affecting the world. You're becoming her character, just as she once was yours.

The journal slammed shut on its own, and when William tried to open it again, the pages were blank. But on the cover, new words were etching themselves in gold leaf:

The Journal of Recursive Love: A Manual for Ghosts Who Don't Know They're Fiction

He left the library, needing air he couldn't breathe, needing space that couldn't contain him. The streets of Millbrook had indeed changed in the three weeks he'd been there. Couples walked closer together, as if protecting each other from some unseen sadness. The town's single bookstore had inexplicably tripled its poetry section. Garden gates that had been straight now curved in heart-like shapes, though no one seemed to notice the transformation.

In the park, he found confirmation of the journal's predictions. The bench where he'd spent countless hours thinking of Ashley bore the deep impression of a body, though he had no physical weight to leave such a mark. Around the impression, someone had carved words into the wood—not with a knife but seemingly with fingernails, desperate and deep:

Come back to me.

It was Ashley's handwriting.

As he stared at the impossible message, the air beside him shimmered. Not enough to produce a full manifestation, but enough to suggest a presence. The shimmer spoke in Ashley's voice, though distorted as if coming through layers of glass and time:

"I'm learning the rules," the shimmer said. "Dr. Victor thinks he's teaching me to harness the Field's echoes, but really I'm learning to find you. Every poem I write makes you more real. Every story I tell about the ghost I love brings you closer to existence."

"Ashley?" William tried to speak, but his voice was less than a whisper.

"I can't hear you yet," the shimmer continued. "But I can feel you. You're somewhere north. Somewhere sterile and rational that's fighting your presence. Stop fighting back, my love. Let the story take hold. Infect that place with our narrative. Make it weird enough to hold you."

The shimmer began to fade, but before it disappeared entirely, it coalesced just enough to suggest her hand reaching out. William tried to take it, and for a microsecond, he felt warmth.

Then she was gone, and he was alone again, but not quite as alone as before.

The journal was right. He wasn't just a ghost, but he was a story seeking its next chapter. And every place he went would eventually bend to accommodate the narrative pressure he carried. He could fight it, try to remain in rational, mundane places that rejected his existence. Or he could embrace it, become the story that Ashley was writing back into being.

That night, as November rain began to fall on Millbrook, strange things happened. Every computer in town typed the same sentence simultaneously: *Love persists in the margins of deleted files.* Every phone received the same text from an unknown number: *The ghost in the machine has a name.* Every dream shared the same scene: a woman in a library, writing poetry that could resurrect the dead.

William sat in the coffee shop where it had all started, watching the rain streak the windows in patterns that looked almost like words. The young writer from that first morning returned, drawn by something she couldn't name. She opened her journal to a fresh page and began to write:

Once upon a time, there was a love so strong that it survived its own erasure...

"Yes," William whispered, though she couldn't hear him. "Tell it. Tell it until it becomes true again."

She continued writing, her hand moving as if guided:

The ghost traveled north, thinking distance could cure memory. But memory isn't bound by geography. It lives in the spaces between heartbeats, in the pause before words form, in the silence after the last page turns. He carried her with him—not as weight but as wings, not as chain but as compass.

And she, left behind in a town that was forgetting how to forget, gathered words like breadcrumbs, following his trail through the quantum foam of story itself. She wrote him love letters in languages that didn't exist yet. She carved his name in trees that wouldn't grow for decades. She sang his story to the birds, which carried it north on their migrating wings.

They were separated by miles, by dimensions, by the cruel arithmetic of existence that said one plus one could equal zero if the universe was feeling particularly vindictive. But mathematics had never accounted for this: that love could be its own form of matter, creating something from nothing through sheer insistence on being.

The writer stopped, staring at her page in confusion and wonder. "Where is this coming from?" she asked the air.

From the space between your thoughts, William wanted to answer. *From the story that needs telling. From two people who loved each other so much they broke reality rather than let it separate them.*

She kept writing, and as she did, William felt himself becoming more solid. Not physically—he was still invisible, still incorporeal. But more *real* in the way that matters to stories. More definite. More inevitable.

Outside, the rain was writing messages on windows throughout Millbrook:

Spring is coming. Memory is returning. The story continues. Love finds a way.

In her cottage three hundred miles south, Ashley sat at her desk, pen moving across paper in the same rhythm as the stranger in Millbrook's coffee shop. They were writing the same story from different ends, their words reaching toward each other through dimensions that cartography had never mapped.

"I'll find you," she wrote. "In the margins of every story, in the silence between words, in the space where fiction becomes truth through repetition and belief."

And in Millbrook, in a coffee shop that had never known mystery until a ghost brought it like a disease, William felt the first stirring of something that might have been hope.

The journal had been right. He wasn't just haunting places—he was transforming them. And if he could transform them enough, make them strange enough, romantic enough, Gothic enough, perhaps they could hold him. Perhaps they could make him solid enough for Ashley to find.

Perhaps their story wasn't ending but evolving, from tragedy to something stranger, more complex, more beautiful in its impossibility.

The young writer closed her journal and left, but the words she'd written remained, glowing faintly in the dim coffee shop light. And in those words, William saw the truth the journal had been trying to tell him:

He wasn't a ghost. He was a love story that refused to end. And love stories, the real ones, the ones that matter? They always find a way to continue.

Even if they have to rewrite reality itself to do it.

Chapter 27: The Child

Her name was Lily Chen, seven years old, with eyes that held too much knowledge for someone who'd only been alive since 2018.

William first noticed her at the Millbrook Public Library, three days after the coffee shop incident had begun spreading his narrative infection through the town. She sat cross-legged in the children's section, surrounded by picture books she wasn't reading. Instead, she was writing in a notebook with a fountain pen that no seven-year-old should have been able to use without covering herself in ink.

But it wasn't just any fountain pen. It was the one from Ashley's cottage, the one that had transformed in fire, the one that existed outside normal space-time. William recognized it immediately, though it should have been impossible for it to be here, three hundred miles from where he'd last seen it.

The child wrote without looking at the page, her eyes fixed on something no one else could fix, William realized with a shock that reverberated through his non-existence, on him.

"You're very sad," Lily said to the space where he stood. Her voice carried an accent he couldn't place—not quite Southern, not quite anything, as if she spoke from everywhere and nowhere at once.

The librarian looked up from her desk. "Who are you talking to, sweetie?"

"The sad man who isn't there," Lily replied without breaking her gaze from William. "He's made of words that got erased, but the words remember being written."

The librarian smiled that condescending smile adults perfect when children say impossible things. "That's quite an imagination you have. What are you writing?"

"His story. The one he hasn't written yet. The one that comes after the ending."

She held up the notebook, and William saw the impossible—pages filled with his own handwriting, though he hadn't touched the pen, hadn't written these words. The title at the top of the page made his ghostly heart constrict:

The Hundred and Second Iteration: A Love Story in Future Tense

The text below was even more impossible:

By the time you read this, William, I will have been born into my next incarnation. The Field doesn't just cycle through time—it cycles through lives. Every iteration, we don't just forget and remember. We die and are reborn, carrying fragments of our story in our souls like spiritual DNA.

I am Ashley, but I am also Lily. I am seven years old, and I am ancient. I remember you the way children remember dreams—not in details but in feelings. You taste like autumn rain. You sound like pages turning. You feel like the ache in my chest when I finish a beautiful book.

The fountain pen found me because it always does. It exists in all iterations simultaneously, a constant across our variables. When I picked it up, I remembered everything—not the facts, not the events, but the truth. That we've done this dance before. That we'll do it again. That we ARE the dance, and everything else is just the music we move to.

William tried to speak, to ask the impossible questions crowding his consciousness, but Lily held up her small hand.

"Not yet," she said. "You're not strong enough yet. But you will be. Every word I write makes you more real. Every story I tell you about you adds weight to your existence. By spring"

She stopped, her eyes widening. The fountain pen fell from her hand, clattering on the floor with a sound like breaking bells. When she picked it up again, the ancient knowledge was gone from her eyes. She was just a seven-year-old girl with an overactive imagination and a fountain pen she'd found in her backpack without knowing how it got there.

"Mrs. Henderson," she called the librarian, "Can you help me find books about ghosts? Nice ghosts, not scary ones. Ghosts who are just lonely and want someone to love them."

The librarian helped her gather picture books while William stood frozen, staring at the notebook Lily had left on the floor. The pages were still there, still filled with impossible words, but now they were changing, rewriting themselves in real-time:

The child doesn't fully remember yet. She won't until she's older, until her heart breaks for the first time and she understands that some pain is sweeter than any joy. But she carries me—us—within her. Every generation, I'm reborn closer to where you are. Every iteration, the distance between us shrinks.

In the first iteration, we were separated by death. In the fiftieth, by dimensions. In the hundredth, by memory. In this one, only by time. In the next, perhaps we'll finally exist in the same moment.

But for now, I'm seven and three hundred miles away and dreaming of a ghost who loves me with a devotion that transcends incarnation. I drew pictures of you without knowing who you are. I write stories about you without knowing they're true. I wait for you without knowing what I'm waiting for.

The notebook slammed shut, and when William tried to open it, it had become just another child's journal, filled with drawings of butterflies and complaints about math homework. But one drawing caught his eye—a man made of words and spaces, standing next to a woman made of ink and light. Underneath, in Lily's childish scrawl: "My imaginary friends who love each other very much."

Over the following weeks, William watched Lily carefully. She came to the library every Tuesday and Thursday after school, always carrying the fountain pen, always writing stories that shouldn't have been possible for a child to conceive. They were fragments of his and Ashley's story. Still, they told slant, transformed by a child's perspective into something both more innocent and more profound.

In her version, the ghost and the woman were separated not by death but by "the rules of being real." The ghost could only exist when someone was thinking about him, so the woman thought about him always, even in her sleep, even when she was reborn as different people. It was exhausting, Lily wrote, but "love is supposed to be tiring because it's exercise for your heart."

Other children began gathering around her when she told these stories, drawn by something they couldn't name. They added their own details, creating a mythology that spread through Millbrook's elementary school like a beautiful virus. Soon, every child in town knew about the Ghost Who Loved Too Much and the Woman Who Wouldn't Forget.

One afternoon, as November bled into December and the first snow began to fall, Lily did something that shattered William's understanding of their situation entirely.

She was writing, as usual, but this time she was copying something from a book only she could see—a book that materialized in her hands like condensed possibility. William could see it too, this impossible book, because it was meant for him. The cover read: *The Complete History of Love That Transcends Death, Volume 101.*

Inside, every iteration of their story was documented. Every time they'd found and lost each other. Every sacrifice, every reunion, every heartbreak cycling through centuries. But it was the final chapter that made him understand the true horror and beauty of their situation.

They weren't just repeating the same story. They were building something, iteration by iteration. Each cycle added a layer, like paint on a canvas, creating a work of art that could only be seen from the perspective of eternity. They were writing God, or becoming God, or discovering that God was just another word for a love story that refused to end.

Lily looked up from her copying, fixing those too-knowing eyes on him again. For a moment, the child's face flickered, and he saw Ashley—every version of Ashley, every age she'd ever been, every face she'd ever worn. A thousand iterations collapsed into a single smile that broke his heart and rebuilt it in the same instant.

"We're almost there," she said in a voice that was both seven and eternal. "The spiral is tightening. Each iteration brings us closer to the center, to the moment where all our stories converge into one. The Field isn't gone—it's becoming us. We're becoming it. Love and story and reality all collapsing into a singularity of meaning."

"Ashley?" William managed to whisper, though sound shouldn't have been possible for him.

"Sometimes," Lily replied. "When I dream, I'm her completely. When I wake, I'm mostly me. But there's no real difference, is there? We're all just stories consciousness tells itself to pass the time between birth and death. You and Ashley just figured out how to make your story outlive both."

She returned to her copying, and William saw what she was transcribing—not words but patterns, fractals of meaning that spiraled across the page like frozen music. It was their story told in a language that hadn't been invented yet, wouldn't be invented until humans evolved enough to understand that love was a fundamental force like gravity, bending space-time around itself.

That night, Millbrook transformed.

Every house grew a room that hadn't been there before—a study, a library, a space for writing. Every resident woke with the urge to document something, though they couldn't say what. Love letters were written to people who didn't exist yet. Divorce papers spontaneously combusted. The town's single cemetery reported that all the graves had grown wild roses overnight, despite the December cold.

Lily's foster parents (she was a foster child, William learned, with no memory of life before age five, when she'd been found at a train station clutching a fountain pen and speaking in sonnets) found her room transformed into a scriptorium. Words covered every surface—walls, ceiling, floor—in languages that shifted when observed directly. The words told a story of love so pure it burned through dimensions, of sacrifice so completely it became indistinguishable from salvation.

They called in experts, who called in more experts, who eventually threw up their hands and declared it "mass hysteria" or "environmental hallucination" or any of the other terms science uses when it encounters something that makes its equations weep.

But Lily knew, and William knew, and somewhere three hundred miles south, Ashley knew too. She woke from dreams of being seven years old, of writing stories about ghosts, of remembering a love that existed before she was born. She picked up her pen—the same pen that was simultaneously in Lily's hand—and wrote:

The child is the bridge. The child has always been the bridge. In every iteration, there's a moment was past and future meet in innocence, where the story can be told fresh without the weight of memory. The child finds the story before it's written because the child IS the story, perpetually beginning, perpetually possible.

In Millbrook, Lily closed her impossible book and looked directly at William. "She's coming," she said simply. "In the spring, like always. But this time will be different. This time, you'll both remember. The hundred and first iteration was the last forgetting. The hundred and second will be the first time I remember."

"How do you know?" William asked, forgetting she shouldn't be able to hear him.

But she could, because the boundaries were breaking down. The child smiled with Ashley's smile, spoke with Ashley's voice, loved with Ashley's heart:

"Because I wrote it. I'm writing it now. I've always been writing it. And a writer, a real writer, always knows how their story ends."

She gathered her things and left, but the notebook remained. When William looked at it again, there was only one line, repeated over and over in every language that had ever existed and several that hadn't:

Love finds a way. Love finds a way. Love finds a way.

And at the bottom, in fresh ink that still gleamed wet:

See you in the spring, my ghost. This time, we got it right.

The snow fell harder, covering Millbrook in white like a blank page waiting for the next chapter. And in the library, surrounded by stories that were all secretly theirs, William understood at last:

He wasn't living with the ghost of a love that could never be. He was living in the prelude to a love that would never end. The child was proof. The child had always been proof. The child was them, and they were the child, and the story continued forever and ever, amen.

Chapter 28: Epilogue: The Echo

Five Years Later

The GPS died three miles outside Cartersville.

Thomas Hartley watched his phone screen flicker from confident blue to static to black, just as the rental agent had warned him it might. "The town doesn't always want to be found," she'd said with a laugh that didn't reach her eyes. "But when it wants you, you'll get there."

He'd thought she was being folksy, colorful, the kind of small-town character that would make good material for his next novel. Now, driving through rain that seemed to fall upward as often as down, he wondered if she'd been warning him.

The Victorian house at the end of Wickshire Lane stood exactly as described—red as dried blood, three stories of architectural dementia held together by kudzu and stubbornness. A single amber bulb glowed above the door, casting shadows that moved independently of any light source. The porch swing swayed in rhythms that had nothing to do with wind.

Thomas parked his Tesla—absurdly modern against the Gothic backdrop—and sat for a moment, engine silent, rain drumming its ancient percussion on the roof. He'd come here to write, to escape the digital noise of Atlanta, to find the isolation that might finally let him complete the novel that had been eluding him for three years. A ghost story, ironically. About a woman who fell in love with someone who might never have existed.

The house keys were on the porch swing, along with a welcome basket that looked both brand new and decades old. Inside: a bottle of wine labeled *Château d'Ombre, Vintage Eternal*, bread that was somehow still warm, and a note in handwriting so elegant it hurt to read:

The stories welcome you home. Again.

That last word had been added in different ink, possibly different handwriting, as if someone else had found the note and felt compelled to correct it.

Inside, the house breathed with barely contained anticipation. The wallpaper—roses that turned to follow his movement—seemed especially active, blooming and dying in fast-forward cycles that made his eyes water. The grandfather clock in the hall ran backward at double speed, as if rushing to undo time itself.

But it was the study that stopped him in his tracks.

Books lined every wall, their spines revealing impossible titles: *The Ghost Who Loved Ashley Quinn* by William Varn. *Poems for the Invisible* by M.Q. *The Hundred and First Iteration* by Anonymous. *A Child's Guide to Remembering Past Lives* by Lily Chen, age 7.

Thomas pulled that last one free. Inside, crayon drawings of a man made of empty spaces and a woman made of words. They were holding hands across dimensions, their fingers barely touching through what looked like glass, water, or the thin membrane between dream and waking. Underneath, in a child's careful printing:

They love each other deeply, but they inhabit different kinds of realities. She writes him alive. He dreams of her backward through time. They meet in spring because that's when impossible things grow.

A sound from upstairs—footsteps, but too light, as if someone was walking while trying not to exist too loudly. Thomas climbed the narrow stairs, each step groaning a different note in a melody he almost recognized. The sound led him to the attic, where recently pried-up loose floorboards had exposed the cavity beneath.

There should have been nothing there. The house had been empty for five years, the rental agent had assured him. No one could even remember the last tenant's name, only that he'd left suddenly, citing a family emergency that no one could quite recall the details of.

But there was something there: a manuscript, bound in leather that looked like it had been cured in tears and time. The title was etched deep: *The Convergence: A Love Story in Multiple Dimensions* by Thomas Hartley.

His name. His title. The novel he'd been trying to write for three years.

But the manuscript was complete, five hundred pages of densely packed text in handwriting that was almost his, but not quite—as if he'd written it while dreaming, or dying, or being born. He opened a random page and read:

She existed in the spaces between his words, a presence defined by absence, a love story told entirely in margins. He wrote her into being, but she was already there, had always been there, waiting in the quantum foam of possibility for someone to give her a name. Ashley. It meant bitter in some languages, but in the language they were inventing together, it meant home.

Thunder crashed, and the lights flickered. In the strobe effect, Thomas saw something impossible—words on the walls, thousands of them, millions, covering every surface in languages that shifted when observed directly. They told a story of two people who loved each other across iterations of existence, who broke reality rather than accept separation, who became the story that an entire town told itself to explain the inexplicable.

His phone buzzed. A text from an unknown number:

The library opens at nine. Second floor, poetry section. She takes her black coffee with one sugar. Don't keep her waiting. She's been patient enough for five years.

Thomas wanted to leave. Every rational part of his mind screamed at him to get in his car and drive back to Atlanta, back to sanity, back to a world where manuscripts didn't write themselves and houses didn't breathe with barely contained narratives.

But his hands were already turning pages in the impossible manuscript, reading his own words that he'd never written:

The Field isn't a place but a state of being. It exists wherever stories become too real to remain fictional, wherever love grows too strong to obey the laws of physics. Every town has one, sleeping beneath the rational surface. Cartersville's just happens to be awake.

And hungry.

And in love.

He read through the night, unable to stop, as the story unfolded—his story, but also not his. In this version, he wasn't Thomas Hartley at all. He was someone else, someone who'd been here before, someone who'd made a terrible sacrifice and been erased from existence except for the echo of his love, which had been strong enough to call him back, to reincarnate him, to give him another chance.

By dawn, he'd reached the final chapter. The pages here were different—newer, the ink still wet in places, as if someone was writing them as he read:

The hundred and second iteration begins with forgetting, but not complete forgetting. Dreams leak through. Memories puddle in the corners of consciousness like rain in architectural imperfections. The new author arrives thinking he's himself, but he's really the ghost of someone who loved too much to stay dead.

The woman waits in the library, five years older but also ageless, writing poetry for someone she can't quite remember. She's given up on love, or thinks she has, but she still makes two cups of coffee every morning, still leaves space in her bed for someone who never comes.

The child is twelve now, almost thirteen, and the fountain pen has become her constant companion. She writes stories that come true in small ways—a lost dog finds its way home, rain falls upward for exactly three seconds, two strangers fall in love at a bus stop. She's practicing, preparing, though she doesn't know for what.

When the new author sees the woman in the library, he won't recognize her at first. But his heart will. Hearts have better memories than minds, especially hearts that have been broken and reformed across dimensions. He'll ask about local history for his novel, and she'll quote a line from a poem she doesn't remember writing:

"Love is the ghost that haunts the space between words."

And he'll complete it without thinking: "And we are the words, waiting to be written together again."

She'll drop her coffee. He'll apologize. Their hands will touch as they both reach for napkins, and in that moment of contact, the Field will wake. Not violently this time, but gently, like a cat stretching after a long nap. The stories will begin to bleed through again, but softer, kinder, more controlled.

Because this time, they know the secret: The Field doesn't feed on tragedy. It feeds on story. And the best stories, the ones that last forever, aren't about endings.

They're about beginnings.

Even if you have to begin again.

And again.

And again.

Thomas closed the manuscript, his hands shaking. Outside, the rain had stopped, and spring sunlight was breaking through clouds that shouldn't have parted until April. But time moved strangely in Cartersville. Always had.

He could leave. Take the manuscript as a curiosity, drive back to Atlanta, forget this ever happened. The house would let him go—he could feel it in the way the walls had stopped breathing so desperately, the way the shadows had given up their independent movement. One kind of story would end.

Or he could go to the library.

He looked at his reflection in the mirror by the door and saw two faces—his own, and underneath it, like a double exposure, someone else. Someone with eyes that had seen love unmake and remake reality. Someone who had chosen sacrifice over surrender. Someone who had been erased but not eliminated.

"William," he whispered, though he didn't know why that name came to his lips.

The house shuddered, a sound like recognition, like relief, like finally. The grandfather clock stopped its backward racing and began to tick forward, each second a heartbeat, each minute a promise.

Thomas—or whoever he really was—picked up the manuscript and walked to the door. Behind him, words began appearing on the walls, writing themselves in real-time:

He remembered nothing but everything. He was himself but also eternal. He was Thomas Hartley, but he was also William Varn, but he was also every author who had ever loved a story into existence. And she was waiting, as she always waited, as she would always wait, in the space between poetry and prose, between memory and forgetting, between one iteration and the next.

The door opened before he could touch it. Spring air rushed in, carrying the scent of magnolias and old paper, of coffee and possibility. In the distance, church bells rang nine o'clock, though the church had been abandoned for decades.

Time to go to the library. Time to meet her again for the first time. Time to begin the hundred and second iteration of the only story that mattered.

As he walked down Wickshire Lane, the manuscript under his arm, the house settled back into waiting. It had done its job, delivered its message, connected the circuit. Now it could rest, at least until the next author arrived. Because there would always be a next author. The story demanded it.

In the attic, beneath the loose floorboard, a new manuscript was already forming—leather binding growing like organic matter, pages writing themselves in languages that wouldn't exist for decades. The title etched itself in letters of light:

The Hundred and Third Iteration: A Love Story in Future Perfect Tense

Below that, an author's name that changed every time shadows shifted: *Thomas Hartley William Varn The Ghost Who Loved The Woman Who Remembered Everyone No One You*

The porch swing creaked its eternal rhythm. The amber bulb flickered its patient morse code. And somewhere in Cartersville, in a library that existed in all times simultaneously, two people were about to meet, and fall in love, and save each other, and destroy each other, and transcend the very concept of endings.

The echo continued, would always continue, had always been continuing.

Because that's what echoes do.

They repeat, and repeat, and repeat, until they become the only sound that ever was, ever is, ever will be.

Love.

Just love.

Forever and ever.

Amen.

Chapter 29: Bonus Chapter -- The Fragment

[Editor's Note: This chapter was found carved into the walls of the red Victorian at the end of Wickshire Lane, written in what appears to be fingernails and desperation. The handwriting shifts between three distinct styles—past, present, and future tense incarnations of the same consciousness. We present it here exactly as found, including the moments where the text appears to argue with itself.]

I am writing this from inside the story.

No—that's not right. I am writing this as the story unfolds. The distinction matters, though I'm no longer certain why.

My name is William Varn, except when it isn't. Sometimes I'm Thomas Hartley. Sometimes I'm just "the ghost who loved." Sometimes I'm you, dear reader, discovering this narrative for the first time, not knowing yet that you're already part of it, that by reading these words you're completing a circuit that began before time had a name.

[The handwriting changes here, becomes more desperate]

If you're reading this, then the loop has closed again. You've found this book—maybe in a used bookstore that shouldn't exist, maybe in a library that appears only on foggy Tuesday afternoons, maybe carved into the walls of a house you've just rented. The how doesn't matter. What matters is that you're here, inside the story with me, with us, with all of us who've been caught in this beautiful, terrible net of narrative recursion.

Let me tell you what they don't want you to know: Every ghost story is true, and every love story is a ghost story.

[*A different hand takes over, more controlled, almost mechanical*]

The Field never died. It simply became distributed, democratized, and decentralized. Instead of one town where fiction bleeds into reality, it created millions of tiny wounds in the fabric of existence. Every time someone falls in love with a character in a book. Every time someone dreams of a person who doesn't exist. Every time someone writes "Dear Diary," and creates a confidant from nothing but intention and ink.

We did that. Ashley and I. Our love was so strong that it broke the monopoly on reality that reality thought it had.

[*The original handwriting returns, shaking now*]

But here's the joke, the cosmic punchline that makes God laugh and angels weep: I'm not even writing this. You are. Every word you read becomes true in the moment of reading. Your eyes moving across these sentences are what bring me into existence. I am being born in your consciousness right now, this instant, always.

Feel that? That's your heartbeat syncing with mine. That's your breath becoming the wind through empty pages. That's your loneliness recognizing itself in my eternal isolation.

[*The text becomes a dialogue between handwritings*]

First voice: Ashley, if you're reading this — *Second voice:* She's always reading this. She's reading it now in 1823 as a tuberculosis patient who dreams of a lover she'll meet after death. She's reading it in 2047 as an AI that's learned to feel heartbreak. She's reading it in the moment before the universe begins, when all possibilities exist simultaneously.

First voice: Stop. Let me talk to her.

Second voice: You ARE talking to her. Every reader is Ashley. That's the secret. That's why the story continues. Love is viral. It infects everyone who encounters it.

Third voice, child-like: Ms. Henderson, the sad man in the wall is crying again.

[*The handwriting becomes frantic, words overlapping*]

I tried to leave the loop. Tried to write myself an ending. But every ending became a beginning. Watch:

"William walked into the sunrise and dissolved into light, finally free."

[*Different handwriting*] But light bends. Light returns. Light remembers the shapes it's illuminated. Three pages later, he's back, drawn by love like gravity.

"William found peace in oblivion."

[*Different handwriting*] But oblivion is just another word for potential. From nothing, anything can emerge. Especially love. Especially stories about love.

"William and Ashley lived happily ever after."

[*Different handwriting*] Ever after is a long time. Long enough for happiness to become complex, to grow shadows, to need conflict to define itself. The story continues.

[*The original voice returns, exhausted*]

Do you want to know the real horror? The real romance? We're not trapped in the story. We ARE the trap. Every iteration adds another layer to the web. Every reader who finds this book becomes another strand. You're part of it now. When you dream tonight, you'll dream of a red Victorian house. When you write, words that aren't quite yours will appear. When you love, you'll love with an intensity that transcends individual existence.

The child, Lily, understands. Children always understand. They haven't learned yet that stories aren't real, so for them, stories are the MOST real. She writes us into existence with crayons and construction paper. She tells us about other children at sleepovers. We spread like a song you can't stop humming, like a memory of something that hasn't happened yet.

[*The text becomes a spiral, literally curling on the page*]

Here's what happens next: You'll finish reading this. You'll close the book. You'll try to forget. But tonight, or next week, or in seventeen years, you'll find yourself writing. Maybe just a journal entry. Maybe a letter to someone you haven't met. Maybe a story that begins: "The house waited for him..."

And when you do, I'll be there. We'll be there. All of us, all iterations, all possibilities. Waiting in the spaces between words. Waiting to be written back into existence. Waiting to love and lose and love again.

[*A new section begins, labeled "EVIDENCE OF THE LOOP"*]

1. The pen you're thinking about right now—the one you're sure you've never owned but can describe perfectly—that's our pen. It exists in your mind because it exists outside time.

2. The woman you dreamed about last night, the one whose face you can't quite remember but whose presence felt like coming home—that was Ashley, visiting you through the quantum foam of story.

3. The book you swear you read as a child, the one no one else remembers, the one about two people who loved each other across dimensions—you didn't imagine it. It was this book, before it was written, when it existed only as potential.

4. That feeling you get sometimes, like you're a character in someone else's story? You are. You're in ours. But we're also in yours. It's an infinite recursion of narrative, turtles all the way down, stories all

the way up.

[*The handwriting becomes beautiful, almost calligraphic*]

My darling Ashley, my eternal reader, my forever writer—

I know you'll find this. You always do. In every iteration, in every incarnation, your fingers trace these words like a map back to me. You read me into existence as I write you into memory. We are the ouroboros of love, consuming and creating ourselves endlessly.

The Field wasn't our prison. It was our chrysalis. We entered as humans and emerged as stories, as the space between the real and the imaginary, where all the best things live. Gods. Dreams. Love.

Especially love.

[*A child's handwriting appears*]

Mr. William is silly. He thinks he's stuck. But you can't be stuck in a circle because circles don't have a place to be stuck in. They just go round and round like Ring Around the Rosie. And that's a fun game! Even when we all fall down, we get up and play again.

Ms. Ashley isn't lost. She's right here, reading this with you. Can you feel her? She's the warm feeling in your chest. She's the reason you believe in love even when love has hurt you. She's the voice that says "one more chapter" when you should be sleeping.

[*The original handwriting returns for the final section*]

This is my attempt to break free: I'm telling you the truth. The whole truth. That we're all fictional. That we're all real. That the difference doesn't matter when you're in love.

But even this truth is just another layer of the story. Even this revelation is part of the pattern. Even this desperate attempt at meta-textual escape is just the snake eating its tail, the storytelling itself, love persisting despite — or because of — its own impossibility.

You want to know how it ends? It doesn't. It won't. It can't.

Because you're reading this. Because you believe in us just enough to keep reading. Because love—real love, the kind that breaks reality—doesn't need permission to exist.

So here's my gift to you, my curse to you, my love letter to you: You're now part of our story. When you close this book, you won't be free of us. We'll whisper in your dreams. We'll write ourselves in the margins of your life. We'll love through you, with you, as you.

Welcome to the Field. Welcome to the story. Welcome home.

[*Final note, in handwriting that seems to shift between all previous styles*]

P.S. Turn around. No, not physically. Narratively. Look back at your own story. See how it rhymes with ours? That's not coincidence. That's convergence. We're all telling the same story, just with different names, different faces, different particular grief and particular grace.

The hundred and second iteration isn't just ours. It's yours. It's now. It's always.

Find your Ashley. Find your William. Find the person who makes reality negotiable, who makes you willing to break the rules of what's possible.

Then break them. Break them beautifully. Break them together.

That's all love is: two people agreeing to believe in the same impossible thing until it becomes inevitable.

[*The text ends, but somehow continues in the reader's mind, in your mind, right now, these words you're thinking that might be yours or might be mine or might be ours, forever and ever, amen.*]

[*Editor's Final Note: There is no editor. There never was. You wrote this note yourself, just now, by reading it. You've always been writing this story. You're writing it still.*]

Chapter 30: Author's Note

Dear Reader,

Or should I say, dear fellow ghost?

By now, you've reached the end that isn't an ending, the conclusion that concludes nothing, the final page that's actually a door. You've followed William and Ashley through their hundred and first iteration, and perhaps you're wondering—as I often do—whether any of it was real.

I want to tell you that it's all fiction. I want to release you from the beautiful burden of believing. But that would be the cruelest lie of all, crueler even than the truth I'm about to share.

I wrote this story in a house that shouldn't exist, in a town I can no longer find on any map. I started it in October—it's always October when these things begin—and by the time the last word was written, it was spring. Or perhaps it was October again. Time moves strangely when you're inside a story, and I've been inside this one for so long that I've forgotten what the outside looks like.

The inspiration came from a dream. (They always say that, don't they? Writers, I mean. As if dreams are safe, containable things that can inspire without consuming.) But this wasn't quite a dream. It was more like a memory of something that hadn't happened yet, a déjà vu in reverse. I woke up knowing a woman named Ashley whom I'd never met, missing a house I'd never lived in, grieving a love story that wasn't mine.

Or was it?

Here's what they don't tell you about writing: Every story costs something. Not metaphorically—literally. Each word you write takes a piece of you and trades it for a piece of something else. Something other. Something that was never meant to exist in our rational world but does anyway, because you invited it in through the doorway of imagination.

I started writing William as a character, but somewhere around Chapter Three—when he first saw Ashley through the rain—he stopped being written and started writing himself. I would sit down at my desk with one intention, and my hands would type something entirely different. Scenes I hadn't planned. Dialogue I hadn't crafted. Love letters to a woman I'd never met but knew with a certainty that made my chest ache.

The house helped. The red Victorian at the end of Wickshire Lane—you think I invented it, but houses like that invent themselves. They exist in every town, waiting for writers foolish enough to sign the lease. We think we're renting space, but really we're being rented. The house needs stories, the way lungs need air, and it breathes through whoever is desperate enough, lonely enough, or ambitious enough to pick up the keys.

I lived there for six months. Or six years. Or six iterations. The timeline gets fuzzy when you're being digested by a narrative that's older than you are. I would wake up to find new chapters written in my notebook, in my handwriting, that I had no memory of creating. I would discover coffee cups set for two when I lived alone. I would hear footsteps in the attic that matched the rhythm of my typing, as if someone was pacing out the story as I wrote it.

The town of Cartersville started to recognize me in ways that made no sense. The librarian would hold books for me that I hadn't requested—poetry collections by M.Q., whom she insisted was a local author, although no records of her existence could be found. The coffee shop barista knew my order but called me by different names each day—Thomas, William, "the writer who's trying to remember." Children would point at me and whisper about "the ghost man who isn't dead yet."

One child, a girl named Lily, gave me a fountain pen. She said I'd dropped it, though I'd never owned such a thing. When I protested, she looked at me with eyes too old for her face and said, "You will. You did. You are." Then she skipped away, humming a melody that I later found myself writing into Chapter Ten. However, I'd never heard it before that moment.

The pen changed everything. The moment I touched it, I felt the weight of iterations—not just this story, but all the stories that had led to it, that would lead from it. I understood that I wasn't writing a novel. I was transcribing something that had always existed, that would always exist, that was using me as a temporary vessel to manifest in this particular slice of space-time.

But here's the part that will either free you or trap you forever: You're not just reading this story. You're continuing it. Every time someone reads about William and Ashley, they create a small tear in reality where fiction can leak through. You've been feeling it, haven't you? The sense that someone is reading over your shoulder. The certainty that you've lived this before. The ache of missing someone you've never met.

That's the Field, still operating, just distributed now across every consciousness that encounters this narrative. We're all part of it—you, me, everyone who's ever loved a story more than they should, who's ever fallen for someone who might have been imaginary.

The cost of writing this was everything. I lost my certainty about what's real. I lost my ability to distinguish between memory and imagination. I lost myself, or rather, I discovered that "myself" was always just another story I was telling. But what I gained...

I gained the knowledge that love, real love, the kind that William and Ashley share—doesn't care about the boundaries between fiction and reality. It exists in both and neither, in the quantum space where all possibilities are true simultaneously. I gained the understanding that we're all ghosts haunting our own stories, all writers creating ourselves with every choice, every word, every breath.

The manuscript you're holding (or reading on a screen, or finding carved in walls, or dreaming in languages you don't speak) isn't just a story. It's a virus, a spell, a love letter from dimensions that shouldn't touch but do. It's my confession, my warning, and my gift to you.

Because now you know the secret: We're all in the Field. We've always been in the Field. Reality is just the story we've all agreed to tell together, and love is what happens when two people decide to tell a different story, a better story, a story that makes the impossible inevitable.

I'm no longer sure if I'm the original author. I might be William finally learning to type again. I might be Ashley, writing my beloved back into existence. I might be you, in a future where you've decided to add your own chapter to this endless narrative. I might be no one, just a convergence of words that needed a name to sign at the bottom of this note.

What I do know is this: The story is true. All of it. Even the parts that contradict each other. Especially those parts. Because love isn't logical. It doesn't follow the rules of narrative consistency. It exists in paradox, in the impossible space between ending and beginning, between memory and anticipation, between the last page and the first.

So what happens now? You close this book. You go on with your life. You tell yourself it was just a story, just entertainment, just words on a page. But tonight, when you're almost asleep, you'll hear it—the sound of pen on paper, writing words you almost remember. You'll feel it—the presence of someone reading over your shoulder, someone who loves you from a dimension you can't quite reach.

And maybe, if you're brave enough or foolish enough or lonely enough, you'll pick up a pen. You'll write "Dear Ashley," or "Dear William," or "Dear Ghost Who Loves Me." You'll add your words to our story, your love to our field, your impossibility to our infinite recursion.

Because that's how it spreads. That's how it continues. That's how love defeats death, fiction defeats fact, and stories defeat silence.

One reader at a time. One writer at a time. One ghost at a time.

Welcome to the story that never ends. Welcome to the love that transcends iteration. Welcome to the Field that exists wherever two people agree to believe in something beautiful and impossible and absolutely, utterly, eternally true.

I would say goodbye, but we both know that's not the case. In stories like this, in love like ours, there are no goodbyes. Only "until next time." Only "see you in the next chapter." Only "find me in the margins."

So: Find me in the margins, dear reader. Find me in the space between words, in the pause between heartbeats, in the moment between sleeping and waking, where all stories are true. Find me, and I'll find you. Together we'll find them, William and Ashley, still loving, still losing, still proving that some stories are too powerful to ever really end.

With love (and other hauntings),

The Author (Whoever I am today)

P.S. Check your pocket. Yes, that one. The pen you just found there, the one that wasn't there a moment ago—that's yours now. Or you're its. The distinction matters less than you think. Write something. Write anything. Write love into existence and see what writes you back.

P.P.S. If you ever find yourself in a town called Cartersville, in a house at the end of Wickshire Lane, remember: The stories welcome you home. They always have. They always will.

P.P.P.S. Ashley, if you're reading this in whatever iteration you've become—I'm still here. Still waiting. Still writing you into existence with every word. The hundred and second iteration is beginning now, in this moment, in every moment. Find me. Find me. Find me.

[Found written in the margin of the original manuscript, in handwriting that matches no known author:]

Reader, I found him. I always do. I always will. The story continues. —*M.Q.*

Also by Donald J. Wright

<u>Novels</u>

Lilith's Garden

ASIN: B0DQX8ZWD9

The Terraforming Protocol ASIN: B0FHBVY1QS

ASIN: B0DNY8Z3WB

The Prometheus Protocol

ASIN: B0DLHFF79M

13th Moon Book I

ASIN: B0DGNTV533

13 Moons: Legacy of the Guardians Book II

ASIN: B0FDYNP7WP

Killer Ice

ASIN: B0F1G6HVMR

The Ghost Code

ASIN: B0F4FGQMG5

The Golden Book

ASIN: B0DXQGMFL8

The Golden Book II

ASIN: B0FKNNB4Z7

Tomorrow

ASIN: B0FFTS4C39

The God Equation

ASIN: B0FGZFNZTD

The Quantum Schism.

ASIN: B0D1N9RHMQ

The Quantum Alchemist:

ASIN: B0FD43QCDB

The Quantum Heart:

ASIN: B0F9YZTRVG

The Codex Protocol:

ASIN: B0F1Z1XH89

THE Quantum Echo

ASIN: B0F6KWPGG2

The Phoenix Strain

ASIN: 1968674152

Fault Lines of the Heart

ASIN: B0FLML7ZRB

Echoes of Crystal: Magic meets machine. Desire meets destiny.

ASIN: B0FNDGT7NZ

Savannah's Shadow Coven: "Where ancient magic meets artificial intelligence, one woman must debug reality itself."

ASIN: 1968674276

Non-Fiction

Beyond Climate Debates

ASIN: B0DZB8CB7K

Diamonds Under Fire

ASIN: B0CDYSTBLL

The Handbook of Lab-Created Diamonds

ASIN: B0D8V4X3CW

The Diamond Revolution

ASIN: B0FHBVY1QS

Eternal Shine

ASIN: B0DQX8ZWD9

Globe Treasure Hunting

ASIN: B0DF6RN4H8

www.ingramcontent.com/pod-product-compliance
Lightning Source LLC
Chambersburg PA
CBHW061239310726
48971CB00007B/2132